God In Wingtip Shoes

God In
Wingtip Shoes

Yvonne J. Medley

www.urbanchristianonline.com

Urban Books, LLC
78 East Industry Court
Deer Park, NY 11729

ISBN 13: 978-1-60162-826-8
ISBN 10: 1-60162-826-9

First Printing April 2012
Printed in the United States of America

10 9 8 7 6 5 4 3 2 1

Distributed by Kensington Corp.
Submit Wholesale Orders to:
Kensington Publishing Corp.
C/O Penguin Group (USA) Inc.
Attention: Order Processing
405 Murray Hill Parkway
East Rutherford, NJ 07073-2316
Phone: 1-800-526-0275
Fax: 1-800-227-9604

God In Wingtip Shoes

by

Yvonne J. Medley

This book is dedicated to my armor bearers, Robert, Sr., Robert, II, Renesha, Rashad, and Rachel, and the second tier, Zachary, III, and Zavier. Also in loving memory to the mighty matriarchs, my grandmothers, Mattie L. Tomlin and Audrey L. Johnson, and my great-aunt, the Reverend Margaret Deans Floyd

"A draw on the challenges of clergy and the church vs. humanity and circumstance, *God in Wingtip Shoes* is entertaining, thought-provoking and timely—especially as headlines sweep. It's a safe vessel through which transparent dialogue can begin for all."

—Dr. Teresa Hairston, founder and publisher, *Gospel Today Magazine*

". . . Well written and interesting. I was left with a desire to read more."

—Dr. Eugenia Collier, author of *Beyond The Crossroad*, writer, critic, and winner of the Gwendolyn Brooks Prize for Fiction award.

"*God in Wingtip Shoes* captures the flavor, the feel, the history, and culture of Baltimore City. It salutes the traditions of faith and the need to practice one's faith, while laying bare the infirmities of religious tradition. This novel is full of vision and introspection."

—Tom Saunders, historian and founder of Renaissance Productions and Tours, Inc.

Acknowledgments

As a Christian journalist and a member of the universal body of believers, birthed in my soul came the obvious—church is God-directed, administered by mortals, many times flawed, but immeasurably worth it. That revelation (and a tad more) provided the inspiration for this story. So above all, to my gracious Lord and Savior, Jesus Christ, I thank you. At the onset, I promised to give You all the honor, the praise, and the glory throughout this journey (triumphs and challenges) and during every opportunity for honest discussion and fellowship. I will continue to do so.

To my earthly lord and savior, my husband, Robert Medley, Sr., thank you for not only cheering me on, but also for your constant love, understanding, and care of me and our children. I believe that's called unconditional love and a rich blessing.

I will forever appreciate my family and friends who truly lived for me ". . . faith is the substance of things hoped for, and the evidence of things not seen" (Hebrews 11:1). Even when I treaded frustration, doubt, and the desire to give up, you carried me until I felt strong enough to keep it moving. Thank you to my sister, Yvette Cetasaan, and brother-in-law, Kwaku, and the baby girl, Jordin; sister-in-law, Cheryl Medley-McKinney; Tom Saunders; Billy Medley; Leon and Patricia Dorsey; Nathaniel Williams; Love and Angela Smith; Cynthia Mazyck; Renée Dames; Chaplain John Lewis; Bishop and Mrs. Forrest Stith; Peggy Evans; and Cornell and

Gloria Evans. Thanks to my parents, Juanita Freeman and the late Will S. Freeman, for making certain I focus on joy, not pain.

Thank you to my resilient literary agent, Dr. Maxine Thompson; publishing editor, Joylynn Jossel-Ross; and Mr. Carl Weber for taking my faith and making it tangible (even if the meticulous process caused me to rub some of the skin off my forehead). Thank you to the editor who got everything off the ground, Karen Sorenson-Bartelt.

To my international encouragers, Katerina Llioglou in Australia, Michelle Higdon in London, Tokunbo Oladeinde, simply a Nigerian Yoruba Queen, and Maysa Elshafei, an Egyptian beauty inside and out, a heartfelt thank you.

Thank you to my literary coaches/angels of the Life Journeys Writers Club; Emily Ferren, director of the Charles County Library System (and her crew); the Lifelong Learning Center; The Enoch Pratt Free Library (Baltimore); author Ann Crispin and her husband, Michael; as well as author and publisher Austin Camacho. You not only encouraged and critiqued, but also imparted wisdom.

To the shepherds who ushered me in His presence, thank you to the late Rev. Mannie L. Wilson, Convent Avenue Baptist Church (Harlem, N.Y.), and the Rev. Dr. and Mrs. William C. Calhoun, Sr., Trinity Baptist Church (Baltimore)—and to the shepherds who keep me in His presence, Pastor and Mrs. Darin V. Poullard, Fort Washington Baptist Church (FWBC) (Fort Washington, Md.). Thank you for sturdy lessons in integrity, love, and patience, as well as grace and mercy. Also thank you for your willingness to address the tough questions. To the FWBC deacons and especially the FWBC Women's Ministry, I'm grateful for your covering, objectivity, and support.

Table of Contents

Table Of Contents

Chapter One

God's Point

1996

"If you can't get with this . . . then keep your money in your pocket and go to hell!" he said. He worked the congregation like a poised stripper at The Players Club. A slight remorse tried his stance, but he fought it. Life and death angled on his shoulders. He let silence notarize his conviction. The congregation hushed when the threat of *hell* thundered from the pulpit.

Earlier, the offering baskets had swept through a third time and fingers had grown weary.

Reverend Daniel Harris was on his perch surrendered to the hymn—*On Christ, the solid rock I stand. All other ground is sinking sand; all other ground is sinking sa . . .*—when he eyeballed the laziness of his faithful followers. That's when he flew to his crystal podium and dangled a little damnation in front of their deliverance.

And so he allowed his scorn to blanket the congregation. Then he smiled. A cloud lifted. Reverend's smile was toothy and soothing—and sexy. Relieved, the congregation forgave him for his blunt statement because he was only trying to make a point. So, like a child forced to acknowledge wrongdoing, the faithful accepted his chastisement and responded with upturned purses and emptied pockets of amens. Thankful, Reverend Harris rewarded the congregation with a song.

He looked over at his choir director and gave her the high sign. Even from a distance, she caught sight of his green-apple eyes gleaming in her direction. She understood.

His eyes were beautiful. His buttercream tint, his brown, wavy hair and curly lashes, his manicured fingernails and his round behind—everything on the reverend was beautiful. He looked over at her, beamed his smile, and said, "Have the choir sing something grateful, Sister Cherry."

Sister Cherry pulled her aging body to attention like a general. She motioned the mass choir, robed in royal blue and frosty white, to do likewise.

Forest Unity's musicians operated on one accord. It was the fruit of their labor. Sister Cherry and the music director, Brother Elroy Sallie, privy to rumblings in the inner-circle pipeline, signaled to each other that the song to sing would be the Yolanda Adams hit, "The Battle Is the Lord's." The first delicious chord rang out. Forest Unity's favorite songbird, and the Reverend's bride, Lori Sparrow, emerged from a curtain of royal blue pleats. Her musical testimony folded into the orchestra's intro. Cymbals tingled, piano keys rippled, and organ chords rolled, while a wide, wispy brush danced atop a circle of drums. Emotions stacked clear to the church's vaulted ceiling.

"What is God's message to you today?" Lori asked in her opening monologue. She sautéed it with a stirring Toni Braxton-type moan as she was known to do. It touched off a multitude of spiritual orgasms. Limbs went limp. Bottom lips loosed. Eyelids blinked in slow motion. The reverend fought the droop of his own eyelids to steal a satisfying glance at Lori's lips and a flashback of the night before. She caught it. She understood. She threw back a sexy switchblade smile. Just then, she resembled a soft, chewy Butterfinger, and he felt famished.

Focus! his inside voice demanded.

Lori kept her petite honey-hued body in the corner of his eye and sang, "This battle ain't yours . . ." Then she shut her eyes and belted the rest to the congregation, ". . . It's the Lord's." The choir cosigned in chorus. Reverend Harris supped on the music ministry.

Unplanned, he spied the usual string of young women sandwiched up front. He sighed. Weekly, these women advertised firm thighs and perky bosoms like sacrificial chicken parts on sale. His brow drooped. *I really don't feel like it today,* he thought. Then his glare boomeranged toward the pew that supported the sanctified mothers of the church, seasoned church ladies who chomped on the chance to give these brazen young hussies a lesson in self-respect and decorum. He chuckled because man-hunting was a year-round sport. He blinked the meaty images from his brain to refocus on his loving members as a whole. They boasted more than 1,300-strong even on Super Bowl Sunday—a coup for a young pastor enjoying his first major appointment. "Thank you, Lord," he whispered.

The sopranos chimed the chorus in perfect pitch. Their serenade came sprinkled with soft hallelujahs. He surveyed his faithful congregation and thought, *I know you'd do anything for me, saints, but I wonder if you really know that I'd do anything for you.* His sentiments tumbled in his mind like socks in a dryer. *And together, we're gonna make God sit up and take notice of the glory we're gonna give Him. This is supposed to be our dream together.*

The singing mellowed to a collective whisper, but the offering collection wasn't finished. Deacon Winston gave Reverend Harris the high sign. Reverend Harris forwarded the high sign to Sister Cherry, who signaled the choir to revive another round of the chorus. This time it climbed an octave. Lori came in with a fresh round of her solo.

The congregation blew a gasket. The Holy Spirit swept through a succession of women threaded throughout the sanctuary. Mother Esther, young Tasha Gold, and three other women sprang to their feet as if yanked by a string. Hands flew up, and their bodies snaked like accordions. Tasha's torso trembled as she mumbled godly praises just before her body hit the carpet. She wasn't the only female lying prostrate on the floor. Attentive lady ushers, decked in winter crème, rushed to the scene to keep their bodies modest beneath huge fire-red cloths.

The Holy Spirit touched the men too. One brother, a short, stocky man, didn't look agile in the secular sense, but the Spirit caught him, and he sprinted around the sanctuary like Simba. And Sister Cherry, a reserved, soft-spoken senior citizen, directed the choir with such passion that she perspired heavily in her robe and nearly lost her raven wig-hat.

A teary-eyed Reverend Harris floated down from his pulpit. He combed the base of the three-tiered altar and glided down the center aisle. All the while, he crooned sentiments of the main verse into a cordless mic clipped to his pinstriped lapel. He was beautiful. He harmonized with his wife as part of a private message that said to her, *Yes, I understand that God will make everything all right.*

Anyone still in command of his or her voice also filled the space with song. The deacons marched like soldiers, collecting the wicker baskets teeming with money. Then, one by one, each man disappeared through an opened side panel along the pulpit. It led to the pastor's study. They'd be sequestered long after sunset, accounting for the money.

"The Forest Unity Church of Baltimore," Reverend Harris predicted from his heart, "will be command-central for God's work. We're gonna make Baltimore sit up and take notice. You with me, Church?" He preached and picked members to whom he'd serve his personal eye-to-eye. Everyone's heart screamed, "Pick me, pick me!"

Approval from his trusted members washed over him like the soapy waves of a bubble bath. During Reverend Harris's three-year tenure, the feeling had grown mutual between the two. And to most Forest Unity members, the reverend was God in wingtip shoes.

Each one of Reverend's personal glances sent electric shocks of glory through the arteries of his privileged supporters.

"Amen?" he shouted to confirm his prophesied future of political power and prosperity. The congregation gave back a resounding "Amen."

Returning to the pulpit once more, he stood solid behind his crystal podium and gradually the space before him tunneled. Every earthly body evaporated from his awareness. His green eyes grazed the church walls as the choir now crooned, "I Need Thee Every Hour, I Need Thee."

Judgment hung low, he thought. He studied the majestic stained glass windows. Most bore gold plaques nailed beneath their frames. The plaques bore witness to dedicated saints who sustained the church decades ago, saints now transitioned into glory. The saints seemed to weep. And he wept dry tears in tortured silence. A prayer of intercession rolled through his head. *I can't let foreclosure happen to this church—I can't let it happen to your saints who put their faith in me. My God, where did that money go? Lord, you've got to step in. I've got to do what I said I was gonna do . . . What you told me to do.*

The reverend stood there gazing into the past of this historic church that shepherded much of Baltimore's northwest side. Its pillars were cemented during the civil rights' struggle of the fifties and sixties. Pint-size patent leather T-Straps and shiny Buster Browns wore thin the burgundy carpet in its foyer. Its pews were the perfect place for community organizing and juicy gossip. The walls of its sanctuary cradled the cries of babies and nursed them on current events.

"You got ta be twice as good ta get half as much as they got in this world," Reverend Charles A. Wicker, Sr., had preached from the pulpit. He stood tall and invincible, protected only by the piety of his long, black flowing robe. The sweat on his shiny brow bore the evidence of his heart's conviction.

"This altar was built to sustain hope and make it tangible," Reverend Wicker often shouted. "God will see to it that you only have success and not failure," he'd preach, "if you place your faith in Him." The children listened because the church was the only place where their hope fed their potential.

During the late sixties and seventies, the same church members who toiled beyond sundown in the kitchens of white suburbia or pushed brooms down busy hallways or clutched the sidebar of garbage trucks before sunrise also tutored children and college students in Forest Unity's fellowship hall—because the schools saw no need to challenge *colored* kids. Forest Unity offerings paid overdue gas and electric bills and halted evictions.

But the eighties drew apathy, and personal struggles retreated behind false pride. The church walls stopped cradling babies. None came. While the old warriors hung on, young families either left the church or re-located above the Mason-Dixon Line in search of new opportunities. Then the nineties ushered in. The Reverend Charles A. Wicker, Jr., a seemingly healthy man in his fifties, dropped dead, right there on the altar. Only ten years prior had he taken over the reins when his daddy died.

Fast-forward to now.

Reverend Harris simmered in his thoughts, *Because of me, Forest Unity stands pregnant with new birth and excitement.* His eyes glazed—and confirmed, *Its walls swell with bounties of new flesh.*

Reverend Harris felt the music massage into his body once more. His head swayed to its rhythm as he begged internally, *You said you'd neither leave me nor forsake me. Ain't that right, Lord? Ain't that right?*

He looked at the congregation and said, "Amen, Church?" And the church said, "Amen."

Chapter Two

A Real Crowd Pleaser/Crowd Teaser

1969

"Dern! That fine little boy sho' can preach!" Sister Cherry whispered into a lean.

"Oooooh, Sister Cherry, you sho' right about that," Mother Hayes chuckled back. They grinned and giggled like two seventh-graders sharing a dirty little secret about this adolescent charmer standing before them.

Both women, planted on the front pew, were part of the sanctified seven; the matriarchal pillars of the church, the prayer warriors with seasoned shoulders on which to lean. They were the uplifters who knew all about life and what it could do to a body's soul. They sat decked out in their white-on-white communion steward outfits. Like a one-two punch, the two matriarchs whispered and primped at their white lace collars. They patted their white Dixie cup hats bobby-pinned to stiff hairdos. And they took a moment to fan out their white ankle-length skirts. When the two refocused on the sermon, they zipped back to their holy shouts and hallelujahs. They never broke rhythm.

And that's what the church ladies, young, old, and middle-aged, had to say about fourteen-year-old Daniel J. Harris. "Little Rev" is what they called him. When

Little Rev shouted, flung sweat, and sprinted across the pulpit, every woman swallowed whole like a stray dog devouring a discarded foot-long. Because there was no denying it; there *was* something sensual about this fine young boy spouting off reams of biblical wisdom with such authority.

In between Sunday services, the sanctified seven, clad in white, waited on him and coddled him. It was the same as serving the Lord. They tiptoed around and busied themselves about his sleek adolescent body mass. If they could have, they would have nursed him. And Daniel was groomed by The Reverend Tommy B. Graystone, aka Big Rev, the pastor of The Bible Deliverance Church of God. Daniel was groomed by Big Rev to accept the brown-skin service the sanctified seven lovingly rendered. It was his due because of his God-given gift. "Let the flock serve God by serving you, son," Big Rev often instructed.

Now, when it came to the young girls—upfront and crammed into the second pew just for an up close view of their preaching buttercream Blow Pop—what else is a teenage boy to do? Daniel obliged them to do whatever they promised to do to earn his attention. Such favor was hard to come by, even for mature saints, and *this* favor was priceless. All that favor might have been considered a sinful pleasure if Daniel (or Little Rev) were of common man-boy status. But he wasn't. And so, he was taught to never allow his mind to go there. It wasn't supposed to.

To manage it all, Daniel only needed to seek forgiveness and repentance. In the pulpit, a separation of temporal and divine was paramount. One's earthly failings must neither compete with nor contaminate one's godly gift. It's a pastor's duty, even for one so young, to do what it takes to lead his sheep to the throne of grace without flawed or pesky interruption.

"Don't ever mix the Spirit with the flesh, boy. That would be blasphemous," Big Rev told him, right up to and through his manhood. And so, in exchange for the power to preach, Daniel learned to manage his life and to keep contradictions locked behind their appropriate doors.

"Lawddd, that boy sho' can preach," said Mother Mattie Tawny, whispering in her sister's ear. Mother Lucille Spears (everyone called her Cille for short) leaned in and whispered, "You sho' right about that, sista. But what he gonna do with all that gift?"

Mother Lucille's comments intermingled with her amens and sermonic hums to her little Daniel's rhythmic praises from the pulpit. The sisters sat on the opposite end of where Mother Hayes and Sister Cherry sat. The entire pew was draped with the sanctified seven. All were fashioned in their white-on-white polyester that cradled the tops of their necks and flowed past the thick of their ankles. Their heads were crowned with the Dixie cup hats, and their legs had been poured into white opaque stockings hours before. Well earned bunions molded the curve of their nursing shoes, which had been meticulously polished white.

The first gathering of The Bible Deliverance Church of God's four-day revival made the Lord, Himself, sit up and take notice. The praise had risen to a fever pitch in its first twelve minutes. This pleased The Reverend Tommy B. Graystone because it confirmed his decision to try out his young protégé. After all, a fourteen-year-old preacher was a sight to behold, especially one who fired up a crowd like Daniel could. Big Rev's ample brown body, draped in purple and gold glory, rested on the pulpit's mercy seat. He feasted on the fever of his flock, courtesy of his protégé. Daniel produced a spiritual spectacle, and spectacles drew crowds. Crowds drew money. And The Bible Deliverance Church of God always needed money.

Earlier that evening before the revival service began, Big Rev told Daniel, "You're gonna do fine this evening. The Lord's showered you with a gift, boy. You've got favor!"

"Yesss, yes, sir," Daniel said. Big Rev caught him off guard with such a bold statement. He gazed into his mentor's eyes and smiled, not really understanding the full meaning of this *gift* Big Rev was incessant about. The two stood face-to-face in the pastor's study that used to be a dusty, dingy stockroom. If either of them looked hard enough, no matter how diligently the church ladies scrubbed it, they could spy a speck or two of sawdust, hinting of its former self before conversion.

Big Rev primped at the seams of his heavy robe, making sure it hung on his frame just right. He inspected his image staring back at him through a cloudy full-length mirror mounted on the brick wall. It confirmed his grandeur. Daniel watched and studied and filed it in his memory bank. Warm surges of his future tunneled inside his chest. His eyes hazed when he tried to assign the sensation to a likeness. Perhaps it was like being cradled in the arms of one of his great-aunts as a lap-baby. Or maybe it was like the time, when he was six or seven, and his mother chased down the Mr. Softy Ice Cream truck to buy him his favorite—chocolate/vanilla swirl, two scoops.

That day was a scorcher, he remembered, and she had burst onto the steamy sidewalk, shoeless, and wearing nothing but a thin white slip under a flinging tattered robe. Everything jiggled as she ran. The image was also bolted to his brain along with Mr. Softy's paralyzed glare and ridiculous grin as his mother approached the truck. Daniel remembered his anxiety, fearing that Mr. Softy would pull off before she got there. He didn't pull off. He never pulled off—if he saw her coming. She returned, panting and glistening, to hand Little Daniel his cone. Then she mounted him on her knee and didn't take her happy eyes off him until he devoured it, lick by lick. She squeezed him and fussed over him all the while.

Pure delight was an understatement for that moment and for this moment in the pastor's study. A moment where only pastors could commune and attend to one another; a moment when what they said was private, like father and son, and no one else mattered.

Daniel prayed as hard as he could that Bryan or another one of Big Rev's eight children wouldn't come barging in. Big Rev and his wife, Millie, had four boys and four girls. Big Rev did everything perfect, Daniel felt.

Satisfied with his own appearance and proud of the lesson he was giving, Big Rev pulled Daniel from behind his towering presence and positioned him in front. Daniel's youthful, slender reflection materialized between the old mirror's cloudy streaks. Like a proud daddy, Big Rev primped at the boy's powder-blue corduroy suit. It was perfect.

"You've been blessed with a burden, boy," Big Rev spoke as he fussed over his prodigy—his surrogate son. "Those people out there will follow you anywhere—and that's okay 'cause you mean for them to follow you. It's the way to God's eternal life," Big Rev said. He smoothed out Daniel's lapel with his huge hands. He took his time. "But the grace you preach about won't be the grace you should expect to get from your followers," he schooled Daniel. "That's the burden you bear because of the gift," he said.

Daniel noticed that Big Rev had gotten a little throaty. He wanted to say something back, but what? To him, Big Rev's emotion-filled words felt like a riddle he needed to solve. Since he couldn't, he tucked the riddle inside his heart. Maybe he'd try to solve it later.

A faint knock sounded at the door and blew up Daniel's ecstasy. *Who's that?* his mind blasted, just knowing it was Bryan or one of those other little snotty-nosed Graystones coming in to mess up the groove. With his back to Big Rev, he shot a narrow-eyed threat toward the creaking door as it opened.

"Oh my God!" Aunt Cille said. Mother Lucille Spears was Daniel's great-aunt. Her body stiffened, taken aback by the venom she saw in her baby boy's eyes, the boy she and her sister, Mattie, had watched come into this world. She gasped a feeble sound. Her smile dropped off her face, which caused her bottom lip to hang open. The second Daniel saw who he assaulted, he reneged on his death ray and replaced it with a smile. But he wasn't fast enough.

"Oh, hi, Reverend Graystone," Aunt Cille said, slow and cracked. Her head was poked in, but her behind failed to follow. Her fingers remained glued to the doorknob. "Fo'give me fo' bargin' in. I waz just checkin' on ma baby and wantin' to see if y'all needed anythang."

"Oh, hi, Mother Spears," Big Rev said. "C'mon in. Come see ya boy." He waved her in, but she was glued. "We're doing all right, Mother, but you can come on in and see for ya . . ."

She disappeared and slammed the door as soon as she was able to move. The sound startled Big Rev. He laughed and said under his breath, "Sweet, sweet, Mother." He chuckled. "Old saints never let you finish what you're sayin'. I guess they figure they ain't got much time to waste. Ha!"

The Bible Deliverance Church of God was Daniel's home away from home for as long as he could remember. It laid the foundation of his formative years. The church was a dilapidated storefront on Baltimore's northwest side and commandeered the only corner within a two-block radius that wasn't claimed by a liquor store, a bar, or the black Moslem temple, down on the far end.

Already, at fourteen, Daniel knew the Bible like he knew the back of his hand. "Just call one out," he often heard Big Rev brag to his deacons. He said it not just about Daniel, but about any one of his blood children as well. "Call out any scripture. I dare you. And I'll tell you what; that child will nail it!"

The deacons would laugh and nod their puppet heads in agreement. "I know you right 'bout that, Big Rev," one of them would shout from the cluster. But the "boy," as Big Rev loved to call him, *could* nail any scripture thrown at him. It boggled the minds of everyone. The boy just inhaled God's Word and held on.

Daniel was about as handsome as handsome got. His buttercream complexion looked sweet, succulent. The sun sprinkled his cheeks with a few sandy-brown freckles, like bits of pecans spread out in a shortbread sugar cookie. He never suffered a hint of an unruly blemish. His big, oval, green-apple eyes pierced and yearned at the same time. They looked through a body's soul and hypnotized. Their jade glow went perfect with his wavy brown hair. When his hair was short, it laid down, but when it was long, it wanted to curl up. That was a problem. While all his buddies ran around sporting their Black Power Afros with black afro pics protruding out of their hip pockets—the ones with the strong-armed handle and a clinched fist that declared, *I pick my hair for the movement*, Daniel resolved to wear his hair short, unkinkable, and wavy. "Mannn, why you wearin' yo' hair like some faggoty white boy? What you got? A process or somethin'?" his boy, "C" playfully teased.

Growing up, Daniel, Bryan Graystone, and a little fellow named Charlie Winston, whom everyone called "C," were the three amigos. Whenever "C" made a joke about Daniel's hair, their small crew of cohorts cracked up laughing. Daniel laughed too, but the jokes cut deep. If the joke wasn't about his hair, it was about his too-light skin, or his pencil nose, or his funny-colored eyes.

"Mannn, you spooky," "C" quipped. The fellas would howl with laughter.

Before the revival got started, the boys hung out on the corner killing a little time. They clowned around in the path of an evening sun that refused to give them any heat to buffer the briskness of December. But they didn't care. Unsupervised spurts of freedom overrode chilly discomfort any day. "C" was on a roll, center stage, so he kept at it. "What, brotha, yo' hair too good for some proud naps?" The cohorts roared, again. "Ain't you heard, black is beautiful, mannn?"

Daniel laughed out loud, but bled internally from the lacerations. He searched his innards for a proper comeback. None came. So instead, he initiated a playful shoving match, when he really wanted to punch "C" square-dead in his mouth. He imagined Charlie Winton's three front teeth, pinkish and hitting the pavement like chewed-up Chiclets.

The cohorts egged them on. The frenzy ballooned and entertained. Overcoats flew open, suit jackets waved about, shirttails appeared, and dust particles arose from the filthy pavement to cling to their church shoes, shined with ample strokes of Vaseline. Then something broke it up. Girls sauntered by.

Even with all that was going on and all that threatened to go on, the girls, three of them total, would not
slip by this tight ball of junior testosterone unnoticed.
The girls chose to walk through and not around. The
lion cubs froze and drooled over their prey. They delighted in the dance of bouncy curls coated with Ultra
Sheen and ear petals adorned with big silver hoops.
Their meticulous once-over flowed to the girls' femi-
nine lips glistening in the descending tangerine glow of
the evening sun. Their nostrils sniffed in a strawberry
scent.

In close proximity, close enough to reach out and
cop a feel, soft tan bosoms with brown puffy nipples
pointed in their direction. It didn't matter that the direct evidence of this womanhood lay secured beneath
fake-rabbit fur jackets, the cubs salivated over their
collective vision. Of course, there were bare female
parts, oval and supple, abounding and begging for
their attention. Male body parts stiffened, but the cubs
were confused as to what to do about it. For they were
not really the hunters; they were the hunted.

One of the strawberry-scented girls, the cutest one
in the bunch, broke stride. She zeroed in on her target,
pursed her red lips, and said, "Hi, Daniel. I like your
suit." Her fellow hunters giggled.

Just then, one of the deaconesses poked her head out
of the church door and called out. "Daniel," she yelled.
A whiff of cold air attacked her.

"Ma'am?" Daniel jerked and answered.

"Get in here, naw. Pastor's callin' ya."

"Yes, ma'am." Daniel's thoughts of girls bungeed to
the ground and the cord snapped. His priority shifted,
and he never looked back at his friends or the girls. He
sprinted for the church doors.

❭ "Bryan, you get in here too," the deaconess ordered. "Time for you to get with the choir, yo' sista Joyce said." Then the deaconess disappeared inside. Her nose was about to run.

"Yes, ma'am," Bryan said. He dropped his lusty thought as well.

"In fact," the old lady stuck her head back out and scolded now, "all you boys, quit cuttin' up and get yo'selves in here. Service is startin' soon." She waited until Daniel and Bryan got inside, then let the door slam behind her. The other boys and the three girls, running—their destination the same—fended for themselves.

Daniel possessed a broad toothy smile that fired off in anyone's direction with the slightest prompting. His smile had the power to sizzle a female heart within ten paces. It drew in the girls, young and old, the way a meat wagon could draw a parade of stray dogs. Big Rev recognized early that the girls dragged in their parents.

All the girls at school and at church had crushes on Daniel. All the boys volleyed to be around him so some of that good fortune could rub off on them. At least they could feed off Daniel's leftovers. Having Daniel featured on the revival program every night was simply a win-win situation—for everyone.

Daniel had already been preaching, a full fifteen minutes, and the church was hot and Holy Ghost rocking. Tiny silver circles dancing in the cogs of tambourines threaded the energy of the congregation. They shimmered and shook with the music like the strobe lights of a disco ball. Hand fans, the ones with the nice black family pictured on the front and the funeral home advertisement printed on the back, fluttered back and forth like a thousand checkered butterfly wings. And the choir, comprised of fifteen faithful die-hard members, wore themselves out singing "Oh Happy Day" and bopping a sleek Temptation Walk, Soul Train-style, up and down the tiny one-way aisles of the church. They were headed, to and from, the offering plates.

The choir kept at it a straight twenty minutes. They kept singing while the ushers and the congregation marched around. Daniel egged on the marching. "Oh yeah," he shot at the congregation. "Look at Sister Cherry marching. Blessed Jesus!" At the hearing of her name, Deaconess Cherry stopped mid-Soul Train Line, threw her head back, and let go a hallelujah scream that pierced the heavens. Her praise ignited a firestorm in two other deaconesses, which caused a domino effect, and the three church ladies became entranced in a Holy Ghost dance. In step, the hems of their white skirts jumped to the rhythm of the drums.

Big Rev stood up and looked approvingly at his son, Bryan, also fourteen, commanding the drums. "Praise the Lord, son," Big Rev shouted. That action ignited three more women, draped in white.

Sweat poured down Daniel's high-yellow forehead as he rippled across the feeble wooden pulpit. He screeched out his sermon at a feverish pitch. He kept his Bible crunched close to his powder-blue vest with his right hand and stroked the stuffy layers of air with his left hand. Somehow, Bryan Graystone knew to accent each one of Daniel's moves on cue. With perfect timing, Daniel pointed his finger at the ceiling—just like he'd seen Big Rev do a million times. Everyone recognized the signature move, and for that reason, they grew to affectionately call Daniel, "Little Rev." The evening was electric. Big Rev was proud.

Chapter Three

Order in the Court

1996

"Look at him. Sitting over there all smug . . . like he ain't done nothing wrong. Or better yet, looking like somebody did something to him. He's got that kind of nerve, you know!" Joyce Graystone said.

"Yeah, girl. But the poopies done hit the fan now. Preacher-man's goin' down! He 'bout ta pay through the butt, this time," said Phadra.

"Yep."

"I mean, homeboy's lookin' at some jail time. And we got ourselves a ringside seat for the festivities!" Phadra whispered her summation of the "festivities" to her girl, Joyce, who leaned heavily on every word.

The packed courtroom buzzed with murmurs, pro and con, on the outcome of the reverend's fate. What Phadra and Joyce had to say simply added a dash more salt to the soup. "Humph," Phadra whispered, looking around. "I'm sure glad we got here early. Look at all these people hungry for rump roast." They chuckled. Joyce's chuckle emerged awkwardly, Phadra noticed.

Phadra talked smack for fun, but she looked corporate. She came polished in a tailored black business blazer hugging a pencil skirt that cut at the knee. Underneath she wore a fitted white blouse that bragged tiny diamond cuff links. To divert potential eavesdroppers away from her brash commentary, she spoke quietly while bending to brush some imaginary lent off her stockings—coffee bean, a perfect match to her velvet-brown complexion. Phadra was aware that the folks around her craved to overhear what Joyce, Daniel's jilted lover, had to say about this latest turn of juicy events. Tidbits like that sat like steak and potatoes on a silver platter. Keeping it on the down-low, Phadra kept her head down while she flexed her tender heel in and out of her new midnight-black pumps.

Joyce's otherwise pouty lips contorted in a vile twist when she said, "Serves him right! That mutha—"

"Hey, hey, heyyyy," Phadra interrupted, cosigning her shock with a bug-eyed stare. "Joyce, sista-girl, don't let him make you lose yo' 'ligion!" She snuck a survey-peek around them both to make sure inquiring ears hadn't heard Big Rev's daughter, his oldest offspring, about to say the mother-of-all curse words in public.

"Sorry, girl. Guess when it comes to Mr. Look-So-Good—girrrl, you know I lose it." Joyce's eyes rolled upward, searching for some relief, but all she found was a throb.

"Yeah. Huh! Pretty-Daniel-what-dey-call 'em! Think dey gonna call 'em that in the pokey?" Phadra said. She laughed louder than she meant to.

"Girrrl, you jokin', but, I swear," Joyce said, "when I see that man . . . I just wanna stick my foot up in his be-hind for what he did to that church . . . for what he did to me. Shoot, for what he did to half these silly-behind women sittin' up in here, lookin' stupid, right now. Shoot, I *even* feel sorry for his silly-behind wife . . ."

Joyce wasn't finished, but her words cut off in her throat. She turned her head, clamped her lips, and blinked her eyes. She fought to control another menacing teardrop. Her fidgety fingers ransacked her purse to extract a tiny mirror. She'd forgotten that it boasted, "Solomon's Island is for Lovers" written in tiny script. Daniel had given it to her a million years ago. She stole a glimpse at her reflection to check her makeup and the firmness of her jelled-tight French roll. Joyce cleared her throat and smoothed the pleats of her lima bean-green dress. Her attire of the day was conservative and cold, on purpose. But it wasn't that big of a stretch from her normal attire. Between growing up in a strict Christian household and now teaching in a middle school filled with hormone-raging little boys, conservative *was* her look. On court day, she went all out with it—crisp and clean with no caffeine—emotionless was her goal. But things grew shaky from the start.

"Where is First Lady Harris?" Phadra asked, scanning the room.

"Huh, the sparrow woman?" Joyce snorted. "That bird flew the coop." They laughed.

Back at the defendant's table, The Reverend Daniel J. Harris sat purposely still, surveying his surroundings. *How come there are no windows?* he thought. He summed up the room to be a huge bland brown and tan rectangle, constructed in smooth oak wood, slathered with a caramel finish. *A coffin*, he thought. *I'm sitting in a coffin.* Harsh overhead globes of light were mounted in the ceiling like soldiers standing in formation. The light unjustly glared at him. He took a second to glare back, but he lost the contest. *I'm sitting in a coffin with lights*, he thought. *Great!*

Eric Johnson, his lawyer, sat dutifully next to him. Daniel watched him jot some crap on a yellow legal pad and slide it in front of him. It wasn't legible because it wasn't meant to be. He wanted to chuckle at its absurdity, but he couldn't because this was his life at stake. So he didn't. Every couple of minutes or so, Eric put his head to Daniel's and whispered some crap. Daniel complied with likewise crap to look conferring and discerning.

"You all right, man?" Eric asked. Daniel deliberated; then he leaned in, nodded, and answered, "Yeah, I'm all right."

Another time, Eric said, "What time is it anyway? What's taking that judge so long?"

Daniel's thought was *The heck if I know.* But he took a moment, studied the diamonds posing as numbers on his watch, straightened his tie, then leaned over and said, "I don't know. Beats me." He was committed to playing out this ritual for as long as it took, until the judge made her appearance.

Upon another survey of the courtroom, he took in the chatter behind him and he thought, *I'm sitting in a coffin with lights and a viewing stand.* He brushed his lapel and straightened his cuff links. "Well, at least I'm casket-ready," he mumbled.

"Huh? You say something, Rev?" Eric questioned.

"Huh? What? . . . No, no, I didn't say anything," Daniel said, slightly irritated.

I guess the bereaved and those doggone player-haters, Daniel rounded up in his head, *are darned anxious to see me lowered in the ground. Well, let's just get on with it,* he thought. *But I'll be darned if they're gonna see me squirm.* He repositioned himself in his chair.

"Huh? You say somethin', Rev?"

Startled from his thoughts, Daniel coughed. "No, no, naw, Eric, man, I didn't say anything."

Daniel cursed himself for giving in and appearing in court. All the other times, he finagled to send his flunkies as proxies. The mere thought of having to sit in this courtroom made him uncomfortable in his seat again. But the plain fact was that he'd spent all his wiggle room the moment the judge put her foot down and threatened him with contempt if he didn't show up this time, in person. So now, here he sat.

This is too much oak, he observed again. He sat erect in his chair. *No sense in looking guilty when I'm not.* His eyes took in the judge's bench, again, the spectators' pews in his peripheral, the counsels' chairs and the tables, even the hardwood floor. The one good thing about it was that it all looked new and polished. When Daniel looked up at the ceiling again he wasn't sure if it hung low, had gotten lower, or if it just felt low. Perspiration cemented the collar of his pristine white shirt to the back of his neck. He tugged at it, but it still choked him. The air grew tight. He became conscious of his tugging making him look guilty. So he stopped.

The sound of his mother's sniffles snuck up from behind. He worked to block it, but it moved in anyway and rested on his earlobes. It crept into his head and leaned on his last stable nerve. Daniel stiffened his gaze toward the judge's bench. *Oh, in the name of heav . . . No, I'm not turnin' around. I'm not. Heck no!* The sniffles got louder. *Doggone it! Here I am with my butt on the line—excuse me, Jesus—and she's beggin' for center stage. I frickin' can't believe it.*

When she got no response from Daniel, Rose Harris stood up directly behind her only child and gently leaned her top half over the wooden banister that separated them. The banister creaked with disdain, but she showed no fear. Every eye behind her lasered their interest in the fullness of her shapely buttock. She was used to the rays. It egged her on.

Still sniffling, Rose accidentally-on-purpose cradled Daniel's head deep into the crevice of her big bosom. His head fit like a glove. Somehow, she managed to also reach inside her bra, her bosom-pockets, to fetch a white lace hanky while she cradled. She patted her eyes. Rose also used the hanky to dab the tiny crystals on her son's forehead. It infuriated him because today, in his mind, perspiration symbolized guilt. She fanned her hanky, and her scent filled the air. The fragrance caused Daniel's nostrils to flare and inhale. Her scent diluted his fury and invoked a brief ecstasy. A fine mist of fresh baby powder weaved a cocoon around their heads. He grimaced to combat it. She took her hanky and gently patted his moist neck. Rose motioned like a geisha comforting her number one. It was her natural way.

For a second, Daniel wanted to collapse into his mother's bosom-fold, close his eyes, and suck his thumb. When the second vacated, he wanted to vomit. "Rose," he said in a stern whisper. He stopped. He took a breath. He forced a smile and started over. "Calm down, Mother," he said. "I know everything's going to be okay. Don't get yourself all upset over this." *Darn it*, he thought, *she played me anyway—always gotta get top billing.*

"Okay, baby," she whispered through pouty, peach-colored lips that tickled and tinted his right sideburn. Mission accomplished. She sucked up her last sniffle, tucked her hanky back into her bra, and sat down.

I'm finished with these bull-crap shows, Daniel's inner voice shouted. *As far as I'm concerned*—he wiped the back of his neck and rubbed the side of his face to erase his mother's touch—*whatever happens in this courtroom today will be my final act—anywhere*, he declared in his head. Then he leaned over to Eric as if Eric were privy to his thoughts and whispered, "I'm sick and tired of putting on shows, trying to make other folks happy, especially when I meant them good."

Eric nodded his discerned cluelessness.

All the intense chatter grinding behind Daniel migrated into white noise, then into nothing. He no longer cared what those familiar voices had to say. *Forget this crap*, he thought. Then something pricked him.

"Hey, Eric," Daniel said into a lean. His lawyer was thankful for another chance to banter.

"Yeah," Eric responded.

"I know Bryan and Big Rev aren't here. They're pissed at me. But is Joyce here? Is she here, man?"

"Yep. Over there, in the corner."

"Darn. How does she look? Who's she sitting with?"

"She's sitting with Phadra. And—"

"Shoot. That means they're crucifying me."

"Don't know about that, man. Looks like she's over there crying."

Daniel threw himself back in his chair. "Mannn, that's worse. You know I didn't mean to—"

"This isn't the time to go into all that," Eric said. "I know how you feel, but we've got to keep focused on the moment. All right?"

"Yeah, man. I hear you. But I can't face her, man. I can't even look in her direction."

It sickened Daniel to think about it, but that was over too. Any hope of squaring things with Joyce or ever holding her in his arms again or ever getting to know her son, it was over.

The bailiff announced, "All rise, please." The judge materialized from her chambers and ascended to her perch on the oak bench.

As she sat down, the bailiff announced her presence in regal fashion. "Her Honor Grace McPhever, the justice of the court." He then announced, "You may be seated."

After everyone settled down in their seats, the bailiff continued. "Will Counsel please state your barristers for the record?"

"Anthony L. Barone for the Prosecution," Barone said, standing.

Harris's counsel stood and responded, "Eric Milton Johnson for the Defense."

From the bench, Judge McPhever spoke, reading and flipping the pages of a thick manila file. Joyce and Phadra faded into the courtroom sea of extras as everyone fixated on the bench. They braced for words to spring from the judge's lips. She said, while alternating her stern eye from defendant to Prosecution to spectators, "This hearing is set to determine if there is sufficient evidence to proceed with an indictment and criminal trial in the matter of the People of the State of Maryland vs. Daniel Judah Harris."

A collective gasp heaved in the courtroom as if all this weren't real until that moment. Murmurs mounted until Judge McPhever beat them down with her gavel. Daniel remained iron-board stiff, determined not to betray his nerves. He sucked in a breath and held it as long as he could.

"Is the defendant ready, Mr. Johnson?" the judge asked.

"Yes, Your Honor," Eric responded.

"Is the Prosecution ready?" The judge looked over at the prosecutor.

"Yes, Your Honor," responded Anthony Barone.

"Then proceed, Mr. Barone. State your case."

Daniel exhaled, then repositioned himself to relieve the flood of humiliation that flushed his face with a ripe apple tint.

The courtroom was otherwise in an amazed hush. Phadra broke silence. "Joyce," Phadra called to her friend.

"What?" Joyce responded.

"You know, I hope Rev gets his comeuppance too. But you have to admit, he really does look kind of pitiful; maybe even a tad bit sorry. I mean, for real."

"Huh! See that, Phadra?" Joyce narrowed her eyes when she said it.

"See what?" said Phadra, playfully.

"See how you tryin' to make a Christian sista cuss all up in here again?" Joyce said. "The only thing that bastard is sorry for is the fact that he got caught with his mess all raggedy and got hauled into court for it. 'Cause you know that brother hates to be embarrassed."

"I know that's right," Phadra said, laughing.

Joyce grunted and said, "That mess, he cannot take. Imagine, stealing from the church like he did. And he don't want nobody to say nothin' about it but amen."

Phadra snickered and chimed in on what became a string of their sanctimonious barbs. "You outta order!" Phadra said in a mocking whisper.

Joyce returned in a mousy tone, "You stompin' on the pastor's vision."

"You messin' with the anointed!" Phadra shot back.

"You downright blasphemous!"

"You headed fo' damnation if you don't give up all yo' money!"

"That ain't no tithe if you still got gas money to get home!"

Phadra's right shoe fell off her foot. When she tried to retrieve it, she inadvertently pushed it under the row in front of her. That was funny too.

"Quit your laughing, naw," Joyce said. "You know you're being disrespectful to the Lawrd."

"Girl, you makin' my side hurt," Phadra whispered. "Question."

"What?" asked Joyce.

"Tell me where the Lawrd at?"

"He over there, ain't he?" Joyce said, jutting her chin in Daniel's direction. "He's over there in that tailored Brooks Brothers suit and them shiny shoes. He sittin' behind that desk, lookin' all cheesy with all his flunky bodyguards and his mama-ho flock behind him."

"Yep!" Phadra said. The barb jogged a memory. "And do you know that I ran smack-dab into Deacon Charlie Winston coming through the metal detector, and he didn't even speak to me? That two-faced bum dodged me."

It was incredible how Daniel and his disgusting disciples did things, Joyce summed up. Like the time they raised money three consecutive Sundays to blacktop the invisible parking lot in front of Daniel's imaginary new church.

"How many of you good brothers and sisters will show your faith by sacrificing a week's pay for God?" she remembered him preaching from the pulpit. Within minutes, bunches of faithful members, some crying, some shouting hallelujah, some waving their hands in the air to the Lord, ran down to the altar to literally throw their money at the shepherd's feet. Sacrifices of twenties, fifties, hundreds, thousands; week salaries, children's tuitions, car notes, dance lessons, dental visits, kidney transplants feathered down on the plush burgundy carpet, right before his wingtip shoes. *It still ain't nothing over there in that dusty lot, but some raggedy-behind gravel,* Joyce thought.

Then came her recollection of a stream of his in-crowd flunkies toting laughs and luggage through the airport when they traveled, three times, to the Holy Land. She almost lost it, again, when thoughts of how Daniel took his main ho, Crystal, to New Orleans to some bogus clergy convention. *The streets must have been crawling with loose tail that time. Huh!* The dagger cut deeper when her father went along. Anger mushroomed in her chest. Her eyes clouded. She fiddled with the pleats in her dress, again. Composure was a scarce commodity today.

"And Crystal ain't really a ho," Phadra said in jest.

"Huh?" Joyce responded. *Did Phadra read my mind?* she wondered.

Phadra went on with her commentary. "She ain't screwing nobody but Rev and her husband. And you know she's the best little executive assistant a pastor could ever have." Phadra laughed.

"You think?" said Joyce. Her eyes blinked more than they should have with that last remark. Her lips resembled an overworked rubber band stretched beyond its limits.

"They need to put that sleazy, greasy, high-yella, grinnin' fake negro under the jail," Joyce said through clenched teeth.

"Oooh, you ain't feelin' no grace and mercy today, is ya, girlfriend?" Phadra said, trying to unsalt the air. "You know the man said he was sorry to the congregation."

"Yeah," Joyce quipped, "being handcuffed in front of television cameras will make you do that. Shoot! I am such a fool. How could I fall for his lies like that? How did I let my guard down that low? I mean, to the ground. I don't understand."

Phadra put her arm around her friend and coaxed Joyce's chin to rest on her shoulder—forget the spectators. A pang of guilt surged Phadra's chest. It was the same guilt that had thinned their friendship over the years. She didn't mean to let their friendship drift like it did. But she felt guilty because her life came together so smoothly, while Joyce's life seemed to unfold into one drama after another. She offered a gentle squeeze of Joyce's hand to soothe her. From here on out, Phadra decided, she would be there for her girl, 100 percent.

"You're being too hard on yourself," Phadra whispered, straight-faced. "You loved him. That's how you did it. Girl, you know that love is stupid! Shoot, even I know that fool is irresistible." Joyce fought a laugh in the middle of her cry. Phadra continued, "And, seriously, you shouldn't forget, he loved you too. Probably still does. He's just unfamiliar with real love."

"Yeah, well, I hope he gets some *real* lovin' in jail," Joyce said. Phadra turned her head and stifled her laugh with both hands.

"Quiet down, please, or we're going to have to clear this courtroom."

Chapter Four

Rose and Daniel at the Crossroads

1960

Daniel's mother, Rose, worked at the Crossroads Bar, right where Fulton Avenue, Reisterstown Road, and Pennsylvania Avenue intersected. It was a Jewish-owned bar, but its clientele were the black folks who lived all around it. The bar buzzed extra when Rose showed up. The owner let Rose bring Daniel to work whenever she wanted because of it. This was a blessing, because otherwise, Daniel had learned to be home alone since the age of six. He was now ten. But all along, bringing her son to work was a job-related perk she earned, horizontally. Daniel was so cute. Down through the years he became the bar's little mascot. He had the run of the place, like he did on the weekends at his great-aunt's house and at church. When it got late, the barmaids made him a bed on the couch in the backroom.

Playing at the bar was fun for Daniel. It was dark and smoky, had a pool table with bright colored balls on it, and some old drunk or another stuffed him with candy and soda, especially if the motive was trying to get next to his mother.

The Crossroads' barmaids were works of living art. They dyed their hair ash blond or fireball red and layered it with sweet scented hairspray. The pretty brown women often adorned beehive hairpieces and pageboy wigs, fancying themselves dead ringers for the Supremes or the Marvelettes. The official dress was miniskirt, tight low-cut dresses and blouses, hip-hugger bell-bottoms, black fishnets or sky-blue windowpane stockings. Their full, soft, supple lips were kissed with lipsticks of candy-apple red, pale orange, and peachy pinks. All night long, Daniel's cheeks provided the canvas upon which they painted their colorful contoured smooches.

At Crossroads, Daniel had not one, but at least four mommas. When the barmaids weren't busy, they spent their breaks picking him up, jostling him on their hips, or cuddling him just because. He was their living doll baby. Daniel's little head cradled atop soft bosoms that felt like warm cotton balls. They looked like frosty giant scoops of ice cream—chocolate, caramel tinted, or vanilla bean, cresting over their cones. Sometimes Daniel purposely buried his nose in the warm creases of cleavage because it smelled so powdery good. It was a perfect place to nap. He loved barmaid kisses and perfumed hugs. His memory of them lingered long after his life left them behind.

Daniel's dinners consisted of soda, potato chips, popcorn, or takeout fried chicken and french fries from Louie's Southern Shack next door. Daniel's barmaid mommas shared no real clue about what was good for him. Unwittingly, they cussed, fought, or necked with the customers, right in front of him. They blew cigarette smoke in his face, and when he was too wound up to fall asleep on the backroom couch, "Well, give him a little Budweiser," one would say to another. "That'll calm him down."

But when Daniel got a little older, around eight or so, he began noticing stark differences between what he heard and witnessed at church and what he saw at the Crossroads. The barmaids were still soft and pretty, their bosoms still smelled powdery good, and they still treated him nice (their "little man," they called him). But these women were bad, according to what Big Rev said. They drank, smoked, and cursed. They paraded their body parts and let men touch all over them.

In Sunday School, Daniel clung to every word. He twisted and rearranged his thoughts to find a clear road out of his confusion. *Is my mother going to hell?* If he was to believe what he heard at church, then yes, to hell was just where his mother and those sweetly scented barmaids were headed. "How can that be?" he asked God in a bedtime prayer.

One evening at the bar, Daniel, barely ten years old, raised himself up, and to everyone's shock, he kicked a man in his shin. He swung at him too because he spied the man reaching over the bar's counter, grinning and stuffing rolled-up dollar bills down the front of his mother's blouse, right down in her crease! Then the man reached out his hand and slyly cupped his mother's powdery breasts. Daniel's little face contorted as he felt his bodily fluids boil over. His mother chuckled and whispered at the man through a smile. *Maybe she just doesn't know any better. She's helpless*, he thought. *She needs me.* Before he could think more on it, Daniel kicked the man in the shin and lunged. It took three guys to pull Daniel away from the intoxicated man. It was like pulling a clawing cat from the limb of a tree. Finally, a huge pair of hands whirled him around in a circle, as if he were the weight of a feather, then bum-rushed him to the front door of the bar. In a cocoon of laughter, some man plopped his protesting little body outside on the cracked front cement stoop like a rag doll.

"Naw, you calm down, little man," the man said, still chuckling.

"Get off me," Daniel shouted, humiliated and tearing up with anger. When Rose appeared, she looked as if she'd been laughing too. The tears he struggled to hold at bay avalanched down his cheeks. She sat down beside him on the stoop, drew him close, and branded his cheek with an orange-blossom kiss. He wanted to pull away, but lacked the will.

"Naw, c'mon baby," she said. It was a whisper with breath that smelled like Christmas candy. He whimpered and rested on her pillow-soft chest. She pulled a white lace hanky out of her bra and from it came a wisp of white crystals that smelled baby powder sweet. Rose gently dabbed her son's tears away.

"What got into you? Why you actin' like that?" Rose said to him, sweetly.

"Momma, that man touched you. I . . . He shouldn't touch you like that."

"Boy . . . Manny don't mean me no harm. You see, I ain't hurt none. Daniel, you shouldn't disrespect grown folk like that," said Rose, trying to convince her son.

Daniel yelled, "Aunt Cille and Big Rev said no man should touch you like that. Aunt Mattie said it too."

Instantly irritated, Rose lashed out. She shouted, "Aunt Cille this. Aunt Mattie that. Naw, you listen here, boy, *I'm* yo' momma, and whether you know it or not, I know how ta take care of you and me. So you don't have ta worry, okay? Naw, you carry yo' little high-yella tail back in there and say you sorry."

"No!" Daniel yelled.

Rose's nostrils flared at his insubordination. "Then you can get on home right naw. Here." She reached

down in her bra for the house key. "And get. And don't
do no stoppin' along the way, you hear?"

Daniel snatched the key. He jumped up off the stoop
and stomped off without looking back.

"You hear me, boy?" Rose yelled again in his direction, but got no response. She didn't expect one. She
stood at the door and watched him stomp his way beyond a line of pristine white marble steps that belonged
to each dingy row house he passed. She watched him
until he turned the corner; then she retreated inside the
bar, shaking her head.

That night, Daniel stayed up to watch for his mother
coming home. He was enraged all over again to spy his
mother and Manny zigzagging down the street, chuckling, whispering arm-in-arm and slobbering all over
each other. When he heard the screen door screech
open and the rusty doorknob turn, he sprinted back to
his bed that doubled as the living-room couch. Their
heated moans and groans staggered by him and into
his mother's bedroom. They fell onto the squeaky box
spring behind the closed door. The noise kept up for
some time.

The next day was Saturday, and he couldn't wait for
one of the deacons to pick him up and take him back to
Aunt Mattie and Aunt Cille's house. When he got there,
he told them what happened. Hurt was in his green-
apple eyes. Anger was in his voice. The sisters angered
too. They'd gotten bits and pieces of the night-visitor
story before, when the boy was too young to really
know what he divulged. But this telling was purpose-
ful and filled with details. "I wanna live here with you,"
Daniel cried.

"Let's see what we can do," Aunt Cille said, pulling
him into a hug. "Let's see what your momma says."

That Sunday after service, they all ate dinner at
Miss Annie's Soul Food Kitchen. Miss Annie's peach
cobblers could soothe anyone's hurts and solve most
world problems. When he got back to his aunts' house,
Daniel changed out of his church clothes and rushed
outside to play. "C", and Bryan, and the boys were on
the porch, antsy and already calling his name. "C'mon,
mannn, what's taking you so long?" one of them yelled
out. The others erupted in laughter. The screen door
slammed and Aunt Cille made a call to Rose.

"Hello, Rose?" Aunt Cille worked to sound gentle.

"Yeah?" Rose was curt.

"It's Aunt Cille."

"I know. How you doin'?" Rose sounded monotone
on purpose.

"Fine."

"How you?"

"Fine."

"Well, listen, Rose, I'll get right to it." Aunt Cille's
gentleness was slipping.

"Yeah?"

"Rose, you know me and yo' aunt Mattie loves you
and we prayin' for ya, chile."

"Yeah, Aunt Cille, I know. But I don't know if I can
make it to chur—"

"Hush, chile, that ain't what I'm talkin' 'bout, though
you know you need ta go. I wanna talk to ya 'bout Little
Daniel. How y'all been doin'?"

Naked, with her half of the sheet pulled up just
over the bridge of her breasts, Rose pulled herself up
against the headboard of her bed. She banged her head
against it in anger for ignoring her first impulse not to
answer the phone. *Crap!*

"Oh, I know what this is about, naw," Rose said,
rudely. "He told y'all about Manny, right?"

"Lawd, girl, you shouldn't have Daniel hangin' round that bar all the time. I done told you that."

"Aunt Cille, did Daniel tell you how he acted? He kicked and hit Manny for no reason. And if that wasn't enuf, he sassed me. But you needn't get in it. I'm his momma. I can handle it." Rose nervously wrapped the light blue phone cord around her fingers as she talked.

"I'm sho' you can, Rose. And I know you his momma. I waz there when you had him. I waz just wonderin', naw, since you there doin' the best you can—raisin' him and all—all by yo'self—while you tryin' ta work—why don't you let the boy come 'n' stay wit' yo' aunt Mattie and me?"

Aunt Cille stammered on quickly before Rose could respond. "I mean, fo' good, Rose. Fo' good. Let the boy stay here and go to school up here and all. I mean, you welcome too, but if you don't wanna, you should at least let him come on."

Rose finally got a word in. "Where all this come from, huh?" she said, not really caring for an answer.

"Listen, Rose, the boy knows and plays with all the kids 'round here, and," she said for emphasis, "he friends with Tommy Graystone's kids at church. So he just asked if he could live here—that's all."

Rose's gut twinged. There was silence on the phone for the seconds she needed to grab for her cigarettes. She knew she didn't treat the boy right. The guilt ate her up alive, but she loved him. Up until now, she thought he'd never ever ask, outright, to leave her side—for good. His stays with his aunts were always temporary—on the weekends so he could go to church with them. It really only took Rose seconds to come to what was best. Besides, Manny had all but moved in anyhow. He didn't care much for children—evident in the abandonment of his own three children, and wife, living just around the corner. And after that fiasco at the bar, she knew for sure that Daniel and Manny weren't going to make it under the same roof.

"Aunt Cille?" Rose called out.

"Yes, chile."

"Daniel can stay with y'all for a little while. I don't care."

"Praise the Lawd, girl," Lucille exclaimed in a sigh of relief.

"Yeah, yeah," Rose shoved her words under her breath. The phone call was over.

Manny, ashy brown and musty, dragged his erectness to the bathroom. Rose crawled over the mess of bunched-up sheets and blankets to sit on the edge of the bed. Hunched over in a fetal position, she rocked and hugged her torso, trying to think. *What in the world have I done so terrible to bring me here? That little half-breed negro is just like his daddy, after all,* she thought. It caused her to rock and sob for the next five minutes it took for her to remember the half-pint bottle of Old Grand Dad lying on the floor next to her bed.

Manny reappeared looking like a satisfied zombie. He offered no notice of her predicament, her red, swollen eyes—no more than a yawn, a fart, and the intention to reclaim his spot in her bed. He fell in, yanked his portion of the covers, turned his back to Rose, and called hogs with the back of his throat. The rest of the afternoon slipped away in a fog of tears, leftover sex, and drunkard slumber until she was due back at the Crossroads.

Daniel refused to go to his mother's house to say good-bye when Deacon Smith made the trip to get his clothes at Mother Cille's request. If she wanted to see him, she had to come to the church to do it, which meant that Daniel saw his mother in his dreams more than he did in flesh and blood.

Chapter Five

It's a Thin Line between Love and Heartbreak

1969

At seventy-nine, Mattie Tawny was considered one of the church mothers at The Bible Deliverance Church of God. She and her sister, Cille Spears, who was seventy-six, watched Reverend Tommy Bryan Graystone grow up in the neighborhood. They even babysat him for his momma, Valdesta. So in 1958, when Tommy came to start a congregation right there on Garrison Boulevard, at his pleadings, the two well-respected sisters, active in community projects, left their church across town on Fulton Avenue to join his.

The sisters lived right around the corner from the church. Tommy knew that if he could get them to join his church, others would follow and bring their families. And it worked. The church gradually swelled from about thirty constants to seventy-five, to one hundred, and then to its present 300.

The Spears sisters were born in the early 1890s in Charleston, South Carolina, on a quartered-off farm their daddy sharecropped. It was a time when small white farmers were doing a little better than they had before, but little had changed for black farmers and blacks as a whole. The farm was just outside of town, north of the legendary slave market that stood in the town's center as a treasured monument to Charleston's heritage. Mattie and Lucille walked by the slave market every day on their way to school. Sometimes they'd even stop to play on its auction block. The splintered wooden platform, upon which beaten and abused black bodies were premiered as chattel, still hung on to its thick black iron chains. The chains were firmly bolted to its base and coiled atop the dusty-red earth like huge, thick black snakes.

Lucille never married. But when she was eighteen, she was in love with a boy named Joseph Deans. She very much planned to marry him. That was back in 1911.

On a sizzling August night, Joe, who had just turned twenty, was brutally attacked and lynched for punching out a white boy. As he walked along a desolate patch of dirt road, the boy, about his age, taunted him, seemingly on the drunken whim of having nothing else better to do.

"Boo, nigra-boy. What you doin' out afta dark? Pretendin' to be a spook?" His words slurred and hiccupped a smelly laugh that was rye and evil. Joe ignored him at first. He shoved his hands in his pockets, kept his head down, and kept moving. But smelly breath blocked his path and the white boy poked him in the forehead with his index finger. Then the boy slapped him. Joe, rebounding, took a quick look around, then punched the white boy in his mouth. The unexpected force knocked the boy on his behind. Joe attempted to take flight, but three more white guys, laughing and snarling, sprung out of nowhere.

"Negro, you gotta nerve attackin' my brotha fo' no reason," one of them said. Only the sound of crickets and lightning bugs abounded. "Give a answer when a man is talkin' to ya," he said twice.

"You gonna get it, naw, boy," said another.

Joe was angry, young, and virile. He steamed. Dust flew up around them during the brawl. For every wild punch one of those wiry white boys swung, Joe landed two solid ones, which was evident by the black and blue badges of honor and busted lips the three Hainey boys and their cousin proudly wore for more than two weeks after the incident.

The Haineys owned the general store in town. The Hainey clan ran the post office, the sheriff's office—and the court.

That night, those Hainey boys dragged Joe into the woods and beat him unconscious. The next day, a couple of little colored boys, barely seven years old, who lived on the farm next to where Joe's family lived, were in the woods searching for blueberries. They ran up on Joe's stiff body hanging from an oak tree. His eyelids were maroon red, puffy, and permanently sealed shut. Drips of blood, until there were no more, had creased a path in both of his dark brown cheeks. The paths journeyed down his chin. His jaw, ripped apart, hung open and broiled in the midday sun.

Now—the young man—who days earlier had celebrated his birthday and was filled with plans of maybe leaving his family's farm to find fortune elsewhere— hung silent, drained of his life. His body was bruised and battered all over. It was nude from the waist down, missing his penis, and covered in bits of twigs and grass and dried blood. Ripped flesh bore curdled belt buckle prints. Flies and gnats continued their feast, winged scavengers circled overhead, while at ground zero a horrid image forever branded the innocence of two young boys just scouting for blueberries.

The two little boys stood there for several paralyzing moments before their stick legs empowered them to run. They screamed out their discovery in all directions. As soon as the grown folks heard their screams, they knew. That dreaded thing had happened once more. Decades later, Mattie and Lucille would shutter and cry the first time they heard the famed singer Billie Holiday label their Joe as "strange fruit." The pungent phrase referred to the lynchings in the South.

Lucille was devastated. She became hysterical in her grief. She demanded to ride with Joe's father to retrieve his body, but her parents, shaken and flooded with fear, held her down in the Carolina dust of their front yard. They wouldn't let her go. She pounded the earth and screamed to the heavens. She wailed and wailed for what seemed like hours until her soul emptied. The commotion drew a small crowd of colored neighbors. Their hearts bled for Lucille. They owned a direct line to her pain. They stood paralyzed, compelled to watch and weep and ask God two questions: why, and why, again.

The night Joe was murdered, he was on his way home from Lucille's house and unbeknownst to both of them, their brief stolen moments under her momma's apple tree seeded a child. Lucille's folks loved Joe as much as Lucille did, but when they discovered that their daughter was in the family way, they forced her to go to the midwife in the next town to get the baby pulled out of her.

"Joe is gone," her momma tried to reason with her. Her father held her tight. "You, lookin' at his baby for the rest of yo' life, is prison, girl. You'll never move on," her mother said. But the young girl's heart never left that moment anyway. Lucille Spears never loved again. She never married. She'd never bear a child.

In Charleston, visions of Joe Deans's lynching hovered everywhere. It was just too much to take. Shortly after the incident, Mattie and Lucille moved to Baltimore because it was northbound. Because it sounded friendlier. Because their parents told them to. A nice porter they met on the train directed Mattie and Lucille to a boarding house for nice young colored women on Pennsylvania Avenue. The proprietor helped them find domestic work.

Twelve years rolled by. Lucille was thirty years old and still in the same woman's employ. It was uptown, in the Forest Park neighborhood in Northwest Baltimore. The elderly white woman, Ms. Pat, had no family close by and lived alone. Ms. Pat did have a lawyer son who lived in New York. He didn't visit much. So, behind closed doors, Lucille became Ms. Pat's family. When Ms. Pat died in the spring of 1923, Lucille was shocked to find out that she had willed her home and all that was in it to her. The three-story Victorian house, skirted front to back with a roomy porch, was more than Lucille could have ever dreamt of living in, much less owning.

It stood on Liberty Heights, not far from Garrison Boulevard. But would Ms. Pat's wishes ever become a reality, she wondered. The area was lily white, except for servants, nannies, and street cleaners moving through and about. It had even been written into the bylaws of the district that only the "desirable" people would be allowed to purchase homes in the area. "Desirable" was code for white Christian families. Not until the stock market crash in 1929 and the lean times that followed would realtors relax their rules to allow a few Jews to move in.

But Ms. Pat's son seemed to be oblivious to all that. He just wanted to be rid of the house and its worries. The transfer went smoothly, without the mention of color or the appearance of Lucille in the flesh at the reading of the will. The neighbors either seemed to go along with the pretense of Lucille keeping house for Ms. Pat's son, or, maybe, they really believed it. Lucille always said it was her prayers that made it all happen. The good Lord owed her one for allowing her to lose Joe. The area remained lily white until the 1950s, when a prominent black high school principal moved in and broke the color barrier. Lucille and Mattie read about it in the newspaper as they sipped on tea sitting on their front porch. It made the front page of the *Baltimore Afro*.

Mattie Spears married Darius Tawny, that porter she'd met on the train the day she arrived in Baltimore. She was twenty-three, and he was twenty-seven when they married. After he steered her on where to live, whenever he was in town, he'd show up on her doorstep, hopeful to run into her. A friendship kindled and over time, love bloomed. The couple rented a cold-water flat over a grocery store on McCulloh Street and grew busy with living and making life do. But Darius was away most of the time, so when Lucille got the house, she persuaded them to come live with her. They did.

The Tawnys had fifty good years together, but they never had any children. Nobody knew why, exactly, except to say that the sisters were so closely connected, Mattie's body just couldn't conceive something that Lucille would never have. Mr. Tawny died of lung cancer in 1963. He was seventy-seven.

Over the years, as the sisters watched the area turn from white to black, they doted on almost every child that crossed their path, always doling out freshly baked cookies and holiday candy. The sisters babysat most of them, consoled some of them (and their parents when the occasion called for it), and vouched for some of them in court when needed. "That chile wasn't born to be no thief," the sisters told the judge, "and that's not what he is, neither."

When the sisters came to The Bible Deliverance Church of God, they brought Daniel along with them. Mother Tawny and Mother Spears were Daniel's great-aunts on his momma's side.

In 1955, Daniel's mother, Rose Harris was a seventeen-year-old Coppertone beauty. She possessed full lips, innocent brown eyes, and soft dark brown pigtails that danced on her shoulders. Her beauty came packaged in a tight hourglass frame that commanded attention early when she was just thirteen. She was the youngest and the prettiest of the three girls her parents birthed and reared. Rose was sent up north from Charleston because she got herself pregnant. The sisters took Rose in, no questions asked.

Rose moved in with the sisters when she was six months pregnant and starting to show. Three and a half months later, she had her baby boy at Providence Hospital, the colored hospital on Division Street. Lucille was the first one to hold her precious great-nephew.

"Nurse, I'll take tha baby," Aunt Cille said when it was apparent that Rose didn't want to look at him. Lucille gave a fragile smile and held out her arms to receive God's gift, tightly wrapped in a pastel blue blanket. With care, she pushed back the blanket to get a good look at his face. She softly cooed and the sleeping baby responded by yawning and opening his eyes. She gasped. "Oh, Lawrd, chile, you see this baby's eyes! You sho' they give you the right one?"

"Yeah," was all the answer Rose could muster. Tears moistened her pillow.

"Huh, I swear befo' God in heaven, this chile been here befo'. His eyes are like glass. They cut a hole right through ya. And why they green?" Aunt Cille's question just circled the ozone, unanswered.

Lucille asked Rose to name him Daniel. It was Joe's middle name, but she explained to Rose that the name "Daniel" meant "God is my judge." Rose really didn't care, so she did what her Aunt Cille asked. Lucille forgave the stark stare of baby Daniel's green-apple eyes and rocked her buttercream bundle close to her heart.

It took no time for Rose's young body to boomerang back into its voluptuous shape, and she began stepping out and tasting the city whenever she could. She loved the attention—the top billing—her body commanded whenever she strolled through the Lexington Market on errands for her aunts or walked up and down North Avenue or on Pennsylvania Avenue, the mecca of black nightlife. But getting out at night was an increasing challenge for Rose because she had to come up with some lame wholesome excuse for going out. Sometimes, a boy from church would ask her out and that was okay. But otherwise, her aunts always wanted her at home or in church with them. When Rose went to church, she felt stared at. The boys salivated. The girls got nervous, jealous, and curious. If true friendship came, Rose was so mistrusting, she'd blow it off. And the would-be friend informed the other girls, "Shoot, she think she's too cute to mess with us. Forget her then."

Things got to a point where Rose could no longer stomach her aunts' strict house rules. And she was jealous of the way they just took over Daniel like she wasn't even his mother. So, she got a job as a barmaid in a little dive on Druid Hill Avenue and rented out a third-floor room in a row house on North Avenue, nearby. She was on her own, doing for herself, but her independence and pangs of responsibility fluctuated.

Over the years, Rose's quick temper got her fired from one bar or another or she'd quit before she thought it through. In between her employment dry spells and her shacking up with some dude to pay the bills, she'd gladly hand Daniel off to Aunt Cille and Aunt Mattie, especially if the dude didn't feel like playing daddy. They were always ecstatic to take him. In fact, even when Daniel was with Rose, they insisted that he come spend the weekends with them. "'Cause, you know that boy needs ta be in church on Sundays," one of the aunts would preach to Rose—on the constant. "And you too, Rose, honey!" they threw in every time they could, but Rose wasn't trying to hear it. The sisters would send someone down to pick Daniel up and bring him to their house. Rose's wild reputation had grown legendary. So whoever the deacon/errand boy was who got the assignment—he was eager to do it. It held the possibility of getting to make a little time with Rose or at least peer into her lust-driven life, if only for a moment.

Once Rose moved out from under her aunts' roof, she didn't have any inclinations about going to church.

"Aunt Mattie, thanks for invitin' me to Women's Day. But you know I can't make it. Ahhh, but as soon as I can get myself together, Auntie, I'll be over there."

"Well, okay, chile. You know Daniel will be reading the scrip—" *Click.* Mattie heard the phone go dead on the other end.

Most Sunday mornings, Rose was so hung over that her body didn't even budge until around one o'clock in the afternoon. "Church is a place for good folks," she said to herself after she slammed the phone down. She rubbed her head in anguish. *Not fo' folks who sleep around, drink, and curse.* Rose wasn't good enough for God, and she didn't see a change coming any time soon. Her fate was sealed, she thought. But her son was another matter. He was pure.

Even though Rose was only seventeen at the time she conceived, she actually believed that she and twenty-one-year-old Jud Hainey were in love. Sometimes—caught alone and sober in her cold-water flat—loneliness drew Rose unwillingly into the hell-draped chambers of her mind. Sour images of their lovemaking flushed her body. Orgasmic tingles, holdovers from their sweaty youthful bodies rippling on a dingy mattress that Jud kept tucked away in his father's dusty storeroom, conquered her, wholly. An even cheesier feeling followed the memory of having her torso bent over the hard metal edge of a display counter. That happened when he couldn't even wait to get her to the semen-stained mattress. Her buttocks bare, legs spread wide, and panties pushed down to her ankles. Jud's heaving body, pumping and panting on top of her. Everything he persuaded her to do came packaged in proposals of marriage and promises of a new life.

"I don't wanna do 'dis," she sometimes pleaded and whined like a wounded dove. The store was dark. Only the streetlights lit their silhouettes rhythmically melted together in a honey-vanilla swirl.

"C'mon, baby," Jud moaned, clawing Rose's body and panting like a thirsty dog. "We luv each other, don't we?"

"Yeah," Rose responded, feebly.

"We gettin' married, ain't we? Or did you change yo' mind?"

"No, no, Jud, I ain't changed my mind. You?"

"Of course not, baby. Well, you gotta do dis-here thin' fo' me. We gonna make each other happy, gurl."

Silence conveyed compliance. Dust and sparks flew about them.

Why such treatment and disrespect of her body and soul, she wondered in retrospect, weren't clues to his lies she'd never know. Jud promised her that they only needed to wait a year or so until she turned eighteen before they could tell everybody.

"Then we can get married and run away to New York or Philadelphia or someplace where colored and white folks can live in peace," Jud told her, time and time again.

"They're places like that, you think?" Rose always quizzed her lover in the manipulated afterglow.

"Oh yeah, Rose, honey, of course dey is," Jud whispered in her ear—she remembered of a particular time. She remembered nestling underneath his body sweat on that dingy, dirty mattress, crammed in that dusty storeroom.

In the clarity of hindsight, she reached for her cigarettes. Lighting up, inhaling with force, then exhaling white puffs of revelation, she whispered to herself, "If only I could have known better, I wouldn't have wasted it like that." Then she made a mental note to polish off the last of that pint of Old Grand Dad sitting on the kitchen table.

Chapter Six

Don't Ask/Don't Tell . . . Don't Work

1969

Why in all Daniel's years hadn't anybody talked about his father? Daniel's buttercream hue didn't match up with his mother's Coppertone skin or his chestnut-colored aunts, he knew. To him, he was a little off from what he should have been. His green eyes and straight hair were different, as was his sharp nasal features. His lips weren't as textured as he would have liked. When Daniel inspected himself in the bathroom mirror, it was like looking at half an image, a puzzle hammered with pieces that didn't quite fit. Where did the ill-fitting pieces come from?

Home from the revival meeting where he preached his first full sermon, Daniel said, using an even tone, "Aunt Mattie."

"Yes, chile."

"Who's my daddy?" he asked.

Aunt Cille, complaining about her stiff joints, had already headed upstairs to bed. Daniel, still wearing his coat, and his aunt Mattie, stood alone. The moment treaded in dead silence. Daniel kept his eyes peeled on his aunt's face during the full reign of dicey minutes, carefully scrutinizing every second for clues. He learned that from Big Rev and Mattie knew it.

"Who's my daddy, Aunt Mattie?" Daniel asked again. "Where is he?"

"Listen, Daniel, that's a very important question and one you deserve to have answered. But it's too late, naw, to talk about it. Can't it wait 'til in the morning?"

Daniel remained silent, scrutinizing.

"I will answer yo' question," Mattie said, "but not ta'night. So you go on and get ready fo' bed. It's late." She framed his face in her hands and kissed his forehead, then headed up the stairs, purposely not looking back.

In her bedroom, instead of going to bed, she eased herself into the huge maple rocking chair Mr. Tawny made for her on their tenth wedding anniversary. She rocked herself in prayer and consultation with God about what to do. *What can I tell that precious boy? I don't want to tell him, I don't know—that maybe nobody knows,* were the thoughts that swirled in her mind and heart.

Sunrise came in a rush. Daniel got up and left for school. His aunt Mattie was noticeably absent.

Aunt Mattie straggled in the kitchen for her regular cup of tea and Cream of Wheat. Aunt Cille had finished one cup of tea and polished off her oatmeal.

"Good morning, sista; rough night, huh?" Aunt Cille said with a chuckle.

"Yeah," Aunt Mattie replied with a sigh. She milled about the sun-drenched kitchen kind of disoriented until she spied her favorite cup already sitting on the counter. Aunt Cille had put it there.

The aunts always saw their Daniel off to school. Daniel had been used to getting up and out on his own since the first grade when he lived with his mother. But at his aunts' house, he grew to expect a hot breakfast, if he wanted it, and crisp ironed clothes to wear.

Aunt Mattie sipped her tea in silence this morning, and Aunt Cille took notice.

"What's wrong, sis?" she asked.

"Daniel asked me something last night—actually, it was this morning befo' we went to bed. And Cille, I kain't think of nothin' else."

Aunt Cille quit stirring her second cup of tea to make eye contact across the kitchen table.

"Mattie, what is it?"

"Daniel asked me who his father was."

"Well, we knew this day would come," Cille said.

"He asked me who was he, where was he, and why we ain't never talked 'bout him befo'."

"Mattie, what in God's name did you say?"

"Well, I stammered and stuttered. Then I came up wit' tellin' him it was too late to start talkin' about it right then. I promised we would talk about it today."

"What? Well, what you gon' do?" Cille asked. "We don't know who his daddy is—do we? I mean, Mattie, do you know?"

"No, but I'm gonna find out," Aunt Mattie said. She took a ride over to Rose's to do just that. One of the church deacons drove Aunt Mattie over and waited for her in his car.

Face-to-face, Rose said, "Aunt Mattie, you gotta know that I loved Daniel's daddy. I loved him. He told me he loved me too."

"Oh, I know that, chile. I know," Aunt Mattie said, gently patting Rose's back to comfort her.

"He promised to marry me, and I believed him." Rose's tears drenched Aunt Mattie's shoulder, and she stroked her niece's hair as they sat on Rose's tattered sofa.

❭ There were fresh tears held at bay all this time. Now, the flood was full force—not even her flashbacks felt this bad. In all this time, Rose hadn't shared any of this with anyone—not a living soul. She was so ashamed and so hurt. She couldn't tell anyone—not even her sisters back home in Charleston. She never talked to them anyway. "They so uppity," was Rose's description of them to anyone who asked why she never seemed to talk about her family. She especially couldn't confide in her parents, who at the time drilled her constantly to find out who the boy was.

Rose's father was hurt, disappointed, and enraged. He would have tried to kill anyone who violated one of his precious daughters, black or white. Rose knew that. She also knew that since Jud was white, her daddy could have been killed too. And she was ashamed to even think it, but she also wanted to protect Jud. She loved him. Maybe things would change. Maybe he would come after her. So, she refused to tell and her frustrated, disgusted parents shipped their daughter up north to her aunts Cille and Mattie. Rose knew she wouldn't tell; she'd never tell anyone. It never even occurred to her that one day her son would want to know.

"I was so young," Rose said, "so stupid."

"Naw, chile, that was a long time ago. I knowed yo' heart was in pieces when you landed on our do'step. Heartbreak ain't nothin' new to a woman," Aunt Mattie said, comforting her niece with the truth.

Finally, Rose's sobbing settled to a slow trickle of tears. Aunt Mattie pulled a powdery scented handkerchief out of her bra and wiped Rose's cheeks. Weary from the stress of it all, Rose allowed herself to be rocked by her aunt. Aunt Mattie started her familiar humming and stroked Rose's hair and neck. The rocking and sweet melody covered Rose's heart like a warm, thick quilt.

"Chile, who is Daniel's daddy? Who fathered yo' baby?"

"His name was Jud Hainey," Rose blurted out.

The rocking stopped. Aunt Mattie knew the name well, *but it couldn't be*, she thought. *He got ta be a old man naw.*

"Jud Hainey? Hainey? You mean the white Haineys in Charleston—what owned the grocery sto'?"

Rose lifted off her aunt's dampened chest and stared at her inquisitively. She didn't expect Aunt Mattie to know who he was.

"It was the Five and Dime store, and the grocery store, but yes, Aunt Mattie, that's his family. Jud helped manage his family's Five and Dime store in town. I worked at the store after school, sweeping up and dusting off the merchandise," Rose explained. Then she realized what all this was referencing, and she looked down at the floor in shame. "Yes, he was white," Rose said, waiting for her aunt's disapproval.

Aunt Mattie grabbed Rose's shoulders and looked directly into her face. "He rape you, chile? That ole man rape you? Tell me the truth."

Rose's lip started quivering again. "No, Aunt Mattie, I told you I loved him, and he loved me too. He promised to marry me."

Aunt Mattie drew Rose close to her chest again and simply stared off into space toward the front window. Now she was the one engulfed in flashbacks. Rose's living room transformed into her parents' front yard on the dreadful day they found out that Joe Deans was lynched. Images of the horrible way those Hainey boys gloated in the days after materialized. Jud Hainey was one of those Haineys who killed the only man her dear sister ever loved. They destroyed her sister's life forever. Could that really be what her dear niece said—that Jud Hainey was Daniel's father?

"Who his daddy?" Aunt Mattie asked. "I mean, Jud Hainey, he got ta be old enough to be yo' granddaddy."

Rose was puzzled by the statement. "Aunt Mattie, you talkin' 'bout Jud's granddaddy or maybe his daddy. You heard of them? All them is named the same—Judah Hainey," Rose said. Aunt Mattie's heart sunk. "My Jud was Jud, the third. He was twenty-one. I was seventeen. Remember when I came to live with you?"

Oh my God, Aunt Mattie screamed in her mind. That boy's granddaddy was the one who killed Joe Deans. "Oh my God!" This time her outburst was audible.

"What?" a frightened Rose shouted back. Aunt Mattie couldn't answer. She just started squeezing Rose tighter and rocking her intensely—to the point that it was uncomfortable. This felt worse than when she was trying to digest Daniel's question. Aunt Mattie felt dead inside. How in the world could the boy she and Cille cherished—how could he have that killer's blood coursing through his veins? Suddenly, the total picture washed clear. Daniel looked like the Haineys. He had Jud Hainey's eyes, nose, and mouth. Now, the portrait was complete. *When Cille finds out this news, it's gonna kill her*, Aunt Mattie thought.

Aunt Mattie gently kissed Rose's forehead, lifted her off her chest, and got up to gather her things. She walked toward the window. Rose was in total befuddlement now. Aunt Mattie stared down at Deacon Joe's car parked at the curb. Quiet tears now streamed down her cheeks.

How can I tell Cille this? She wondered. *How will Cille look at Daniel from now on?*

"We can't always rule over our hearts. But I ain't gon' lie to you, chile," Aunt Mattie said with her back turned to Rose, "this-here thing is bad—really bad, and it's gonna take all our faith to pull us up out of this. I

tell ya, chile, I don't know what the Lord wants us to
make of all this. But I tell you this, li'l girl, it's time you
find yo' faith in the Lord—'cause you gonna need it—fo'
Daniel's sake, fo' yo' sake, and fo' yo' aunts' sake. You
hear want I'm tellin' ya?"

"Yes, ma'am," Rose said, hearing her, but not understanding her.

Aunt Mattie kissed Rose on the forehead, wiped her
cheeks with her fingers and the palm of her hand, and
turned to leave.

"Wait, Aunt Mattie!" Rose turned and ran back into her
bedroom. She went to her top bureau drawer, scrounged
around behind her underwear to pull out Jud's aged,
black-and-white, wallet-sized photo. She returned, cradling it with both hands.

"Please, give this to Daniel when you tell him, okay?
Aunt Mattie, please tell him I love him. I'm sorry.
Okay?"

"Okay, Rose, okay. Bye, chile."

It was a long walk down the steps and a long ride
back home. Aunt Mattie wrapped the photo in a tissue
and placed it in her purse without looking at it. She
wasn't ready to look at it yet. *Just think, having to see
that face—after all these years. What is God thinking?*
she thought.

Aunt Mattie gently tapped on Deacon Joe's passenger window. The good deacon let go one last big snore.
He snorkeled, then rubbed his face to wake up enough
to lean over and unlock the car door. He cranked the
handle upward and shoved the door open to let Aunt
Mattie in. The rehearsal in her head about what she
would say to Daniel, how she would say it, and how
much to reveal commenced almost immediately. One
thing for sure she hashed over in her head as she gazed
at the passing traffic was that *He's gonna wanna know
as soon as he gets home.*

***

Daniel was silent. His face was blank. For a few seconds he couldn't think. Then his thoughts began to kick in. *A white man! How am I gonna grow an Afro if I'm half-white? How am I gonna shout "Black Power" if I'm half-white?* Actually, Daniel hadn't planned to do any of those things right at that moment. But what if he wanted to? He couldn't. He would be a fraud. How was he going to brag on how Jesus was black if he was half-white? How was he going to feel every time someone said something about white people? How was he supposed to be half-white and half-black? No one ever talked about his father because he was white. It must have been a big secret because he was white. That everybody, Big Rev and the rest, was laughing behind his back. He couldn't wait to get upstairs and resurvey his face again. To find the puzzle pieces—that were white.

"That's why y'all never talked about this, huh?" Daniel asked his aunt, later, when she'd hoped the matter was settled. "Where is he now?"

"Still in Charleston, I guess."

"He knows about me?"

"I, I . . . I don't know, son."

"What does he look like?"

Aunt Mattie reached in her dress pocket and held out its contents. Slowly, he extended his arm out and took possession of the package. Tiny white dust particles from the tissue broke loose and began to dance and gleam in a funnel of sunlight streaming from the bedroom window. He unwrapped it with caution and sat down on his aunt's bed, not saying a word, just studying the photo. Now, his puzzle was complete. He held the missing pieces in his hand.

"Can I have this?"

"Sho', son," Aunt Mattie said, not looking at the photo. "That was a gift from yo' momma. She told me ta give you that."

"Thanks," Daniel said. Then he raced toward the bathroom.

His aunt yelled down the hall, "Yo' momma told me to tell ya that you could talk to hur, if you wanted to."

He didn't respond. She took note that Daniel, so stunned about his father being white, she guessed, never even asked his name. Mattie was relieved. She plopped down in her rocking chair and dabbed her forehead with her hanky. She was drained.

She mumbled to herself, "Lord, I sho' hope this doesn't come up again, for a while yet, anyway. I don't know how I'm gonna bring this to Cille." She pondered for minutes more, then shook her head fervently with a decided thought. "No. No," she said to herself. She stopped rocking and looked straight up to God. "Lord, fo'give me, please. Sweet Lord, fo'give me. But I think I'm gonna have to take this one wit' me to the grave."

Chapter Seven

Lookin' for the Right Stuff, Baby

1993

"You really think I could handle it? I mean, a big church like that?" Daniel asked, surveying his mentor's confidence in him.

"Sure, you can handle it," Big Rev said, rocking his body mass in his burgundy plush swivel chair. It creaked a little. "Look, Forest Unity Memorial Church needs a new senior pastor, and they need one now—before things fall apart over there. They called me to get my input, and I'm tellin' you you're what they need. That's why I called you in here, boy!"

Earlier, Daniel had watched his mentor take his good time to walk the length of his office and plant himself behind his cherry wood executive desk. It caused him to reminisce about the construction of the pastor's study in Big Rev's new church, a real building that was meant to be a church. His thoughts took him back to when he helped Big Rev decorate it; the rug, the lamps, the pictures on the wall, everything had to be worthy. And Big Rev loved gold. Everything had to be trimmed in gold; his car, his Rolex watch, his pinky ring, his preaching robes, and his wife, Millie—she was trimmed in gold jewelry. Big Rev only called in his wife to put the final touches in the office. So it was just the two of them making the important decisions, as in this decision to become Forest Unity's senior pastor.

The intimacy of the pastor's study was never stronger. Daniel smiled when Big Rev finally settled himself. The desk and chair were custom-built to accommodate his six foot four, nearly 350-pound stature. Ordinary chairs murmured and complained when Big Rev rounded their vicinity. *He can put a-hurtin' on some furniture*, Daniel snickered to himself.

"Hey, Pop, how are you doing these days?" Daniel said, changing the subject so he could think. "You still pumping that iron?" Daniel knew Big Rev loved to talk about how good he looked for his age. It was a shame there wasn't an audience around.

"Ha. You better know it, boy, every day except Sundays and Mondays," Big Rev said, stroking his chest.

"Yeah?" Daniel said. Daniel stretched out like a peacock, showing off his chest, saying, "I ain't doin' bad, either. I'll be hitting forty soon, you know." Daniel positioned his arms, spread-eagle, when he said, "Yep, in two more years. I should make a banner—stretch it across the choir loft." He laughed.

"Boy, you wish you gonna look this good when you hit sixty-three," Big Rev bragged. "Put up your banner then." They both laughed.

Age worked in Big Rev's favor. The signature lines ingrained in his face announced his wisdom and bragged his cunningness. Age turned his hair, sideburns, and perfectly trimmed goatee, silvery, sprinkled with pepper crystals. All of it perfectly accented his smooth chocolate skin. On Sundays, dressed in a fine midnight-blue tailored suit, Big Rev looked regal and rich even before he opened his mouth or waved his hand to give some peon a command. He looked majestic and Jesus-like whenever he picked up a little child to hug. Just one of his huge boat-hands completely cupped an infant during a christening. When Big Rev entered a room, his aura announced him. And all who shared the space knew immediately a king had come to grace their presence.

Their playful banter suffered a brief interruption when the phone rang and Big Rev had to take the call. The voice on the phone was yelling.

"You need to come down here, Rev, and set this brother straight," shouted Short-man Carl, one of Big Rev's trustees. "I mean, Brother Reny is tryin' to rob his own church. He's charging us an arm and a leg for fixin' the furnace!"

Daniel overheard Short-man Carl's rants, and it tickled him. He thought, *Huh, senior pastor shoes, senior pastor sludge.* He worked to minimize his smirk.

Big Rev's full attention was now directed into the phone. "Brother Carl, first of all, calm down, man. You're shoutin'." Big Rev looked over at Daniel, smiled, and winked. The lesson was that Big Rev commanded respect in all situations. And if folks needed to hold up and regroup, well, then, so be it.

While Big Rev doused the fire, Daniel eased back into his chair and conjured up childhood images with a smile. Comical ruckuses like that happened all the time when he was a kid, and this current ruckus led him to thinking about the time Big Rev almost beat a pimp down in the street for disrespecting him in front of his wife. First Lady Millie had to squeeze up in between them to calm the situation down. But there were other moments too. Special moments like being hoisted up to the sky as a boy in Big Rev's arms; sitting at Big Rev's dinner table with the rest of his children, feeling more like his mentor's flesh-and-blood son, than some kind of fatherless charity case, which he sometimes felt whenever his emotions played tricks on him. And then there were their times together in that dusty, dingy storeroom, preparing to preach. The privilege was too great, he remembered and still felt so, today.

"The furnace needed repairing, right?" Big Rev said smoothly into the phone. "Brother Reny fixed it, right?" There was a pause. "Well, pay the man, Carl. Respect the brother for his weekday talents. He's gotta eat too, ya know." He paused again. "Yeah, well, I've got to go. My boy, Daniel, is here. I'll straighten that out later—we'll go to the congregation if we have to. Bye." The call ended.

Daniel was all ears and nearly slurping like a puppy dog. When Big Rev refocused, he was amused. "You got it like that, now, Pop?" Daniel asked.

"Yeah, boy, we're doing all right these days." He relaxed himself against his chair. "We used to short-change saints, here and there, back in the old days. I'll admit it—to you." Big Rev let a mischievous grin slip in. "We had to. Them folks throwing twenty-five cents in the collection plate wasn't getting it."

"Yeah, I got that," Daniel said, chuckling.

"But today, folks are a little better about turning it loose—about tithing. And there's better ways of doing things, collecting, and paying out. But you've got to be careful too," Big Rev said, leaning forward to make a point, "because these saints, today, will take you to court! You don't want none of that!"

"Shucks, I know that's right," Daniel cosigned.

The coveted position over at Forest Unity became available because its senior pastor, only the second pastor in the church's history, collapsed and died one Sunday right in the middle of his sermon. The Reverend Charles A. Wicker, Jr., a mere fifty-three years old, was soaring high in the Holy Spirit when his spirit departed his body and went up to meet the Almighty, face-to-face.

The church happened to be packed like a tight bushel of corn that Sunday, and Reverend Wicker was just about to bring the Prodigal Son home when he ascended.

Big Rev telephoned a close friend, Forest Unity's Deacon James Stone, as soon as word got out that the senior pastor position was up for grabs. He never asked anyone to consider Daniel for the job, not directly, anyway. He just happened to point out what a crucial time this was for Forest Unity Memorial Church. And how a gifted up-and-coming pastor, like Daniel, one who could pull in a crowd and hold'em until either the full measure of the Holy Ghost ushered in or until everyone's pockets emptied out, was a good thing, "Because it takes a lot of flowing capital to run a big church like that. Ain't that right, Jimmy?" Big Rev asked.

Later that evening, a handful of stuffed shirts assembled around an oblong mahogany table in Forest Unity's conference room. It was a closed-door meeting. Deacon Stone took it back to the board of trustees of Forest Unity that Daniel Harris, over at The Bible Deliverance Church of God, could be persuaded to step in as an interim pastor.

One trustee said, "He can preach, yeah. But he's kinda young, ain't he?"

"How old is he now?" inquired another.

"Thirty-eight or thirty-nine? I know he ain't hit forty, yet," the first trustee said.

One of the deacons cleared his throat and countered, "Look, maybe we need some young blood around here."

"Well . . ." pondered a founding member. And then there was a round of contemplative silence.

And so, before long, without much more bend than that, the stuffed shirts came around to Big Rev's point of view.

***

Back in Big Rev's study, the desk was all that separated these meeting of the minds as the two mused
back and forth on the possibilities of Daniel taking over
the great Forest Unity Memorial Church.

Its congregation was at least 500-strong, layered
with doctors and lawyers, all types of professionals,
and lowly dedicated saints. For Big Rev, the fellow-
ship/business opportunities derived from his church
and Forest Unity being joined at the hip would spring
eternal. Power, wealth, and, prestige would abound
if he and his protégé mastered the helm of two of the
most notable black churches in the city. For Daniel, it
was the spotlight he had waited for all his life. He had
been groomed for it. But even at that, the question still
loomed, could he handle it?

"Really, Pop, you think I'm ready for a move like
that?" At this point, the possibilities began to ring
clear, but he just wanted to hear Big Rev say it aloud—
one more time. Daniel loved praises.

Big Rev leaned forward in his chair for that eye-to-
eye he liked so much. It honored his allies and intimidated his opponents. "Son, they'll appoint you on my
say so."

"You mean to tell me, they don't have anybody over
there capable of taking over?" Daniel asked Big Rev.
His green eyes bore a concentrated seriousness, now.
This was hard to believe.

"Apparently not, son." Big Rev's eyes bore a Cheshire-
cat grin and aimed it straight-ahead. He made no effort
to hide it, knowing his boy would decipher it correctly.

"Nobody's waiting in the wings?" Daniel repositioned himself in his chair to leverage his point. Ques-
tioning Big Rev even in the slightest degree made him
uneasy. He cleared his throat and added, "All I need is

some little whiny, whimpy backstabber tryin' to sabotage everything I do because he got passed over."

"There's no one," Big Rev assured him, which wasn't altogether true. "But even if there was," he said to Daniel, giving him more eye-to-eye cat grins when he said it, "who cares?" Big Rev fumbled with some papers on his desk as if what he had to say next wasn't that important. "Backbone isn't that strong over there. Shoot . . ." He salted his comment with a dry laugh and an extra rock in his swivel chair. "How long you been pastoring with me in this church, boy? Since you were fourteen years old, right?"

"Right." Daniel was eager for where this was going.

"There ain't never been no shortage of backbiters and spoilers in this church, and I know I taught you well on how to handle 'em." This time, Daniel let escape his own dry laugh, signature to Big Rev's. The statement threw him back to a couple of those lessons.

Big Rev ruled unruly saints with an iron hand. *Big man don't play, that's for sure*, Daniel reminded himself. That assurance flexed the stress from his chest. He uncrossed his legs and let his body enjoy the plush office chair in which he sat. *Yeah, I got this.*

Big Rev ran it down. "Don't let the troublemakers talk. And turn the weak ones into your leaders. Tell the crowd to be obedient—to you and to God—because that's what it takes to run a successful, growing church. Boy, you know that."

Daniel's intense concentration barely gave him time to nod, swallow, or interject his chorus of "ah, huh's."

"Do that and everything will fall in line without much trouble, son. Believe me, you *can* handle it," he said.

Choir rehearsal commenced in the sanctuary. The harmonizing seeped gently through the wood grain paneling of Big Rev's study. The sound was heavenly to

Big Rev, but it was noise to Daniel and he got twitchy. He knew that Joyce was front and center directing the choir. He could hear her voice, delivering instructions about this and about that. Even with all those singing voices, he could still isolate her sound. Always could. Always would. Knowing that he and Joyce were in such close proximity, together, with Big Rev in the mix, heated his blood. His hairline grew moist. He knew that at some point, he was going to have to get up, summon the strength in his legs to make a quick exit from Big Rev's office, walk through the sanctuary, past Joyce and the choir. And he was going to have to accomplish it like it was nothing—no big deal. He was going to have to move like making love to her wasn't the drug he craved, like she wasn't the love of his life, like their secret love affair, being the on-again, off-again emotional roller coaster that dramatically spent their precious younger years wasn't his fault.

Daniel walked by the heavenly cherubim, and his heart ached. Joyce was startled by the sight of him. On Sundays, the two of them geared up for the performance of their lives—acting as though the other didn't exist—but the unprepared moments, like this one, still presented challenges. Shaken by his presence, she tried not to freeze in some benign direction, meant for the altos. She froze.

Lord, I can't wait until I get to Forest Unity, was the thought that scurried through Daniel's mind as he hightailed it out of there. He threw up a polite wave and barely an eyelid in the choir's direction.

Chapter Eight

The Installation

1993

"Praise the Lord, Church, for giving us such a wonderful day on which to celebrate this momentous event." Reverend Daniel J. Harris began his little speech softly and controlled into the microphone affixed atop his new sleek fiberglass podium. It replaced the solid oak podium—the one used by the late Reverend Charles A. Wicker, Jr., and his father before him. The new transparent podium adorned the church's new symbol of praying hands angled beneath the golden outline of a king's crown. He aimed to own the space.

In the few minutes prior to the service, in the pastor's newly decorated study, Big Rev and Daniel had debated the pros and cons of Daniel coming out in the full glory of his velvet black and gold "bishop's robe," they chuckled, or whether to make his debut in his crisp midnight-blue, Brooks Brothers suit.

"Naw, naw, naw, boy, just wear the suit, I'm tellin' ya," Big Rev advised.

"What? Pop? Is that you talkin'? Mr. Tradition himself?"

Mentor and protégé stood layered behind each other, surveying Daniel's reflection in the full-length mirror, giving the matter satisfying thought.

"Yeahh," Big Rev conceded with a slight smile, "I know, boy. But the suit . . . that gold tie . . . and them gold cuff links . . . It says change and prosperity. We can give tradition a rest for today."

Daniel smiled at himself in the mirror, purely delighted with what he saw. He primped and talked. "Pop, you know that robe we picked out cost $1,500 and now, you're saying, don't wear it?" Daniel spoke with jest in his voice, but this was incredulous all the same, he thought.

"Yeah, boy, I know. But you ain't preachin' today. Save it for when you preach your first sermon—as their permanent pastor. Don't throw all the treats out there at once," he joked. "Save some for later. Ain't I taught you nothin'?" They both laughed and kept looking in that mirror. Daniel was ashamed to think it, but he hoped Bryan and none of the other Graystones busted in, breaking up the groove in there. They didn't.

Daniel never doubted his mentor's vision. During the pomp and circumstance, all the dignitaries—the clergy—emerged on the pulpit robed in full regalia. They all took their seats. The mayor of Baltimore and an invited state delegate were honored guests as well. After a moment or two, Daniel, straight-backed, chin up, cuff links ricocheting bright electric bolts of light throughout the crowded sanctuary, made his slow-motion entrance wearing that tailored midnight-blue suit. The congregation erupted like fans at a Luther Vandross concert.

The service continuing, Daniel said at the podium, "Today, we, as a unified body of Forest Unity Memorial Church, embark on history." He spoke a little louder now. "I want you to know that I am honored . . . no . . . more than honored. I am honored and humbled by your decision to install me as your senior pastor, your willing servant—and shepherd of this branch of Zion."

His welled-up eyes bore down upon the congregation. He felt thankful, but he felt ready too. Anyone else might have been nervous before they spoke on such a day, but he wasn't, not in the least.

Standing on the pulpit, his innards warm, Daniel gushed. He heard the echo of his amplified voice when he spoke. His words hit against the flutter of church fans, the ones with the attractive African American family on one side and the funeral home advertisement on the other.

He relished in the hearing of Big Rev's voice covering him like a warm blanket. "Go 'head, boy, bless God all you want to."

All eyes had landed on Daniel. They bathed him in consummate glee. His heart wanted to break from his chest and dance. "I can hardly contain myself," he said to the congregation as if it was privy to his private jubilee and thoughts of accomplishments.

Jubilation erupted throughout the church. Daniel struggled to continue his opening remarks. "Church, Church," he called out, smiling and enjoying, but the overwhelming shouts, claps, and praises overtook the power surging through his microphone. Before long, the musicians jumped in and began to play the Holy Ghost shout song. Church members sprung from their seats like they were on pogo sticks. Some took to the aisles; still others set off in relays around the rim of the sanctuary. There was hootin' and hollerin' and Holy Ghost dancin' everywhere, all in perfect sync to the lively music. It was fifteen minutes of a rousing good time. Elated, even Daniel did a jig, as he was well known to do.

Deacon Charlie Winston, also newly installed on that day, rushed to his side and mapped out an imaginary chalk line of safety. Finally, panting, Daniel urged himself to slow down and regain his composure. On cue, someone handed him a soft, beige, lemony-scented hand towel. He brushed his face, breathed in its glory, and used it like a furry striptease boa to unveil a fresh signature smile.

"All right, y'all, all right, naw. Settle down," Daniel said into the mic through winded breath. "All right, y'all. Saints, y'all know you cuttin' up, naw." He laughed again. His sheep laughed too. "Today, as you install me as your pastor, I want you to know that you are also giving honor to the one whose shoes I dare to fill; the beloved Reverend Dr. Charles A. Wicker, Jr."

Reverend Daniel Harris intended to engrave his indelible impression on the church. And his vision was to take Forest Unity Church of Baltimore into the future. He tweaked the church's name slightly because he said the word "Memorial" made it sound like the past or that death loomed. He planned to transform the church into a spiritual and political powerhouse. Big Rev anointed the vision.

"You know, boy," Big Rev said to Daniel one afternoon, also prior to the big day, "God might have a lot more in store for you than preaching and just leading this congregation." The two sat cozy in Daniel's study. They had lunch catered for their private talk to discuss some groundbreaking ideas.

"Whatya mean, Pop?" Daniel asked, knowing, full well the answer.

"Boy, this church and this community, shoot, this city needs some new leaders around here. Some fresh black leaders."

"Yep, I've been thinking that myself," Daniel could have said, but he stopped short and stuck a fork full of Miss Annie's peach cobbler in his mouth instead.

"You do Forest Unity right, boy, and you could run this entire city one day. You seen all that gentrification going on downtown—throwing good, decent, struggling, hardworking black folk out of their homes so they can upscale the Inner Harbor."

"Yeah, I see it," he swallowed, nodded his head, and laughed. *"White folks are tired of commuting from the suburbs—they wanna live where they work naw,"* Daniel said.

"Huh," Big Rev laughed. But it was one of those this-ain't-funny laughs. He had finished his meal, pushed the tray away, and rested back in the La-Z-Boy reading Daniel's face. *"Look here, boy, you got a platform. Now, you need a plan."*

Daniel listened intently.

Big Rev continued, "Start building up your constituency right here in this church. Get rid of all those haters—you know what I'm talking about, and preach your plan from the pulpit. Your people will get with you."

"I already been chewing on it, Pop."

On that day, Installation Sunday, Daniel had planned to share with the congregation his total vision about wanting to build a bigger church on a bigger parcel of land that he had his eye on.

"Don't divulge too much too soon," Big Rev always warned him. "Better not give your sheep too much to graze on because troublemakers can cause a ruckus."

He and Big Rev spotted the desired real estate one day about six months earlier. An old dilapidated school, Lemel Middle School, closed for years, had finally been torn down.

"Yep," Big Rev said to Daniel over his BLT special during yet another lunch meeting, this one at Miss Annie's. *"I talked to Councilman Ruby. He told me that*

*they're selling the land, cheap. And they're lookin' for
a minority buyer."*

*"Oh yeah, Pop?" Daniel was intrigued over that and
his quarter-pound hamburger.*

*"Yeah, boy," Big Rev said. "If we want it, we gotta
move quick."*

*"Yeah?" Daniel said, dabbing grease off his lips with
a well-used napkin.*

*"That's right! Dope fiends are using that prime piece
of real estate for their social club. The community's
gettin' pissed about it and callin' for some heads over
at the State House." He laughed. "It's election year, ya
know."*

Daniel laughed too. "I know that's right!"

". . . Church," Daniel said after the guest preacher
of the hour, the Reverend Archer, concluded his sermon, "I want you to do like Reverend Archer preached.
Today is a new day. We're going to spring forward by
upgrading this place, inside and out. Because, Church,
you know as well as I do, we're putting a heavy burden
on this edifice. We've grown to about a thousand members and two Sunday services just in this short time I've
served as your interim pastor." He shook his head in
amazement.

"Church, we've accomplished a lot in a year." The
congregation erupted in agreement-applause. Daniel continued as soon as he could. "Yes, brothers and
sisters, we need to give thanks for our success, but we
need to do more. We need to stand ready to minister
to all those still coming into our fold. With your tithes
and offerings, we can do it. In a couple of Sundays,
we're going to implement sacrificial offerings to complete some needed work around here." He searched
the crowd below to check for signs of dissenting eyes
and/or approving nods. A few amens surfaced around

his words, so that was enough for him. "We'll explain that more in the coming weeks. Remember, this is your church, your house, and we need to support it, keep it strong. The Lord loves a cheerful and obedient giver." A few more amens surfaced. "Seek ye first the Kingdom of God and all His righteousness. And all other things shall be added unto you! Isn't that what the Good Book says, Church?" He flashed his intoxicating smile at the encouraging response.

Daniel summoned the praise and worship team back to the front to render a couple more songs during the last offering call—this one, announced by one of the deaconesses, was to demonstrate a show of faith in Reverend Harris's remarks on renovating the church. "Let's kick-start the giving," she encouraged. "For where your treasure is, there will your heart be also. Amen, Church? Matthew 6:21. Amen!" Her comments drew heartfelt handclaps.

Prior to Installation Sunday service, the visiting preacher and the church made a deal for his payment. "Reverend Archer," Daniel said to him, up close, "it's quite all right for you to raise your own offering." Daniel smiled. Reverend Archer, smiling back, understood. "Our folks are quite God-fearing and generous, I'm sure you'll find," Daniel assured. The comment earned another smile from them both.

The tithes and regular offerings, mandated for the church's upkeep and salaries, took place early in the service. The take was $10,529. Just after altar call, while the church still rode high on emotion, Reverend Archer announced, impromptu, that, "For all who want a special blessing from the Lord, for all who need an immediate answer from God to a heart-wrenching problem, come down right now and bless God with at least one hundred dollars." Reverend Archer announced, "I promise you'll be blessed beyond measure. God will bust that thing you've been battling with wide open."

As the choir sang, Reverend Archer bargained downward whenever the marchers grew thin. He bargained down from one hundred dollars to fifty dollars to twenty-five dollars. Finally, he said, "Just give what you can." Each time the amount became more manageable, more people journeyed to the altar. Flowing tears drenched the cheeks of some as they made their way. Others sprinted to get in on the marked-down sale of a much-needed blessing.

In the pastor's study, after service, the church administrator handed Daniel a slip of paper bearing the tallies for the regular offerings, totaling $10,529, and another slip of paper bearing the total for Reverend Archer's impromptu offering collection. It was an impressive $25,000. Big Rev, standing near, stole a peek at the totals and offered Daniel his I'm-proud-of-you look. Reverend Archer finally entered into the study, still wiping sweat off his face. Just then, Daniel got a revelation.

He turned and whispered to his church administrator, "Make Reverend Archer's check out for $5,000—even." The extra funds, Daniel's revelation told him, served as God's confirmation for his vision. Big Rev, observing and overhearing, gave him an approving thumbs-up, solidifying the revised deal.

Chapter Nine

Serving the Least of These, Lessons from the Master

1969

The neighborhood lingered in the aftermath and battle scars of Dr. King's assassination for some time. Big Rev was sick of looking at the despair. He harbored, more and more, his visions of finally outgrowing his little storefront church. "By 1970," he'd prophesize in his sermons, "God will deliver us out of this meager existence and into the abundance of His grace."

He declared that the day would soon come when they would vacate 612 Garrison Boulevard for a grand church structure more fitting of his holy robes and their fervent prayers. But he never divulged the whole truth, not even to his wife, Millie, that, really, he was sick of stepping over smelly, nagging winos to get to his church. He was sick of bell-bottomed pimps wrapped in fake furs, purple pleather pants, and jive talk. He was sick of their whores who combed the streets with sin.

The clusters of able-bodied men cluttering up the street corners in the prime of day embarrassed Big Rev. They embarrassed the African descent of his manhood. The neighborhood scene as a whole flooded him with every emotion except grace and mercy and forgiveness. Sometimes that fact shamed him, but most times, it fueled his focus to get the heck out.

A Friday night function at the church came seasoned with the same disgusting cast of characters. Sometimes they showed off for the church members heading in and out of service. That's when the loud cursing and fistfights were plentiful. Some applejack hat, platform shoe-wearing slug would shout, "You actin' like that in front of these nice church folks!" His cohorts cosigned with laughs and vulgar remarks.

"Yeah, Leroy, whadya say that fo'?" the yucks abounded.

Blond-wigged whores doubled over in amusement. Their belly flab convulsed up piercing cackles. Leroy the pimp relished in his five-minute comedy act, strutting around in scuffed-up, square-tipped white platform shoes. His dirty burnt-orange pants and a snag-ridden burnt-orange leather jacket once perpetrated as a suit. Leroy looked like a confused rainbow.

The street corner often reeked with the aroma of reefer, spilled beer, and urine. A specially potent blend emanated from the nearby alley. On a sweltering day, it competed with the mouthwatering aromas emanating from Miss Annie's Soul Food Kitchen. Miss Annie's was next door to the church and was a favorite spot after the service. Annie Winston, the owner, and her family were members of The Bible Deliverance Church of God. Her husband was a deacon there. Her son, Charlie, everyone called him "C," was the same age as Daniel and Bryan, who was Big Rev's oldest son._

Secluded in his study, policing the goings-on from his window, Big Rev turned to consult the sacred portrait of Dr. Martin Luther King, Jr., hanging on the wall. There was not one better to represent or attend to the trials and tribulations of oppressed black people than the black preacher, Big Rev considered. *But Dr. King couldn't have been reaching out to these people, bebopping up and down the street like fools and aimless peacocks.* His thoughts circled time and time again.

Still, Big Rev pushed his congregation to involve themselves in street ministry. On Sunday mornings, he preached his heart out about saving the lost souls of those on the streets around him, but deep down, their sinful dispositions sickened him. His feelings were a decadent contradiction to his faith. That too made him angry. He felt guilty because when he first felt the Lord's call to ministry, all he wanted to do was serve and help the people around him. He didn't like feeling guilty.

"You can't lead your people if you don't love them," he heard the Father God say a thousand times in his head. "And you can't be their pastor if you're not willing to serve them." The declaration thundered in his brain, but the fight to prevent his heart from hardening remained a constant internal battle.

The nights in his small section of Garrison Boulevard were a multitude of opposites. On one corner, the militants distributed Black Power newspapers, tough talk, and sold bean pies. On the other corner, the liquor store did a brisk business with people stepping and creeping with their Mad Dog 20/20 and Malt Liquor 40 ounces, snug under their chicken-wing arms.

Mr. Ugly's Bar sat smack-dab in the middle of everything. It was a white brick building with bold black lettering that sucked up all the clientele the liquor store missed. But the strangest neighborhood component was the modest funeral home adjoined to Mr. Ugly's. The funeral home sprung forth a cool irony. Passersby could see long black limos parked out front of either establishment, and it took more than a minute to figure out which group of customers was being served. Was it the grieving folks, dragging themselves in and out of Brown's Funeral Home, or was it the folks stumbling out of Mr. Ugly's Bar?

Once Big Rev officiated a funeral at Brown's Funeral Home as a favor (a big favor) to a longtime church member whose son had gotten himself shot up by the cops. The young man, in his twenties, was a popular neighborhood numbers' runner.

During the funeral, only a thinly plastered wall separated the bar from the funeral home. Next door, noisy people cackled and salted the funeral with party music from the jukebox. Big Rev towered over the cheesy podium that nearly touched the wall. He tried to mask the invasion in disguised passion for the deceased, who was laid out inches from his elbow. But the noise poured in anyhow.

In between the eulogy and the sentiments of grieved family members, he even heard clanking glasses and muffled curse words. His eyeballs swelled out of their sockets with rage. In his mind, what he heard desecrated the living and the dead. The only outrage to top it, he marveled, was how the intrusion only seemed to bother him.

Daniel spent his formative years studying Big Rev's world and how the reverend operated in it. The intense study wasn't intentional, but as a fatherless boy, it just was. Daniel watched how Reverend Tommy B. Graystone lived like a king. In his home and in his church, Big Rev's word was bond without challenge. He never even raised his voice unless he was preaching. He spoke in respectful, controlled, but firm tones, and he always seemed to anticipate the next move that others plotted to make. He was sly. Sharp. He was the master motivator.

Big Rev quietly played the faithful members of his congregation like pawns in a chess game to get them saved by God, Daniel surmised. And those who rebelled were branded as troublemakers—but not by Big Rev (he didn't have to), by his faithful followers whom he served. If one of the trustees or deacons got riled up in a meeting or wanted to do things differently, Big Rev calmed them down with a special tone in his voice reserved for soothing the angriest beast. He played to their concerns and got them to come around to his way of thinking. Then he'd slap a "Praise the Lord" on it. The disgruntled never even realized that their minds had been changed. Big Rev was just smooth like that.

Now, while Big Rev may have held a secret disdain for the sinful ilk running around loose on the streets, he did love his congregation dearly. He never looked upon the coercion of his members as selfish manipulation. He considered it his way of offering spiritual protection like a father would do for his son. Every Sunday and during every Wednesday night Bible Study, Big Rev preached and taught his heart out to his beloved people. From the pulpit, he gave them hope for life and for eternal life. "As long as you devote your life to Jesus," he preached.

Big Rev was savvy with finances. Millie's salary as an English teacher covered their mortgage, and Big Rev's church salary covered the utilities, the car note, and such. The church showered them with everything else they needed. They also knew how to save a penny. Big Rev was not only watchful of his personal finances, but also the church's finances. He personally accounted for every dime the church took in. And every church dime went to church business/upkeep, events, and neighborhood projects or missions. Soon, Big Rev's vision of moving his church out of that old storefront finally became a reality in June of 1970. He celebrated his fortieth birthday that year.

White flight was full-blown during that time in Baltimore. A huge Lutheran congregation had decided to move out of Baltimore City to Baltimore County in Catonsville. Its building was huge and sat on the hill of Hilton Road and Liberty Heights. Big Rev heard about the white church's plan to move from one of his members who worked for the city. Through a special minority business program, Big Rev was able to secure a mortgage cheaply. Within nine months, with a tremendous blessing from God, The Bible Deliverance Church of God had a new home.

Chapter Ten

Straight Up from the Lord!

1996

"What happened over there this time?" Big Rev asked with great concern.

"Gray', mannn, you should have seen it. It was a sight to behold," Elroy said with a sarcastic chuckle and a hard-sounding slap on his thigh.

Elroy Sallie and Tommy B. Graystone had been buddies and confidants for most of their lives. They grew up in the same neighborhood together. When Daniel took over at Forest Unity, Big Rev sent Elroy over there to look after him. "Keep a low profile, but stay close. Protect him, if he needs it," Big Rev told Elroy during a late-night phone conversation. "You know how those young cats are when they start fillin' out their britches," he said.

"Yeah, man, I got you covered," Elroy responded back. They both laughed that private, knowing laugh that men do. Elroy and his family joined Forest Unity that next Sunday. They all stood close to one another at the altar absorbing the handclap praise their joining caused. Elroy took the deacon's microphone and explained to the congregation, wearing a straight face, that he wanted to support the young man's efforts. Plus, his daughter, who was nineteen, loved Daniel's preaching so much that the only way she'd go to church was "to go wherever the Reverend Harris was preaching." That prompted a good-natured chuckle throughout the congregation. "So, with Reverend Graystone's blessing," Elroy explained, "me and my family left The Bible Deliverance Church of God to be with Reverend Harris." And that was his story for publication, and he aimed to stick to it. Deacon and Mother Cherry made close to the same speech.

"So, what happened over there, man? Spill it already," Big Rev asked, slightly irritated at the suspense his buddy tried to build. Inside, he was on edge, but outside, he remained cool—even as the two buddies flung their sweat and grunted, trading turns on the punching bag at Goldbloom's Gym.

"Okay, Gray'. Mannn, get to this." Elroy swallowed hard. "Church was going along as usual, right? Preachin' hadn't started yet, but Little Rev had come up to take his seat in the pulpit." Elroy wagged his arms for accent as they walked over to the weights. "The choir had finished about its third song; emotions were high; folks were prayin', shoutin', praisin', the whole bit," Elroy said, waving his arms all around his head, using the full space, painting the full scene.

"Yeah, yeah, yeah, I got all that, Elroy. What the heck happened?"

Elroy started laughing again, but struggled to get out what he itched to say. "Gray'," he said, "when the choir settled down, this woman stepped out of the choir . . . I'd seen her before a couple of times, but I don't know her. She's new, you know what I mean? Anyway, the broad came down front in the choir loft, cryin' and, I guess, in the spirit and whatnot, and she demanded to give a testimony."

Big Rev interrupted him, "Well, Elroy, what she say?"

"Gray', that woman stood there in front of everyone, and you know stupid ole Deacon Cherry gave her the microphone, free and clear. I mean, he took his hands off it," Elroy said and he broke out in a contagious laughter.

Big Rev started smiling and shaking his head again. He restrained any full laughter because he didn't want to get Elroy off course with the story.

Elroy struggled on. "You know as well as I do, Gray', you ought never give somebody carte blanche over the microphone like that, especially when you don't even know what they're gonna say. So, like I said, she had the mic. So everyone could hear her real good. She stood there and announced that she had gotten it straight from the Lord Himself that she was going to be Mrs. Reverend Daniel J. Harris. And that it was going to happen within the next six months. And that—that was the beginning and the end of it."

"What, what? Naw, she didn't say that, Elroy." Big Rev's mouth fell open.

"Oh, you heard me, brother," Elroy said, licking the gossip juices off his lips.

Big Rev shook his head. Elroy Sallie laughed as they each straddled a weight bench. Big Rev was furious and nearly sent his hand weight upside the head of the guy on the next bench.

"Hold on there, partner. What you tryin' ta do, bust a window?" Elroy said with a snicker.

"Elroy, Elroy," Big Rev stopped his weightlifting and said, "C'mon man, what happened after that."

"Gray', it was about twelve hundred people in that church, and you could have heard a pin drop for a good ice-cold five minutes. No one knew what to say, and there wasn't an amen to be found. And . . . you know all them other young girls didn't like that testimony one bit."

"Oh my God in heaven," Big Rev said. "I told that boy he's got to watch what he's doing. He's got to be careful!" His voice was loud and echoing.

"That's an understatement, Gray'. It's gettin' so that if you want to find a young single sista in Baltimore on a Sunday, you'd better get up and go to a Forest Unity Church service. Them gals are in there fighting, tooth and nail, for prime seating in them front pews. And when it's all over, they look like sardines in a bent can. That's until they get up, you understand. Then, they busy shakin' boobs and butts; whatever they got. I mean, it's breasts and tail all over the place. They wearin' miniskirts up to their cracks and blouses cut so low, I swore I thought a saw a nipple Sunday before last," Elroy said, laughing again, running his long fingers in a mockingly dainty gesture across his chest to aid the visual. "Gray', . . . them women are doing everything but throwing their panties up on the pulpit.

"My wife wouldda shot me between the eyes," Elroy said, "for sure, if she knew I saw that testifying woman's panties too. Shoot, come to think of it, I don't think she was wearin' none!" Both men burst out in a howling laughter, shaking their heads.

"Boy, you crazy!" Big Rev said.

"I swear, man. It's the truth! And don't think that the deacons and Daniel don't talk about it too. I heard that they see everything I saw that day and then some—on a regular basis. It's gettin' that crazy up in there. It's gettin' so that a Holy Ghost dance at Forest Unity is quite a peepshow."

"Yeah, I hear ya," Big Rev said. "I haven't visited in a while—tryin' to give the boy his space. I'm gonna have to invite myself over there to preach soon. So back to the choir-woman-heifer; what happened after that?" Big Rev asked.

"Oh. Well, after the ice-cold five," Elroy said, "you know Little Rev; he's still cut from your mold."

Big Rev smiled a bit at that remark.

"Little Rev is smooth as he wanna be with that tongue of his. He's slicker than goose crap," Elroy said. Elroy Sallie and Big Rev chuckled under their breaths at the pure decadence of it. "Daniel got up slow, gave the congregation a big old smile. Then he called the woman down from the choir loft and gave her a big hug. He whispered something in her ear, and she blushed and smiled. Then he eased the microphone out of her hand, you know, like it was his third leg, and returned it to Deacon Cherry. And told Cherry's stupid behind to sit down. Daniel sent the gold digger back to her place in the choir; then he moved to the podium and said, 'Well, if the sister said that the Lord told her something . . . nobody . . . not you or I, can refute that. So we'll just let it be and put that in the Master's hands, all right?' There was some cosigning from the congregation.

"'But,' Little Rev told 'em, 'what I can tell you is . . . that the Lord has not come to me with the same message. . . .' Gray', you could almost hear an audible sigh released in the sanctuary. Then folks started to laugh. '. . . but, hold on now, hold on,' Little Rev said, 'I don't know what the Lord will say to me. But I do know that when He speaks to me, I want to be obedient to His will. So until such time, Church, I'll keep you posted.' Then he smiled big, down in the direction of the front rows. Kinda like a fox-in-the-henhouse grin. That's when everybody threw out their amens and hallelujahs."

Big Rev, with Elroy following behind, moved over to the treadmill and started clicking buttons. Before he jabbed the START button, Big Rev said, "I'ma have ta talk to that boy about those women. Sooner or later, that crap's gonna hit the fan and fly right up in his face."

Daniel was rounding out his third year at the helm of the Forest Unity Church of Baltimore and things were going well, he thought. Any jitters he may have harbored at the beginning of his tenure had dissolved. The new administrative staff was in place, especially the tireless Crystal Mercer. She was proving to be the best administrative assistant there ever was. She and her husband and their three children joined Forest Unity about six months before Reverend Wicker died. Immediately, Crystal and her husband, Lee, became active members. Crystal was a stay-at-home mom and often volunteered in the pastor's office. She got to know Reverend Wicker's right-hand woman, Mrs. Gentry, very well.

Mrs. Gentry had worked alongside Reverend Wicker as his administrator almost from the moment he took over for his father. She was a wise, dedicated, stout, gray-haired woman, perhaps hedging toward her sixties, when Reverend Wicker died. Mrs. Gentry was best friends with Beola, Reverend Wicker's widow. Her husband, Otis, was just as close to the late reverend. Often, more times than not, the Wickers and the Gentrys spent their Sunday dinners together, mostly at Miss Annie's Soul Food Kitchen.

Change happened fast at Forest Unity in the three years Daniel was pastor. Mrs. Gentry rarely agreed with the new way things were being handled. She also rarely kept her mouth shut about it to Daniel. But she was a diplomat. The wise old woman always waited until they were alone to express her concerns. He always listened with a smile; then he proceeded to do whatever he had planned to do in the first place. Like the time Mrs. Gentry objected when Daniel decided that the deacons should be the ones to handle the money instead of the finance committee.

"The deacons should supervise the Sunday collections too," Daniel said during a closed-door meeting with his deacons. Mrs. Gentry waited until the proper time after all the men had filed out of the pastor's study. She tippy-toed in and sat herself down. Then she patted that tightly wound bun hairpinned to the back of her head as if nothing less than an earthquake could jar it loose. She politely reminded her new pastor that since he had grown up in the church, he should know that handling the church's finances wasn't the proper duty of a deacon.

"A deacon is supposed to be your spiritual armor bearer," she said. "And the spiritual role models of the church, a moral compass of support, if you will," she explained. "I know it shouldn't happen, Reverend Harris, but the enemy often sneaks in where there's money involved, and the Bible says that your deacons must always be beyond reproach," she added. Then she went to quoting scripture like she always used to do.

Mrs. Gentry looked at the boy she'd come to know as a man with loving and affirming eyes, sincerely wanting to steer him in the way that he should go. She said to him softly, but sternly, "Deacons should be serious. They must not be liars, heavy drinkers, or greedy for money. And they must have a clear conscience and hold firmly to what God has shown us about our faith."

It wasn't the first time Mrs. Gentry didn't get any satisfaction from her private consults with Daniel, but the deacon/money incident would be the last. As administrative assistant, Mrs. Gentry was privy to every decision made and nearly everything that was said behind closed doors. When she couldn't effect a change by appealing to Daniel, she secretly told Mrs. Wicker and the Wicker clan all the goings-on behind the scenes. That never failed to cause a rumbling stir at the very least and, at the most, produce showy protests during the church meetings. The Wickers still had the power to cause splinters in the house and to encourage the large tithers and contributors to hold back their financial support. People were starting to talk.

"This must be a unified body of Christ," Daniel proclaimed from the pulpit one Sunday morning. "And God will see to it that this branch of Zion will not be pulled apart. If you're not happy here," he scolded, "you can leave. You can either get with the vision that God has laid on my heart for bringing in new disciples, saving souls, and healing the sin-sick, or you can exercise your Christian good elsewhere." That got amens and applause from all around the sanctuary, mostly from the new members, now in the majority at the church.

In 1995, on a Tuesday, about 9:00 P.M., Mrs. Gentry, along with every member of the Forest Unity Church Finance Committee, received a phone call from Crystal. The newly upgraded executive assistant to the pastor politely informed them that their services were no longer needed. Termination was effective immediately. Mrs. Gentry hung in there at the church awhile longer, still teaching adult Sunday School, still praising the Lord on Sundays, but in private, she collapsed in Otis's arms and cried that her spirit felt trapped in a hazy bubble. Finally, when her good friend Mrs. Beola Wicker left the church, so did the Gentrys. There was no hoopla or fanfare about it; they all just faded away. While a few of the old finance committee members resolved to remain at Forest Unity idling and exercising their staunch protest, most of the old-timers, like the Gentrys, chose to drift off into the sunset as well.

The new trustees were on fire and on board with everything the pastor suggested. And something must have been right because the membership and church's income increased threefold. Daniel was set to accrue a record $100,000 salary. He convinced the trustees that his boy and right-hand man, Deacon Charlie Winston, needed to be available to the church full time. So Charlie, thirty-seven, quit his job at the post office, three years shy of retirement eligibility, to accrue a full-time salary at the church.

Charlie, or "C," as Daniel called him in private, was set to make an estimated $85,000 yearly salary, which was an increase from the post office. No one on Daniel's administrative staff pulled less than $55,000 a year. Everyone had generous and comprehensive benefit packages. "If you want a machine to run efficiently," Daniel said during a church meeting, "then you've got to treat it good and oil it well." He added, "These people, including me, are your servants in the body of Christ, and we are available to you 24/7." At least they were available to him 24/7. And that counted for all the volunteer laborers in the vineyard as well.

A couple of new Christians who flocked to the church manicured the lawns of Daniel's new home. A cute baby Christian with a petite waist and sturdy nutmeg thighs named Faith, with whom Daniel shared a momentary tryst, worked in a salon. Even when the tryst ended, Faith continued to serve the Lord by serving her pastor. She came to his house once a week to cut his hair. The new member auto mechanic took care of Daniel's BMW, and the mothers/sisters of the church came over to clean his house and cook his food. They grocery shopped and picked up his dry cleaning. One of the attorneys who belonged to the church, Eric Milton Johnson, Esq., owned a law firm downtown. The church became the firm's pro bono client. Eric would later help him acquire the land for building a new church.

Everything has two sides to it, and the truth was that doing for Daniel garnered a good measure of personal success for others. If one owned a salon and it was public knowledge that it rendered personal service to Daniel, women flocked to that salon, hopeful that the personal connection rubbed off on them. Perhaps they'd get some insight on how to walk through the door of Daniel's private life; likewise with Jaray's Foreign Auto Parts and Repairs and Miss Annie's Soul Food Kitchen.

Miss Annie's now had three locations in Baltimore. The law offices of Eric Milton Johnson, Esq., and Associates had more paying business than it could handle. Daniel's endorsement had the Oprah touch. It spun gold for his entrepreneurial sheep and the goodness of it was that most of the people who prospered sincerely wanted to serve God by serving His anointed—even the nutmeg girl. Reciprocal service was all good in Daniel's heart as well. He had learned early on that when the sheep took care of the shepherd, the shepherd was supposed to take care of his sheep. Daniel Harris was groomed to be taken care of, but he took care of his flock too.

To the best of his ability, as much as he could accommodate his 1,800-member congregation, he was at its beck and call. He made hospital visits. He officiated every funeral that took place. He dedicated all the babies to the church. He set up business hours during the day to take phone calls and to pray for people with strenuous personal problems. And he tried to counsel young couples who wanted to get married in his church. He used the Bible as his guide because personally, he was ill-equipped to give advice on relationships. At home and in the office, his phones rang 24/7.

Daniel did grant himself Mondays off, and no one, just about, was allowed to interfere with that. He learned that cardinal rule from Big Rev. But for the rest of the week, if he wasn't asleep, Daniel was on call and so was his staff.

Chapter Eleven

Monday Morning Meetings

1996

"Hello?" Daniel said. *Who in the world* . . . was his thought.

"It's me," Big Rev boldly clarified.

"Oh, hey, Pop," Daniel said with gravel in his voice. "What's up?"

"What's up with you, boy? You ain't up yet? It's nearly noon!"

"Pop, it's Monday. You know it's the only day I get some rest." He sat up and slid to the edge of the bed, rubbing the irritation out of his eye.

"Yeah, yeah. Anyway, what's your day like?" Big Rev cleared his throat when he said it, code for *I don't really care what your day is like.* Daniel understood. "Come over in an hour. We got things to discuss."

Sleep was good and freshly earned. They relaxed themselves in it. The morning sun shined down on their entangled nude limbs from the skylight. Had the sun's rays been stronger, more concentrated, perhaps it could have burned a circle right through Daniel's left butt cheek and scorched the right side of Crystal's pelvis, right where his sweaty body had collapsed hours ago. A few hairs over and the rainbowed sunrays could have seared a hole in her sticky triangular jungle. But the phone had rung.

"Darn," Daniel whispered in disgust after he hung up the phone with Big Rev. He wiped his eyes again and shook his head. Half the top sheet was wrapped between his legs. With full clarity about him now, guilt rushed in. Crystal was just beginning to show signs of life. His grumbling interrupted her lust nap. Her eyes blinked open. She moaned and rolled over beside him and attempted to grab his flesh. Daniel pushed her arm away. He inadvertently threw his half of the sheet over her head on his way to the bathroom.

"Huh?" Crystal yelled out once she freed her head from under the cream satin sheets that she'd bought him. Looking slightly Don King-ish, but cute, she flung wild strands of her hair away from her eyes and yelled, "I guess the meeting is over!" He didn't look back. Didn't respond. She sat up in the center of the bed staring in his direction, listening to the toilet flush and the shower spray begin. The Monday morning meeting was over, indeed.

"Oh, this is some bull, and I don't need it," she said to herself. Now, she was disgusted. She scoured the floor for her bra and panties. Her dress lay draped on the chair. "I'll just use the downstairs bathroom," she called out. Still no response from Daniel. Crystal complained to herself, clomping down the spiral staircase. "Schizophrenic bastard. That negro's got at least three crazy-behind personalities," she diagnosed. "I got feelings too, you know. Heck, what's he actin' so witchy about? I'm the one who's married—leaving my kids, takin' all the risks to be with his yellow heinie. Shoot." Then she yelled upward toward the staircase, "Holier-than-thou jackleg!" With that final revelation and an angry shriek into the ozone, she slammed the bathroom door behind her.

"Well, son, glad you could make it," Big Rev said when Daniel appeared at the threshold of Big Rev's living room. He always did that. He always issued commands to his subjects; and then when they complied, he acted like they had a choice in the matter.

Even with just an hour's notice to work with, Daniel dressed sharp. He wore a jeans outfit, pants and vest, with a dark blue muscle T-shirt underneath to show off his abs and bulging biceps. He had on a pair of casual dark blue loafers.

"What's this all about, Pop?" Daniel said, sitting down across from Big Rev.

"It's about that little show that went on over there at your church."

"What you talkin' about?" Daniel said, truly clueless.

"That choir lady making her little testimony. Don't tell me you've forgotten about a thing like that already!"

"Oooh, mannn, that!" Daniel erupted in laughter, partly to defuse the situation. "Huh, news travels fast," Daniel said. Big Rev smirked. He fought a visible smile. "I handled it, Pop. That wasn't nothing. You know them women, Pop. They get crazy sometime."

"No, no, I don't know them women, but evidently, you do. Or you think you do. You cuttin' it too close over there, son. I hear they runnin' wild over there. You can't keep peeking at every little booty that's shakin' in your face and not expect them gals to get unruly."

"I don't peek at every little booty," Daniel laughed.

"This ain't funny!" Big Rev said angrily. Even so, the thought of booty-peeking gave them both a smirk.

Daniel's forehead furrowed. He murmured and complained. "Shoot, Pop. I'ma man. I ain't no saint, like you! Yeah, I popped it once or twice, but I didn't give her no false hopes. She knew what was up. She just decided to go crazy after we did it. Tried to force my hand or some crap like that. But I handled it. I handled it," Daniel said.

"Pop . . .," Daniel stood up and walked around the couch to show his protest. But the conversation stopped abruptly when the vanilla-cream French doors flew open and Millie came waltzing in holding a tray with a pitcher of iced tea, two glasses, and some sandwiches on it. In her mind, anywhere there were two or more gathered, refreshments were needed. She gently set the tray down on the coffee table with a huge smile. Then she walked around the couch, her arms outstretched and waiting for her hug.

"Hi, baby," she said as she squeezed Daniel around his middle and reached up to kiss him on his buttercream cheek.

"Hi, Momma Millie. How you been today?" Stepping back, but still holding on to Daniel's hands, she looked up to survey his frozen expression. Her smile camouflaged her insight. She looked at Daniel and frowned. He looked down at his shoes, ashamed of whatever she spied.

While all that was going on, Big Rev had taken to looking over some papers he had stacked next to him on the end table beside his La-Z-Boy.

With her smile gone, Mother Millie whispered to Daniel, "You come and see Big Rev more often, you hear?" Then she said something curious. "You need him."

Before Daniel could respond with a trite and confusing, "Yes, ma'am," she stepped back again and responded in her normal voice.

"You look good, son," Millie said. "How's things goin' over there at that big church of yours?" Pride forced a girlish chuckle.

"Fine, Momma Millie. Everybody's asking about you. They're all glad you're out of the hospital and feeling better." She had a thankful look on her face, thankful to God for healing her body after a gallbladder operation.

"Yes, son. God is certainly good." Daniel's innards flushed warm at the rawness of the thought. He lobbed back the standard Christian answer, but it filled his heart to say it just the same. A pure thought of God and His goodness did him like that.

"All the time, Momma Millie, God is good!" Daniel said. He reached to hug her again.

"Well, sweetheart, we haven't seen you in a while. So, come over here more often, you hear?" Millie said, like she hadn't said it minutes before.

His back straightened with respect. "Yes, ma'am, I will." Millie disappeared out of the room.

The tension returned. "Sit down, boy. Don't talk over my head like that." Big Rev spoke softly, but it was tight. He didn't look up at no man except God. Daniel collected himself, sat down, and pushed himself back on the couch, sulking.

"Pop," he asked in a restrained tone, "what you got up at Forest Unity, seeing-eye dogs? You checkin' up on me?"

"Yes. That's right. And evidently you need checkin' up on. 'Cause you got some lousy armor bearers over there: hear no evil/see no evil. Them fools you got over there are so mesmerized by your bull, they'll fall for anything," Big Rev said. He yanked his La-Z-Boy to the upright position to get directly in Daniel's eye. Then he threw his huge hands up in the air. "I don't know why them women you pokin' don't flap their gums even more—and call you on your mess, outright. But this little episode . . . women prophesying and betrothing over there . . . was a warning, son—a warning from God Almighty. And the only reason you got a warning is because you're an anointed son of God, even *with* all your bull!'"

Daniel wanted to stand up again. He was furious at Big Rev's gall, calling the kettle black like that, but all he could do was twitch around in his seat. He sat back, threw his arms across the back of the couch, and said, "Well, well, well, ain't this something comin' from you." His voice was smooth. He looked his mentor in the eye. "Don't forget, you're the master. I'm just the student. Are you forgetting that you lead your people around by the nose? And you slam me 'cause you say that's what I'm doin'?"

Big Rev never lost his cool. "Son, I'm tryin' to protect my people, lead them to Christ. I'm not perfect. I never said I was."

Daniel kept his peace, but his eyebrow raised at that comment because that wasn't altogether true. Plenty of times, especially from the pulpit, Big Rev had implied that he was perfect, preaching about how he was never wrong—about anything.

"But I ain't got all these sideshows goin' on around me like you do. Daniel, you got a circus goin' on over there. Jiggling body parts flying around during the preaching; scorned women lodging threats; funny record keeping; money collection scams; and protestors from the weeping Wicker leftovers; and son, you're the ringmaster. You're losing control of the show. People are starting to talk over there." He wagged his finger. "And this little stunt that harlot pulled . . . like I said . . . is a warning from God."

There was a long silence in the room. Daniel looked down at his shoes, acknowledging the truth to what Big Rev was saying.

"Okay, Pop, suppose you're right. What do you suggest I do about it?"

Satisfied, Big Rev said, "Well, son, you've got several problems brewing over there. We'll talk about that later." Daniel just stared. Big Rev continued, "About the women . . ."

"Yeah?"

"Get married."

"Huh?" he said, playing dumb.

"I ain't tellin' no joke. You a grown-behind man. You can't keep runnin' around masquerading as the world's oldest virgin. Besides, some people are even sayin' you're gay. And these women out here, they don't care if you're straight, gay, or slightly bent. They're looking at you like you're a prized piece of meat on a stick. Get married and that will calm down at least some of those other rumors out there."

"I ain't no homo, doggone it!" His green eyes flared.

"Calm down, son. Don't get excited. But you are turnin' into a ho-monger." He smiled a little and kept talking. "And sooner or later, hear me what I'm sayin', a scorned woman will be the one to take your kingdom down—and you with it. You think you can handle a stint in jail? You won't be the first poor fool it happened to."

"So what do you want me to do again?"

"You heard me, you little smart-aleck," Big Rev laughed. "Get married."

Just then, a faint knock happened upon the door. "Come in," Big Rev demanded. The doors fanned open and there stood Joyce, a creamy chocolate soda poured into an hourglass figure. Daniel stiffened and tried hard to cover it up.

Joyce saw Daniel's electric-blue Beemer in the driveway and quickly thought up an excuse to break in on them. She rushed over to her father.

"Hi, Daddy," she said, bending over to give her father a hug and Daniel a view.

Daniel indulged in a liberal survey of Joyce's perfectly round backside, showing off a white pair of skintight Capris. He couldn't help himself.

"Hey, Sister Joyce," Daniel said in a mockingly playful way as soon as he summoned the power to speak.

Joyce turned in his direction. "Oh, I didn't know you were here," she said. She fake-rushed toward him to render the same innocuous hug. He rushed to his feet, ready to receive and yearning to give. Her body made his warm. His body did likewise to her. To let go took some effort on both their parts. Big Rev took the opportunity to tear into his sandwich and swig down his iced tea.

"One of y'all turn on the TV, please." Impatient, Big Rev said, "Hand me the remote." They fumbled to pull themselves together and comply with Big Rev's demands. "Eat your lunch, son," Big Rev said to Daniel, who complied with that too.

"Baby girl, you gonna join us?" Big Rev said, catching Joyce off guard.

Joyce quipped, "No, sir . . . Daddy. I just stopped by to pick up Momma. We're taking Li'l 'D' to the mall to get some new clothes. That boy's growing out of everything as fast as I can buy it for him." She let out a nervous laugh. Her eyes purposely avoided Daniel's direction. And he avoided her. "Well, see you two later," she said, and she was gone.

The mention of Joyce's son webbed Daniel in years of whispers—swirling rumors about the boy's true lineage. Then he picked up his sandwich and started eating to catch up with Big Rev. The conversation moved on to some court TV program Big Rev enjoyed watching. Trash TV was one of his few vices. Snippets often found their way into his sermons.

"Look at that," Big Rev said, pointing at the television. "Look. At. That! Look how that girl's lettin' that bum get out of payin' child support. I outta bring that up on Sunday at my church. You outta carve some of that out for your big fancy church too." Big Rev laughed. "These young girls out here just refuse to use the good sense God gave 'em." Daniel pushed out a cheesy laugh.

"Ha-ha," Big Rev cackled, "them fools that show up in that courtroom are crazy. How do they get themselves wrapped up in all that mess?"

Daniel got up and walked over to the bay window. It framed a cloudy day as well as his cloudy thoughts. Facing the window, Daniel said, "The heck if I know. Only the Lord knows."

Chapter Twelve

First Love

1973

Daniel turned eighteen in September of 1973. He and Bryan graduated from Forest Park High School and moved onward to Morgan State as did a bunch of their friends. Daniel lived full-time with Big Rev's family, now. He and Bryan rode the city bus to campus together. The mother-sisters were getting up in age. Aunt Mattie was eighty-three. Aunt Cille was eighty. Big Rev had a talk with them during one of his sick-and-shut-in visits. He made personal visits to the mother-sisters because of their close relationship.

"You might as well let the boy stay with me, full time," Big Rev laughed. "He and Bryan are always together at our house, anyway."

Daniel's great-aunts nodded in agreement. "Really, all my kids are still at home. Even Joyce." He paused. "You remember, Joyce, my oldest."

"Oh yeah. How old is she now?" Aunt Mattie asked.

"She's twenty. You remember she got married to that nincompoop, Mark Haskins." Big Rev let the miserable flashback sit on his brain for a moment. Then he added, "He wasn't no good. We got it annulled, and she's back home now." Big Rev tried hard not to go off into a tangent about what a big mistake that was. Thoughts of it still ruffled his feathers.

"How's she doin'?" Aunt Cille asked.

"Oh, she's still moping around, snottin', snifflin', and blowin'," Big Rev said with a slight chuckle. "It *was* her first love, you know. Lord only knows why."

"Oh, that's a shame, but you know these young folk," Aunt Mattie said. "She'll get over it soon enough."

"I know that's right," Big Rev said, finished with the thought. "So Daniel can come stay with us? Join the Graystone clan, can't he?"

"Why, sure," Aunt Cille said. "We know you've done right by him. Praise the Lord! All these years, you've been like a father to him, already."

On Big Rev's way out, he joked, "So our Daniel will just be number nine in the Graystone clan! Always room for one more."

Daniel metamorphosed from baby-boy cute to manly-handsome. The boy was fine enough, but as a young man, he was intoxicating. He'd capped six feet four as did Bryan, who possessed his own ample measure of seductive power. Daniel's green-apple eyes, sharp chin, and sandy brown hairline, his build and facial structure, were cut straight from the cloth of his white daddy's image. Daniel loathed it. He felt it made him stand out among his friends like some kind of freak. The only thing different from his daddy was his buttercream complexion.

Little girls, big girls, women, females, they swarmed around Daniel like buzzards circling their prey, and if they needed to, they rushed to place their bodies at his disposal because he was more than just a satisfying scratch; he was a trophy catch. Daniel was learning how to handle the attention his looks and his position in the Graystone family wrought. In the very beginning, Daniel was like Adam, just frolicking about the garden, naked and happy. As long as he hadn't taken that first bite out of the apple, he didn't seem to have much of an appetite for apples. But apples dangled in front of him in bunches. So what's an Adam to do, he thought, but eat—so he partook of the fruit. His eyes were still mainly fixed on getting what he didn't have, which was a father. And as the years went on, he came closer and closer to that end. Although he had Big Rev's love, he would never really have his blood. He couldn't shake the insecurity of it. In the passing years, Daniel looked more and more like his blood daddy. It angered him.

Daniel listened intently to Big Rev's sermons about fallen female serpents and how they could ruin all the lives around them. That was true, he surmised on his own. *Look how Rose ruined mine. She made me half-white. She gave me a father who didn't want me. She had sex with men she wasn't married to. They groped and fondled her in public. She drank, smoked, and showed off her body to everyone. Then, she abandoned me.* Women like her could not be trusted, he learned. A man had to beware of female serpents. Should he encounter one because they were only good for one thing, he must repent and realize how that's not the anointed side of him succumbing to her bite, but the weak, fleshy side of him. He must cleanse himself of the touch.

Daniel also understood how women like that were good tools for getting what he wanted, what he needed. And he could peg their insincerity the minute they looked no deeper than his exterior and started pawing for his attention. They helped him through school in exchange for his fleeting affection and stolen kisses and sex sworn to secrecy. A public show of affection was good for a great deal, he discovered. Boy-toy duty always seemed to reap the biggest payoff. It was all a necessary exchange that secretly reviled him. Oh, he would marry someday, he knew that. Preachers should be married, but his heart would probably not govern the union. He hadn't devised a system, yet, for figuring out how to trust a woman. Until he did, he could never submit his heart into a woman's fold, just his penis. If he ever came close, he decided, he'd just conjure up drunken images of his mother or the sweet scent and cotton feel of those soft powdery busty barmaids who were all going to hell.

Early morning, Daniel had just finished repenting on his knees about some late-night floozy when he suddenly noticed Joyce's total beauty. Her bedroom door across the hall was slightly open as she stood in a stream of morning sunlight flowing from her bedroom window. Its harsh glow outlined her shapely silhouette and framed it in the contour of her thin, pale-blue nightgown. Her back was turned to the door. She was on the phone.

"Well, one thing I know," Joyce said to her best friend, Phadra, "What I *do* know is that I ain't never going near this kind of pain again."

There was a pause. Daniel stood frozen in his tracks, taking it all in.

"No, Phadra, I mean it this time. I'm never getting involved, and I'm surely never having sex with any man, ever again," Joyce said, pausing and shaking her head no to whatever her best girlfriend's opposing argument was. "Yeah, I know forever is a long time, but that's what's up. Look, I'll talk to you later." She sucked up a few sniffles. "Yeah, yeah. I'll see ya."

Daniel's original plan was to scurry down the hallway on his way downstairs and out the front door when his accidental glimpse and eavesdropping freeze-dried his tracks. He saw Joyce's beauty, which was a heavy revelation in itself. He hadn't noticed it before now. But in that moment, he saw even more. He saw her heartbreak. It was deep heartbreak that somehow connected with his own.

Living in the house, Daniel witnessed Joyce's brief marriage and the breakup, but it never really entered into his domain of concern. That day, his heart grieved her sorrow. His body became warm with the desire to . . . to . . . he didn't know what, just then; it just desired. When she looked up and noticed him standing there, she gently patted her tears with the damp tissue she held on to and smiled nervously at him. For the precious seconds that they were eye to eye, his insides quivered. To put an end to the awkwardness, his mind commanded his feet to flee from her sight. *Request denied*. His body remained frozen in time.

Joyce was caught off guard and slightly embarrassed. She stood frozen as well. She had worked so hard to hide her heartbreak, to put on like she was over it. But at that moment, she was too weak to hide it or explain it. All she could do was smile; and then she vanished from his view.

Daniel's insides melted with a passion he'd never quite felt before. He'd never looked at Joyce as anything other than a sister figure. She looked and treated him like he was one of her bratty younger brothers—a body to be whacked on the head if he got on her nerves or swatted at like a bothersome fly. In an instant, a change was set in motion. Now, Joyce was inside Daniel's tight circle of special women. Women who were nothing like the ones Big Rev massacred from the pulpit. She was like the mother-sisters and like Big Rev's wife, Mother Millie. They were perfect in God's eyes. However, *this* perfection now seeped into Daniel's bone and his soul quite differently. This perfection left him breathless—not in charge. It made his loins throb.

Daniel turned and ran down the stairs befuddled with an awkward clump. He almost tripped over the last two steps. He tried to process what had just happened and tumbled right into Big Rev's huge, towering torso blocking the front door. Big Rev never jerked, never budged, but turned around to catch his "son" before he hit the floor. Laughing, Big Rev said, "Boy, what in the world's gotten into you. Stay on your feet, son."

"Ahhh, yes, sir," Daniel said, trembling and speechless for anything intelligible to come out. He just stood pasted in the doorway, watching Big Rev walk the driveway and fold himself into a waiting car. One of the deacons awaited to chauffer him to the church.

Bryan appeared out of nowhere, slapped Daniel upside the back of his head, and raced past him out the front door. He yelled back, "Well, come on, 'D.' What you waitin' for, the bus to come to you? Come on, man." Quickly, Daniel resettled his backpack and his loins.

On the bus, Daniel kept replaying the vision of Joyce's smoky silhouette in his mind. It was a brisk late October morning. Standing on the corner watching his white breath sail in and out of his mouth, Daniel had more than one reason to pull his coat close. It was a good thing too because he kept pitching a tent in his pants and he was powerless to stop it. On the crowded No. 52 bus, Bryan led the way as they wobbled-weaved their way to the long pea-green seat in the back and took it over.

"Hey, 'D,' Chocolate Storm's gotta gig on Friday."

"Huh?" Daniel still resided in the Twilight Zone.

"Mannn, I said . . . we gotta show ta do on Friday. You comin'?"

"Yeah, man. Where?"

"On campus, fool! Those Gamma dudes, they throwin' a party. Mannn . . ."

Daniel gazed out the bus window, looking at pictures in his head, but he struggled to keep an ear on Bryan.

"Yeah, yeah, man. What time?" Then he turned and looked at Bryan as if to pacify him for just a moment. Perhaps he'd stop talking and let him get back to his daydream. Thoughts of Joyce captured Daniel's focus all that day. He couldn't wait to get back home. He had yet to know it clearly, but he had just encountered his first love.

Chapter Thirteen

Dry Bones

1975

It was Christmas, and the year seemed to have whisked by. Daniel and Bryan were on winter break from Morgan, which meant that they were halfway through their junior year. At The Bible Deliverance Church of God, lavish decorations hung throughout its foyer and huge fellowship hall. Both held a towering Christmas tree garnished with colorful glittering bulbs and stars. Beneath the trees were three giant opened boxes, so that members could drop food products into one, toys into another, and clothing donations into the third box. All would be distributed throughout the neighborhoods and at a community Christmas party. The church's giveaways were legendary and very much anticipated by those in need.

There wasn't a Sunday or weekday function that the boxes weren't filled to the brim. The Benevolent Committee did a great job keeping track of all the items and cash and making sure they got to the right place. The committee did a great work in general throughout the community year-round. Big Rev said that as long as he was pastor, he didn't ever want to hear of someone being set outdoors or their utilities being shut off in the Forest Park Community—ever.

Nativity scenes, large and small, decorated small wooden tables dressed with hay. Silver tinsel and tiny angels dangled from the ceiling. It was the works! It was picture-perfect for the coming of Christ. Christmas was just a few days away, and everyone was in the mood of giving and getting. Tuesday night Bible class was as good as it ever was. Joyce taught the class and taught it well.

Whenever she had to be in the public, she made a special effort to put on her happy face or at least her look-I'm-normal face. She'd learned to hide her depression pretty well, but heartbreak was still sewn into the lining of her skin. The advancement of time had yet to make living easier. Her insides still hurt. Still felt hollow. She still mourned the death of her marriage though it had been dead and buried for two years now. The only thing that time seemed to do was to heap mounds of guilt on top of her mound of sadness and emptiness.

Joyce repeatedly asked herself how could she be a Christian and be so joyless. How could she carry such a negative attitude for this long? Surely it meant that she was not accepting the punishment God had laid out for her. She'd slept with her husband before they were married, sinning against both God and her father, and now it was time to pay up—plain and simple.

Bible Study started promptly at 7:00 P.M. That meant folks started to trickle in at about 7:05 P.M. By 7:15, it would be ready to go. Daniel and Bryan were always on hand a half hour to about fifteen minutes early to place Joyce's handouts on the chairs and put out any books or extra Bibles for folks who didn't have one. After class, they'd clean up for her too. Every now and then, Big Rev made a guest appearance to see if things were going okay.

"Okay, everybody, settle down, settle down. We're about to begin now," Joyce said, using her loud talk-over-her-junior-high-school-class voice. She quickly scanned the church's fellowship hall for someone to pray. "Sister Meeks?"

"Yes, Sister Joyce."

"Won't you open us up with a word of prayer this lovely evening?"

"Why sure. Everyone please stand," Sister Meeks kindly requested.

After prayer, Joyce began. She went into automatic pilot mode. "Tonight's lesson is titled 'Dry Bones. Can They Live Again?'"

Daniel and Bryan sat in the next to the last row of folding chairs. They had on their church behavior, so their usual fooling around was at a minimum. The minute Joyce uttered her topic, Daniel, in his spirit, caught an immediate connection. Her sadness was no longer a secret to him. He knew she was dry bones, and he wanted to breathe life into her.

"Do you see on the first page of your handouts . . . It says to turn in your Bibles to Ezekiel, chapter 37, verses 1 through 14," Joyce announced. As the shuffle of turning pages fluttered in the air, she said, "When you've got it, say 'Amen.'"

After a couple of seconds, the "amens" rang out against the twirling silver angels hanging from the ceiling. The Bible Study had officially commenced. "The very name 'Ezekiel' means 'God Strengthens,'" Joyce commented.

The lesson moved on, Daniel even contributed to the discussion, relating its message to the birth of Jesus and such. He loved hashing over God's miracles and had fallen into the zone.

Finally, Joyce declared, ". . . Well, I guess we'll wrap it up here, Saints, and pick it up some more next week, after Christmas."

"Hey, man," Bryan whispered to Daniel, while nudging him in the ribs too hard on purpose. "Can you cover for me tonight? I got ta make a run, young blood."

"Yeah, man? Where you think you going?" Daniel said, joking sarcastically.

"Boy, I got this sweet thang to see before it gets too late."

Daniel was intrigued. "Yeah? Who?"

"Sharon, man. Sharon Freemont. You know her. She joined the band." Bryan whispered even lower when he said the word "band" even though no one was really around to hear them. "And mannnnnn . . ." Bryan lamented. His private thoughts took over. Daniel read his mind. Sharon was hot. He didn't need to say anything else. Later, the two would become a hot, hot item.

"Oh yeah, oh yeah. See ya later, homie." There was schoolboy snickering. "I got this. I'll catch a ride with Joyce," Daniel said.

"Yeahhhh," Bryan said, his smile and tone confirmed their lusty thoughts about Sharon. "Later, dude. And ya know," Bryan said, stroking his imaginary mustache like a pimp, "I'ma be where I'm at!"

The fellowship hall had cleared out. The saints may have taken their sweet time dragging themselves into Bible Study, but on a frigid Tuesday night like that one, they headed for the door like they had a collective hotfoot. When Daniel looked up, it was just him, and across the room, standing over by the piano, was Joyce with her back turned.

Another fit of depression had attacked her without notice and tears began to well up in her eyes. These fits seemed to occur more during the holidays, and she was losing control over them. This episode was a close one. The Bible Study lesson hit her too close to home. Her only defense was to swing around toward the wall and grab her trusty, crumpled up tissue out of her pocket. She tried to wipe away the evidence as quickly as possible, but it was too late.

"What's wrong, Joyce?" Daniel's words, though he tried to speak them soft and low, startled her.

She jumped, but she didn't turn to face him. She felt the closeness of his body standing behind her, and it gave her chills. The vibration of his tenderness tickled the back of her neck. Her tears tumbled down her cheeks instead of ceasing, in spite of her command to do so. Gently, Daniel handled her shoulders and slowly turned her around. Her head just cleared his chin, and she let it fall on to his chest like it was too heavy to hold up any longer. She didn't look up at him, she just couldn't. Her arms fell to her sides. They felt heavy too. Her tissue fell to the floor. Daniel harnessed her whole body in his lifesaving embrace.

For two years, Daniel pined after Joyce. It salted his constant torment of not completely belonging to anyone and the rejection of his parents. He had imagined a chance to hold her for so long. This moment, inside the fellowship hall of The Bible Deliverance Church of God, welded the hearts of two broken souls.

In the silence he stood there, holding her. He was in it for as long as she needed his protective covering. She sensed it and melted in his arms. The warmth of their contact seeped into her empty innards and forced out a stream of anxiety from her soul. They stood there for just about fifteen ample, soothing minutes.

Daniel's passion thickened and rose—not only his carnal passion, but also the passion he'd been nesting for her all this time. He didn't try to restrain either like he had done in the past. Normally, Joyce entering a room had the power to arouse him. This time, he pushed his feelings up against her. It was time that she knew. Joyce felt it, and she didn't budge. Daniel prayed to be her protector, to mend her heart. It seemed natural just to stand there and stroke her hair. It seemed natural to also hold her tighter. It seemed natural to let her feel him. She received all his "naturals" in silence, and when she finally lifted her arms to clutch the back of his overcoat, he knew that was his invitation to come into her heart.

Without thinking, he held her head back, just a bit, to look at her, face-to-face. Her eyes were saturated, and he caught a fresh salty tear with a gentle kiss on her cheek. She had the look and the vulnerability of a little girl. Their eyes remained fixed on each other until she reached to kiss him back. His lips were the softest thing she'd ever experienced. He used them to press open her mouth and searched for her tongue with his. When he found it, without realizing it, she moved her hands inside his coat to hug him tighter and feel him more. He was the lifesaver she had searched for in the middle of an ocean of pain. With both hands, she held on for dear life. In that moment, she'd forgotten who he was, who they were, where they were. She'd forgotten that she was twenty-two to his twenty. She wasn't thinking about how good he preached or that he had been like a little brother to her, living in her parents' house. She did not consider that her father was grooming him to, one day, come into his own as a holy man or that he was off limits. Two years prior, when she spied him peeking into her pain, something had changed for her as well.

Later, when it was much too late, she'd think, *My God, if this isn't blasphemous, it has to be borderline incestuous*. Right then in the fellowship hall, what she did know was that her bones were beginning to surge with the breath of rebirth.

When the kissing ended they both knew that if they stopped to think about what had happened they could lose the flow of emotion. Neither of them wanted to risk it. They were too needy. So they didn't. They moved forward.

"Daniel?" Joyce whispered.

Daniel put his two fingers on her magenta-colored lips to halt her speech. Then he removed them slowly and renewed his passionate kiss.

"Joyce, can we go home now?" he said seductively.

The double meaning was clear. She whispered back, "Yes. Let's."

They awkwardly broke their embrace and struggled to go back to business as usual. They moved about embarrassed, but still thankful for what had just happened. Daniel grabbed the box holding her remaining handouts. She grabbed her purse and keys and went to flick off the lights in the fellowship hall. He walked behind her. She locked the doors of the church, double-checked them as her force of habit taught her to do, while he moved steadily to her car.

She unlocked the car doors, and Daniel threw the box of materials in the backseat in a hurry. Quickly, he sprinted to the other side of the car to open her car door and help her in. It was something he would never have done as her bothersome little brother, but stepped up to do, hopeful to be her lover. Joyce stopped, looked up at him, and smiled. He smiled back, slammed the door too hard, and sprinted back to the passenger's side. Not a word was spoken during the short ride back to Big Rev's house. Didn't want to break the spell.

The house was overrun with siblings alternating in and out of the bathroom and heading for bed (they were running late as they sometimes did). Big Rev was sitting in the dining room doing some kind of paper-work or something. When he heard the door open, he yelled out, "Joyce, is that you?"

"Yeah, Daddy," she responded. A rush of chilled guilt washed over her body.

"Me too, Pop," Daniel said, dipping into the same pot of guilt.

"What took y'all so long?" Big Rev asked. Joyce was startled and dumbfounded by the question. She was speechless and suddenly couldn't look Daniel in the face.

"We stopped at McDonald's," Daniel bellowed out without hesitation.

"Oh," Big Rev said, as they moved through the hall-way. "Mother left some food on the stove for y'all."

The night turned into midnight. Inside, the house was completely still. Outside, the wind howled up against the brick and mortar. Joyce was lying beneath a thin veil of sleep, fighting dreams about what had happened at the church when a streak of hallway light entered into her bedroom. This time, it was she who peered at Daniel's silhouette appearing in her view. He stepped in, wearing only a T-shirt and his boxer shorts. The door gently closed, and she heard him lock it. He stood there breathing in his dream-turned-reality.

Hot emotions flooded her as he lightly walked to-ward her bed and, at its foot, mounted it on his hands and knees and prowled on top of her like a panther sa-voring his fresh bounty. Joyce felt his skin. She felt the length of his member drag itself along her thigh. It was heavy, thick, and moist. Her body flexed and pulsated to its touch. His blood flow increased each time she exhaled a breathless gasp. He gently released his body weight upon her and caressed her flesh without saying a word. Daniel rubbed his hands up and down her silky nightgown to discover bare baby-soft skin underneath. It was like he was finger painting. His nostrils now feasted on a fragrance of sweet cherries layered on her skin. He lifted himself just enough to reach for the hem of her garment and pull it upright and over her head.

He whispered, "Do you know how long I've loved you?" He covered her lips with kisses that worked their way down to her neck and chest. He was on a mission. Her tears started to flow again. He drank the salty nectar and decided that it was the best he'd ever had or ever would have. Her heartfelt tears beckoned for him a second time that night.

Chapter Fourteen

Making Love Not War

1976

Joyce began to pull herself together, thanks to Daniel's love. Her tears had finally dried up, and she enjoyed the surge of blood pumping in her veins, resuscitating life. Joyce's smile and sweet laughter returned to fill the Graystone house. And while Mother Millie and Big Rev didn't quite know what or who to thank, they noted the welcomed change. They were equally thankful that Mark was finally out of their daughter's system.

Daniel was infatuated with his reciprocated love from Joyce. Clowning around one night, he whispered in her ear, "Girrrl, I could pour you into a Dairy Queen cone, lap you up—you—and the cone." She giggled like a schoolgirl, and they started up, again. And that's how it was for Daniel, basically.

Joyce, on the other hand, often in the glare of daylight, was confused and guilty about the relationship. She knew she needed him—tremendously. She got that. And she loved him too. But the relationship was a secret, and secrets wore her out. And this was stranger than living married with Mark in her parents' home, having sanctioned sex down the hall from her parents. This was she and Daniel living as outlaws, having sex down the hall from her parents. Who knew scenarios could get worse, she thought.

"This is awkward as hell," Joyce said to Phadra on the phone. Her girl Phadra was the only other human being in the world whom she confided in—who knew the whole tawdry deal. "I mean, Daddy couldn't stand Mark, and all, but at least we *were* married," she said. "This—this is outright fornication. It's cold, hard-core sin."

"Well, okay," Phadra conceded kind of sarcastically, "but if—"

Joyce cut her off, "If Daddy finds out, he's gonna kill 'D'; and then he's gonna kill me."

Phadra started laughing. She noticed that her laughter collided with Joyce's silence. So she regrouped. "Girrrl, he ain't gonna kill you," Phadra assured; "'D,' maybe. But as for you, after a good tongue-lashing and the appropriate length of silent treatment—'cause we all know Big Rev—when he gets through with you, you'll just *wish* you were dead." Then Phadra turned it serious. "But girl," she said.

"What?"

"Remember how your tail was draggin' behind your hind leg? And how you were wantin' to throw yourself off a bridge, and all that? Girl—you lovin' Daniel and him lovin' you back." Phadra paused. "Girl . . . is it worth it? Answer me that," Phadra said.

Joyce took a minute to suck in a couple of deep, contemplative breaths. "Yeah, Phadra. God, please forgive me. Yeah, girl. Every bit of it." She rolled her eyes up in her head and grinned an orgasmic reflection. Recomposed, the two best buddies said a little more on something else; then the conversation was over. They'd meet up later to hash it out, again, repeating themselves, much with the same results.

Daniel's night visits were on the regular and somehow, for both of them, the risk was a necessary evil, like eating a pint of butter pecan ice cream in one sitting and denying it. It's wrong, but sometimes, necessary.

Occasionally, Daniel and Joyce got creative and took a drive across town or even to the Eastern Shore to hit a motel, but they had to be careful even with that too. Big Rev's church members were everywhere, and they were mouthy. "Oooh, if they ever caught wind of this down at the church," Daniel teased during one of their motel-no-tell adventures, smirking and looking around bushes.

"Shut up, boy," Joyce whispered, chuckling and hurrying inside their motel room at the Dewy Drip Inn, a dive across town in East Baltimore that advertised *Clean Sheets* on the marquee. "You think this is funny, but it ain't," she smirked. They swooshed themselves inside, stumbling over each other, giggling and double-locking the door. The night's end confirmed for them both that it was worth at least a gallon-size consumption of butter pecan ice cream.

Upon their return home, if Millie or Big Rev or any of the Graystone siblings were still up and roaming around, comments would be made on how good the group movie outing had been, and how generous Joyce was to let her little brother tag along.

By the summer of '76, things still moved rather smoothly between Daniel and Joyce. Big Rev didn't seem to have a clue about anything. But one particular night forced the revelation of needing a more stable change of venue. Daniel was on his way into Joyce's room when Big Rev opened the door of his master bedroom and appeared in the hallway. Daniel had his hand on the doorknob, dressed in his T-shirt and boxers, and was totally focused on what waited for him on the other side of the door. He didn't hear the door open, and he didn't see his mentor.

"Where you going, boy?" Big Rev's heavy whisper scared the daylights out of Daniel. His fingers gripped the doorknob harder and froze around it as if they were blocks of ice.

"Joyce said she saw a mouse or something," he responded quickly, but nervously. He was getting better and better at deception. "I was goin' in to find it."

"A mouse! We ain't got no mice, boy," Big Rev said. "Lemme go in there and see what's goin' on."

He pushed Daniel out of the way and entered the bedroom with Daniel following close behind, praying to God that Joyce was presentable. She was. She'd heard the commotion outside the door and had slipped into her nightgown and robe. Big Rev investigated and found no mouse or anything else.

"All right, all right, ain't nothing here. Y'all go back to bed and get some sleep," Big Rev commanded. Daniel and Joyce felt like two year olds with their hands caught in the cookie jar.

Joyce made a swift retreat back to bed, but not before locking the door. Daniel scurried back to his room like the imaginary mouse Big Rev almost snagged. The next morning, when he could, Daniel whispered to Joyce, "Motel tonight?" They had played around with the idea before. That close call set it in stone. Joyce looked at him and smiled.

As cunning as Big Rev was about everything, one would think that he would pick up a clue here and there, but the thought of Daniel and Joyce *knowing* each other in the biblical sense was so remote, it hadn't even grazed his radar screen. All the men/dogs he had to protect his four girls from prowled and scratched *outside* his door . . . or so he thought. They did not lurk or live under his roof. The only people sanctioned to have sex, make love, in his home were him and Millie.

This was his domain, his castle. And his favorite time for making love was on Sunday—the best day of the week.

In Big Rev's mind, foreplay commenced from the time Millie got her healthy, voluptuous body ready for Sunday School, early Sunday morning. She knew it too, and she made it a striptease event in reverse. Millie was caramel drenched and full-figured in every sense of the word. Sure, she had put on a few pounds over the years, but what she had and the way she carried it made her pleasing to look at. To a real man, Big Rev often joked, she was perfect in every way. Millie knew how to please her man because Big Rev taught her how. The two of them played out the Bible teachings on submission to the hilt. There wasn't anything she wouldn't do at his asking. And she was confident that there wasn't anything he'd ask for that would put her in harm's way. They were clear on that.

Millie was a smart, intelligent woman. She was respected in her profession and a powerhouse in her church and community, so being subservient at home did not threaten her one bit. Her strength and confidence made her even sexier, more tantalizing in Big Rev's eyes and his heart. She always knew she was on stage when it came to her role as Big Rev's wife. She played that to the hilt as well. She relished dropping everything to wait on him and tend to his needs, especially while the public studied her movements. She taught the young women around her to do the same for their husbands.

Big Rev played his role well too. He treated Millie like a queen. He opened doors, protected her, and praised her from the pulpit. And for all intents and purposes, how they treated each other wasn't an act. Big Rev knew that his wife's love and service to him was an intellectual choice as well as a spiritual choice. One she had made because she loved God. "I'm not talking about that barefoot-and-pregnant stuff," Millie said, while teaching her Tuesday night mentoring class to the teen and young-adult females in the church. It was dubbed, *How to Become a Virtuous Woman*. Barefoot-and-pregnant thinking nauseated both her and Big Rev. Neither of them had a tolerance for stupid people and/or people who wanted to live lost, and not by scripture. "There's a big difference between intellectual submission and blind, ignorant, and uninformed worship," Big Rev asserted from the pulpit.

Millie got up early on Sunday mornings, always allotting herself enough time to slowly get dressed in a sensual way. It got her husband all hot and bothered without fail. After that, she would adorn her favorite apron, turn into the mother/nurturer, and prepare a full breakfast for everyone in the house. Then it was off to church. At church, Millie was friendly but reserved. She was a lady. In the middle of Big Rev's sermons, he'd cut to his wife, sitting on the right end of the third left-hand pew. She'd shoot him a look that only he could decipher. It had the power to nearly throw him off his thought right in the middle of his sentence. They'd laugh about it later. He loved it. For him, fidelity was wrapped up in making the right partner choice as well as an earnest commitment to God. It was simple black-and-white logic. He preached that from the pulpit too. He loved Millie and, to him, no other woman measured up.

Once they got home, he grabbed the Sunday paper and headed straight for the master bedroom. She directed the children to do what needed to be done to heat up or finish dinner. Millie was old-school. She did the major dinner preparations on Saturday night. Then she headed upstairs right behind her husband. The story for publication was *to change her clothes.* However, the odds of all eight Graystone babies being conceived on the Lord's Day were pretty strong.

The close call of Big Rev almost discovering Daniel and Joyce's midnight meeting also prompted Joyce to finally look for an apartment and move out. Now the lovemaking was really on. It had gotten so plentiful until neither of them had put much thought on where all this was headed. Neither of them was comfortable about making their romance public, either.

Joyce had moved out, but Sunday was still family time and all were present and accounted for come dinnertime. The Graystone offspring, and Daniel, secretly called the dinner table "the round table" because that's where all the inquisitions were initiated. One Sunday, at the dinner table, Big Rev made a remark that changed the course of Joyce and Daniel's path forever.

To Joyce, Big Rev said, "Girl, I'm glad you're feelin' much better these days."

"Yeah, Daddy, I'm doin' all right," she lobbed back, reaching for the corn bread.

"But when are you gonna start entertaining the affections of somebody new?" Big Rev said what he said without a smile because what he really meant was, "What I'm telling you is an order, not a request or a question. Go out and entertain the interest of somebody new."

"It's time now," Big Rev said without looking at her. He cut his meat and continued, "You been respectable. But that doesn't mean you're supposed to be alone for the rest of your life." Translation: *You're twenty-six now. A woman your age should be married. If you stay unmarried any longer, you could end up being a spinster, or worse than that, people might think you're a homosexual.*

Could this mean that Big Rev was ready to pass on his control of Joyce to someone else? That's the notion everyone who sat around the dinner table pondered, including Millie. Initially, they kept eating, pretending not to listen. Daniel was deeper in his ponderings than everyone else as this affected him most directly. Big Rev was giving permission to his firstborn to date and get married again.

Everyone stopped what they were doing and stared at Joyce, eager to hear her response.

Daniel shuddered at the thought that perhaps this would be the time when he found out that she had been seeing someone else and he didn't even know it. *Lordy*, he shouted in the silence of his thoughts, *what is she gonna say?*

"Ahhh, yeah, I've been thinking about it, Daddy—" she responded with ease, without giving up direct eye contact to anyone around the table.

Big Rev cut her short. "You know that young man you work with . . . you know, that teacher?" Big Rev turned to Millie for help in remembering his name. Before she could speak, it came to him. "Derrick Ellis. You know him, sweetheart. He teaches math or something at your school. You know, he joined our church. He's got a fine family; pillars in the community. I think his father is a big official down at city hall." Big Rev went on and on about the man's lineage and how it reflected well upon the church.

Darn it, Joyce thought to herself. *I knew he had a master plan.*

Everyone was staring again. This was juicy.

"He came up to me after church today and asked me about you," Big Rev said as he ate.

"Yeah?" Joyce said, looking as unconcerned as she could.

"Yes," Big Rev said. "He wanted to know if you were seeing anybody. And he did another nice thing. He asked for my permission to call on you. Approach you."

Millie released a huge grin into the room.

"Suck-up," Joyce's inner voice said.

"As a matter of fact, Daddy, I am kind of seeing someone at the moment," Joyce said. A chilly fluid surged Daniel's body. He dabbed his forehead with a biscuit.

A secret relationship? The incredulous thought sprinted across Big Rev's face. He didn't like it and decided to ignore Joyce's absurd comment. "What you think about Derrick?" That question came with a direct stare, no smile.

"I don't really know him, Daddy."

"Well, get to know him, okay?" Big Rev said. Everyone, including Joyce, understood that it wasn't a request. It was a direct command.

Chapter Fifteen

Dilemmas and Decoys

1976

Derrick Ellis was twenty-eight years old, single, and well-grounded. He also taught third grade at the same school where Joyce worked, Garrison Elementary. He was handsome enough, tall, body-builder thick with a cinnamon complexion, and he didn't seem to have any obvious character flaws.

Joyce knew just who Derrick was because he'd been trying to get her attention for some time. She also understood why he decided to enlist her father's help—because he wasn't getting anywhere. The tactic had been done before. That Monday, as coincidence would have it, Derrick and Joyce shared lunchroom duty in the cafeteria. The pursuit was on.

"Church sure was good yesterday, huh, Joyce?" Derrick said, shouting over the concentrated buzzing of children's chatter and clicking plasticware that filled the cafeteria.

Joyce smiled and thought to herself, *Of course, it was good, you doofus. My daddy was preaching, I was directing the choir, and my brother was playing the drums. What else do you think, I think?* Out loud, she said, "It sure was."

Feeling proud that he had broken the ice, he made his move. "Hey, Joyce, you think maybe sometime you'd like to go to a movie or have dinner with me?" He'd hinted around asking Joyce for a date before, but could never get it to hit ozone. This time, his question was a direct hit. Talking to Big Rev must have given him the courage, Joyce assumed.

"Derrick, that'd be fine . . . sometime," she said.

A big smile consumed his face. It was a pretty handsome smile, Joyce was forced to take note. "Great. How about this Friday?" His words rushed out. She smiled.

Eager and taking the church schedule into the account. Nice. You get points. Derrick knew that Tuesday was out of the question because of Bible Study. Wednesday was out because he ran his Boy Scout troop meeting. Thursday was out of the question because of choir rehearsal. Saturday was questionable, at least for the first date, because Sundays probably started at dawn for the Graystones. And Monday stinks, worldwide.

She pondered on purpose while he stewed.

"How about Friday night?" Derrick said again, making it more specific. Now he was brandishing a slight cheesy look, Joyce noticed.

How cute, she thought to herself and chuckled.

Joyce said with a smile, "I'll give you my number when school's over."

Without thinking, Derrick blurted out. "I got it!" His smile locked in the cheesy position now. He couldn't have scraped it off with a chisel. Joyce looked at him, momentarily stunned. "I mean, your father gave it to me . . . I'm sorry . . . He said you wouldn't mind." Joyce wanted to be mad, but his boyish eagerness was too cute and flattering. She always liked that in a man.

Desperate to recover some dignity, Derrick threw in a clever, ". . . but I said I wouldn't use it before I got your permission." She giggled as they moved over to either side of what had to be the largest, smelliest, messiest garbage can in the free world.

They policed the careless discard of half-eaten contents clinging to messy lunch trays. The children's aim left a lot to be desired. As Derrick and Joyce left the lunchroom, parting down separate directions of the hallway, he yelled, "I'll call you." She smiled and waved. He called that night, after an hour or two of staring at the clock, waiting for a respectable time to act.

The date was dinner at Miss Annie's Soul Food Kitchen. Their conversation was fruitful, entertaining, and grown-up. Derrick shared interesting tidbits about himself and his family and appeared genuinely interested in Joyce's future, her career. "So," he said, chomping on Miss Annie's homemade cheese biscuits, "do you see yourself as a principal someday? Or have you thought about a career in music, since you're so good with that choir? I imagine you could write your own ticket."

Joyce put her fork down and chewed on the delight of deliberating Derrick's question and his full attention. "You know I love those little brats at school," she said. "Lord only knows why." They laughed, allowing the commonality to inch them closer together.

"Because," he cosigned, "you couldn't tolerate those monsters unless they shared your DNA and/or you loved to teach them."

"You've got that right," Joyce said, laughing. Thinking, she added, "Lord knows, I'd like to make some real money in music or in education one day." They considered the possibilities in unified silence. She liked the way he never took his eyes off her lips, like they were dessert. Breaking the silence, she said, "Perhaps the Lord will see fit to allow me to combine the two, kids and music together—and build a good career out of it." He smiled and nodded. Joyce looked into his sandy-brown eyes and said, "I'm hopeful." They ate.

The movie was the Gordon Parks's film, *The Learning Tree*. Joyce was surprisingly comfortable and impressed. The evening was going well. Halfway through, he slipped his muscular arm around her shoulder. He allowed his firm thigh to weight itself against hers. His thigh, she noticed, produced a funny combination of a granite-inside-a-pillow feel. The sensation did something sensual and assuring to her insides. *Oh, Lordy* and *Uh-oh*, composed her most intelligible evaluation of the situation. She knew that complications threatened to brew inside her.

"My date with Derrick was actually pretty good," Joyce told Phadra after Bible Study. Folks milled about them, trying to get a handle on the conversation and horn in. Though Joyce was trying to keep her business close to her vest, she took notice of the freeing feeling associated with being able to talk about it in public— if she wanted. "We really did hit it off," she said to Phadra. Derrick, Joyce realized, possessed a maturity level that Daniel lacked, minus his Holy Spirit. And it was relaxing to have a risk-free date and a public show of having a life. She couldn't say all that to Phadra, there in the eye of the church public. But when she looked at Phadra, she chuckled, knowing that she didn't have to explain a thing. Her girl got the picture— the *whole* picture.

"Are you going out with him again?" Phadra asked eagerly as the two headed for their cars.

"Girl, back up. You all-up-in-grill," Joyce said, playfully. "You gonna trip over somethin'."

"Woman, answer the question," Phadra said, wiping her mouth.

"Yeah, yeah," Joyce responded contemplatively, "if he asks, I believe I will go out with him."

Phadra smiled her approval. She said, "It's your world, girlfriend. I'd go for it." They got in their respective cars and drove away.

Daniel didn't like it at all; he let Joyce know during their next rendezvous. "You running around with that hammerhead is stupid," he yelled at her during what she perceived to be a temper tantrum. "You, on a date, is driving me crazy," he shouted.

But Joyce calmly explained it to him. "I have to show Daddy that I'm dating someone, complying with his wishes and moving on with my life," she said. "It also works to keep him away from suspicion, you know, about us," she added. "I'm not planning to have sex with Derrick or anything." In a sarcastic vein, she watched his countenance struggle to absorb a readjustment in his rethinking.

She had kissed Derrick on that first date, but she didn't see a need to divulge all that to Daniel. It was pretty good too, she was forced to note. *For a muscle head*, she thought to herself, *those lips were nice and soft*. No need to divulge that either. Joyce really had no desire to go any further with Derrick. In spite of what she had done with Mark and what she was doing with Daniel, she believed wholeheartedly in abstinence before marriage. Daniel and Mark were just exceptions to the rule. Exceptions for which she routinely asked forgiveness. She was heading into her late twenties and had only been with two men. Some of her high school girlfriends ventured much further than that. Some had even fallen off the hand-count. But she hadn't. *Doesn't that count for something, Lord?* she prayed.

Joyce knew that Daniel asked for forgiveness too. They both felt that God had a special heart for love. And every day, Joyce realized the favor God had placed on Daniel's life for him to be able to preach like he did—and she didn't want to mess with his anointing or hers in music and teaching. She assumed Daniel hadn't been with anyone else since he had been with her, or had he expected to be. So at least they only sinned with each other. But they hadn't talked about their future; just their here and now, and how to keep it under wraps. Deception was stressful, she noticed. Derrick was a great diversion and a respite from keeping secrets and feeling guilty. But she hadn't figured on *liking* him. *Am I cheating on Daniel?* she questioned. *How far can I take this?* she wondered. No immediate answer arrived in view.

The months marched forward and in the course of playing around with Derrick as a decoy, Joyce accidently proved to herself that she had more in common with Derrick than with Daniel, and she liked being with him more and more. Yet, there remained a special place in her soul where only her feelings for Daniel resided. She could control her feelings for Derrick. She liked that too. But her passion for Daniel was too strong. That made her uneasy. She could play it straight with Derrick; no premarital sex. Daniel's touch she had to have. However, the longer they kept their relationship a secret, the wider the improbability stretched about them ever coming clean—especially to Big Rev. So Joyce kept things moving slowly with Derrick.

Irritated, Derrick broke it off a couple of times—especially after their *relationship* hit a year. Not only was he a grown man, he was a desirable man, heavily sought after, especially at church and in the school in which they taught. "I don't need to sit around here playing the Virgin Mary game," he told her, eye to eye, during one of their familiar touchy-feely moments that had gotten a little too heavy. His car windows had fogged up. Her forehead glistened. He spoke, while she panted to catch her breath and rebutton her blouse. It had taken all the energy she had to predict the quick intentions of his big sturdy hands, trying to beat them to the goal like a soccer champion. Making it worse was her growing desire to give in to his hands, his arms, and his lips—and just enjoy.

Joyce kept silent, hopeful her look conveyed her apology to him. It didn't. Derrick politely clarified, while pulling out a handkerchief to wipe his forehead dry, "I do this for you because it's you I want—not because I have to. You've been married before," he said, shaking his head. "You ain't no Virgin Mary. And I ain't Joseph, waitin' to pop a cork. I don't understand the game you're playing." Then he mentioned something about needing to sow his wild oats. "Even if you don't," he finalized. He would do nothing in her face, of course, he promised, but he had to do some sowing, just the same.

Whenever these relationship ruptures would happen, for publication, one of them would say, "We're friends. We're just taking a break. We're still good friends." Joyce and Derrick played that scene repeatedly as the months scooted into years. Only every now and then, she'd let herself marvel at how indecisiveness and unresolved dilemmas had such ability to waste a person's time.

By 1985, Joyce and Derrick started seeing each other again. Soon, it was assumed to Derrick, the church folks, and to Big Rev that they were being exclusive. Thoughts of marriage teased the air. The addition of sex sweetened the deal—for Derrick.

During all this time, Daniel could not be seen twiddling his thumbs either. He perfected his experience at feigning public relationships while making passionate love to the one he truly loved. The only thing the other women he openly dated seemed to crave was to be seen in public with him, and perhaps a little trophy sex—which, he gave in to, especially when he wanted to make Joyce jealous. None of those women could ever keep their traps shut. Bragging and being brazen was part of the payoff. If any of these women hinted marriage, it was for the prestige of getting close proximity to a "first-lady" position, and not true love.

Daniel studied his suitors from the pulpit. They'd turn their noses up at other, more monetarily blessed brothers. Brothers who, he knew for a fact, were sincere and upstanding, but who just didn't have a spotlight shining down on them.

Daniel could show up two hours late for dinner, and it was all right. He could openly show his interest for other women, and it was all right. *Would they get buck naked and run up and down in the middle of traffic if I asked them to?* he wondered. *Sure they would!* They made his innards sick. Besides getting Joyce jealous and his manhood memorialized when he was bored, especially during the cooled-down periods between him and Joyce, those women served no real purpose at all.

In 1986, the month of January came and went. But Joyce's period was a no-show. She couldn't believe it. *How could I have been so relaxed about juggling two men?* she hashed and rehashed. Joyce got confirmation from an out-of-town doctor. Phadra went along for support. Phadra was the only one in the world Joyce had confided in. Phadra knew about the love affair with Daniel. She knew about the baby, and she knew about Derrick Ellis too—that now Joyce was torn between two loves.

Secretly, Joyce wondered if Phadra wasn't the real reason this happened to her. Phadra married her high school sweetheart when she was nineteen. She and Anthony had four beautiful children who were growing up nicely, and Anthony treated Phadra like his queen. Phadra adored him. "Maybe I just wanted some of that too," Joyce told herself one morning, sitting on the edge of her bed, wrangling with the top of a huge bottle of prenatal vitamins, deciding whether to take them. They looked like horse pills. "That's how I made this horrible mistake. I wanted Phadra's life," she said to herself on another day after lifting her head out of the toilet due to the debut of morning sickness. Looking at herself in the bathroom mirror, her facial expression conveyed how she knew she was grabbing at silly straws.

"If I have this baby, I'm doomed," she said. Her stomach rumbled again. "I'll disgrace myself and my family." Her eyes watered. "If I have an abortion, I could ruin myself for life, besides going straight to the toilet-lake of fire," she said, rushing back to her latest confidant: the toilet bowl. The dilemma kept Joyce up most nights, tossing and turning in lose-lose options.

She and Derrick happened to be hot again, going good. Marriage was being discussed—between Derrick, Big Rev, and her mother. It wasn't out of the realm of possibilities that she could get married and have babies, cute babies, with Derrick. The idea grew on her fast like fungus. There was one thing she knew for sure; if she killed the life that was inside her, as wrong as it was for it to be there, God would punish her forever.

Sex with Derrick was nothing like the passion she shared with Daniel. Either way, both soaked her in shame, but shame was a familiar state of being she shared with Phadra on the phone one day. "What difference does it make what I do?" Joyce confessed to her friend.

"Girrrl, you are not the awful person you keep thinking you are," Phadra argued. "You're too hard on yourself, I keep telling you. Cut it out, girl!" But Phadra's arguments swirled in one ear and swirled out the other. Soon the phone call was over.

When Joyce told Derrick that she was with child, he was ecstatic. Daniel was stunned and heartbroken at the news of Joyce and Derrick's engagement. When he heard about it, he tried repeatedly to see Joyce to talk her out of it. But she avoided him at every turn until one evening, Joyce finally agreed to have dinner with him on Solomon's Island.

"Joyce, what's goin' on? What do you think you're doin'?" He was intense.

"Look, Daniel, I love you. You know that, but I can't keep going on like this. My life is in limbo. We're two grown folks who can't seem to make a public commitment."

He held her hand tightly as they strolled along the sandy beach after dinner. The sex they had at the Solomon's Inn beforehand was unforgettable at the very least. The sound of foamy, rolling waves of the Chesapeake Bay, catching the warm glow of a rainbow-drenched sunset, served as a backdrop for their confused emotions. That last comment she made jabbed him in the gut.

"So, what do you want from me?" Daniel asked. "You doin' this to get back at me?" He knew he shouldn't have gone there, but he was desperate. Stunned that the lovemaking didn't do it for three solid hours, all through dinner and beyond, he tried to convince her that marrying this "Derrick-character" was a bad idea.

"You haven't given me an alternative idea," Joyce said. Her stomach churned with the pressure.

"What do you want from me, Joyce?" There, he said it again.

Joyce stopped walking. She turned and looked at him. Silence filled the circle of their private aura for a minute or two, or three. "Poor little Danny-boy. Still thinks the whole world revolves around him." She pursed her lips. "You mean to tell me, you honestly *don't know* what I could possibly want or need? What we should want, *together?*"

Joyce knew Daniel loved her. The fact that neither of them could rise above their connection during all these years was proof of that. But that wasn't the point. Now, Joyce needed a lot more than a love addiction. She needed more than making love with the one man who made her insides curl with desire—just by walking into the room. She needed the support of a man-spouse, the approval of sanctioned motherhood, and a public show of love as well.

Daniel remained silent, but he held on to her gaze. It was all he had. He wanted his look to tell her how he felt. The fact was that he loved her so much; he loved her shadow. He wanted to drop at her feet and beg. But what good was that if everything around them crumbled? Look where that kind of love got Rose. His poor Aunt Cille spent her life trapped in a time warp of hurt because she loved too much. And he was on track to get somewhere—to earn the respect he so longed craved. And he couldn't lose Big Rev.

Finally, Joyce broke loose from his grasp and his gaze. Then she looked at him and said one more thing. "This is about so much more than you." She released his hand, turned, and walked away. Without looking back, she backtracked the length of their journey together, alone, on the sandy beach that helped to culti-vate their love. Joyce walked back to the restaurant's parking lot. She got into her car and drove away—on her way to meet Derrick. Daniel just stood there, and he let her go.

Chapter Sixteen

The Graduate and the Blowup

1977

May 17 was graduation day at Morgan State College as well as a scorcher. A laughing sun sold wolf-tickets threatening to cook anyone who dared to linger in its presence.

The Graystone household was cool, grateful, and all a-buzz. Bryan and Daniel had earned their bachelor of liberal arts degrees and it was a big thing.

It was also going to be the day Bryan had decided to stop lying, stop avoiding, and come clean with his father. His passion was music, not theology—not the pulpit. Big Rev had Daniel to fill that legacy, Bryan concluded, and he should be satisfied with that.

Growing up, right through their teens, Bryan and Daniel stood like brothers, minus any unhealthy rivalry outside of the stuff brothers usually move through. Not even when folks started calling Daniel "Little Rev" did any serious rivalry bubble up to the detection of the naked eye. All eight of the Graystone children loved music and could play instruments and sing, while Daniel was only rhythmic preaching. Bryan was a genius on the drums. He got the girls because he was the drummer boy and not, necessarily, because he was a preacher's kid—a PK by blood, which still presented itself as a related bonus. Bryan's primary focus was on musicianship—not on ministering like his dad. Daniel had imprisoned himself in a constant prove-mode, be it noticeable by Bryan or not. But Bryan lived with nothing to prove (except that he didn't want to be a preacher). He formed his band, Chocolate Storm, during his senior year of high school. It became a regular at the Arch Social Club on Pennsylvania Avenue, a night spot that once bolstered Billie Holiday, Duke Ellington, and later, start-ups like Earth, Wind & Fire on its marquee. Bryan lied about his last name and his age to get the steady gig.

"Mannn, what am I supposed to tell Pop when I come in without you?" Daniel said panicked one Friday night. Lying to Big Rev gave him hives.

"I don't know," Bryan jabbed back, "just think of something. You tha master," he added with a dry laugh. "Quit actin' like a punk." He laughed again. Daniel didn't. He just stood frozen, staring with his mouth open, like it helped him think better. They discussed the matter while standing on Daniel's great-aunts' porch. Bryan was waiting for a ride downtown from one of his bandmates. So the deal was that while the Graystones thought Bryan was over at Daniel's house, the mother-sisters assumed that Bryan went home. "The plan's magic," Bryan assured him.

Bryan knew that he could never admit his true passion to his father. "The big man just doesn't like original ideas unless they're his own," Bryan joked to Daniel behind Big Rev's back. It was a shared opinion. So having Daniel running around in the pulpit being "Little Rev" actually took the pressure off him having to follow in his father's footsteps. It was the perfect smokescreen to help Bryan disappear from church music and phoenix into a purple haze of funk music—his first love.

Sly and the Family Stone was Bryan's favorite group.
Bryan's tall, slinky body was a match for Sly Stone's
physique. He grew a big black floppy Afro, just like his
idol. It framed his strong male Nubian features well.
Traits he inherited from his father, dipped inside his
mother's caramel skin tone.

On Morgan State's graduation day, Bryan and Daniel
spent the eve on campus for the host of on-campus par-
ties that begged their attention. That morning, while
the Graystones prepared to head for the college, Bryan
and Daniel struggled to wake up from a busy night and
predawn activity. Once they pulled themselves together,
they emerged on the balcony of a friend's dorm room
almost simultaneously, filled with anticipation and
memories of last night's celebrations.

Their youthful muscular bodies moved in slow motion, weighted heavy in thought and hangovers. They
stood there divinely cloaked in traditional black-on-
black graduation gowns. Each black mortarboard
adorned a sleek twisty tassel of blue and orange. Each
young man's tall, flowing silhouette stood crowned by
the morning sunlight, gathering the possibilities of a
bright future. Their daydreams rippled in the breeze.
Today, there was no room for any doubt about success.

Daniel was headed for his master's in theology, continuing on at Morgan. And so was Bryan, plus continuing his concentration in music. Big Rev had planned
their futures well.

"Mannn, Daniel . . .," Bryan said. He was the first to
break into their meditative silence while standing on
the balcony surveying the perfectly manicured lawn
some levels beneath them. ". . . I thought this day
would never get here."

"Yeah, man, I know what you mean," Daniel agreed.

"Naw, naw, no . . . you don't," Bryan said.

Daniel, puzzled, looked at Bryan. He inspected Bryan's sharply chiseled face. Bryan's eyes scrunched in the sunlight, but he still owned the same stern, determined look of his father.

"What you talkin' about, brother?" Daniel asked.

"I got plans, 'D,' and they don't include no theology, no preachin', none of that stuff. No offense, man, but Pop's got you for that stuff. He don't need me."

But Daniel did take offense. His cheeks flushed a reddish pink. In all these years Daniel had never heard Bryan express any animosity toward his presence or toward his close relationship to Big Rev. In fact, he'd always expressed the opposite. Attention spent on him always gave Bryan room to pursue his real love. Daniel knew that was music.

"Mannn, you know better than anybody the band Chocolate Storm is hot. We're real hot right now," Bryan said.

"Yeah, I know that, but . . ."

"But what?" Bryan was in defensive mode now. He didn't care about the preaching stuff, but don't play down his music. That was another thing. He shot back, "But *what*, 'D'? That's my hobby? You're wrong, 'D.' Dead wrong."

Daniel stood speechless and staring.

Bryan continued. "This guy came to see us play last month, man. And I'm tellin' you, this dude's got connections. He said he wanted to be our manager. He wants to take us places. The dude said he'd been checkin' us out for a while."

Slightly wounded about the fact that this was all news to him, Daniel was intrigued. Why hadn't he heard any of this before now?

Bryan continued. "So he helped us make a tape—you know, an original demo tape."

"And what happened, man?"

"What happened?" Bryan repeated sarcastically. "What you think the heck happened? We blew up, man! We blew up. This other dude, Raphael Mason, took it to his record label and they wanna sign us."

"What you gonna tell Big Rev?" Daniel asked. "Pop don't know nothing about this, right?"

"Yeah, well, there's a lot he don't know, huh?" Bryan looked at him out of the corner of his eye. His smile was crooked and sly when he said, "He don't know you been gettin' it on with my sister either, now, does he?"

Immediately, Daniel started choking on spit and coughing.

"Cool out, cool out, bbbbrother," Bryan said. "I was pissed at first," he continued, aiming an upturned eyebrow at Daniel. "I started to blow your spot up. But I saw that it was cool. I know you love her."

Daniel, who had been holding his breath, exhaled.

"I'm gonna tell him, today, back at the house," Bryan said, moving things back to him. "In two weeks, Chocolate Storm's headed for New York, mannn, to record. If I have to, I'll move up there, mannn, for good; me and Sharon and the band." With that, Bryan turned and headed back into the dorm room. It signaled the end of the conversation. Daniel followed him inside.

The graduation was held outside under two very huge cream-colored canopies spread out on the football field. One was for the graduating class and guests. The other served as a covering for the stage, lined with dignitaries. It was barely 10:00 A.M., and there wasn't a hint of shade to be found except under the canopies. If it hadn't been for the pride and the sheer determination it took to make that day a reality, the graduates, the dignitaries, and the guests would have all melted into a gigantic, extremely well-educated pool of alphabet soup. But proud chests and bigheads could bear anything on graduation day. Neither rain, nor broiling sun, not even dry, stale academic humor could keep this crowd from it.

The day was going great. Millie prepared a special meal for the occasion.

"You make sure you boys get to the house by six sharp, you hear me?" She issued her demand in between her hugging and kissing on Bryan and Daniel. She was so proud of the two of them she could hardly stop herself.

"Come on, Mother," Big Rev said playfully, "you gettin' the men all painted up with lipstick. And it's not *your* lipstick they wanna be painted up in." Everyone laughed. Millie slapped her hand in his direction.

"Remember, six o'clock for dinner. We're a family! We gonna celebrate together, hear me?" Millie shouted at the boys, while Big Rev did his best to direct her toward the parking lot.

"Yes, ma'am," the boys said in unison. Then they were off. Their unzipped graduation gowns caught the wind and flowed like Batman capes as they made their escape.

The dinner meal was a magnificent spread like the spreads Millie laid out during Thanksgiving and Christmas, but even better. Turkey, two hams, meatloaf, and big, round, juicy crab cakes spilled over from the main dining-room table to a side table. Collard greens seasoned with smoked turkey wings, string beans with pearl onions and little white potatoes swimming around in them, cabbage, corn pudding pie, candied yams, garlic mashed potatoes, dirty rice, corn bread, and more were in abundance. An additional separate small wooden table was garnished with sweet potato pies, apple pies, bread pudding, a three-layer coconut cake (Bryan's favorite), and a huge peach cobbler (Daniel's favorite). The menu was filled with all of Bryan and Daniel's favorites. At six sharp everyone gathered, Big Rev blessed the food and blessed the great potential in the room, and the celebration was on.

The first, second, and third helpings flew around the table almost without the aid of human hands. Silverware and ice-filled glasses clanged with jubilee, and after the customary silence that happens when everyone consumes those first couple of delectable bites, idle chatter began competing with the consumption of good food, unlimited.

"What you boys got planned for this summer?" Big Rev said in between his bites and swallows. He knew what they had planned because he planned it, but he wanted to hear it anyway.

"I'm gonna work at the church, Pop. You remember? I got office hours now. I'm gonna work with the youth group too," Daniel said, happily eating away.

Bryan pretended not to hear the question for some moments. He kept his head buried in his plate; his hand crushed his napkin for gumption.

"What about you, son?" Big Rev said, talking to Bryan.

Bryan sucked in a deep breath; he set his fork down, then exhaled. "Well, I plan to kick it around with the youth ministry. You know, help 'D' out. Work with Joyce, teaching music to the kids. I think we got some future drummers in that church, Pop!" He laughed.

Big Rev smiled his pleasure and ate.

"Annnd, in a couple of weeks, I'm headed up to New York." Bryan picked up his eating. The clan around him fell silent. They were all ears.

"Head to New York?" Big Rev let go of his knife and fork. "What's in New York, son?"

"You know, Pop, my band—"

"No," Big Rev snapped. Mother Millie, Joyce, and the younger siblings, who, for the most part, had been relegated to silent extras in a movie, alternated their stares between Big Rev and Bryan, sitting across from each other. Millie's expression said that she was clueless about what Bryan was about to say, but Daniel, Joyce, and the teenage siblings knew there was an explosion on its way.

"My band, Chocolate Storm . . . We're pretty good, Pop," Bryan said, "and we got a recording contract. We're gonna cut a record. For real!"

Big Rev remained cool. He sat there purely unenthusiastic. He picked up his knife and fork and stabbed a fresh gash into his meat, leaving all the spectators hanging. Daniel's stomach soured with Bryan's disappointment. He hurt for him. Bryan looked down at his plate and just stared at his food. Then he grew angry.

"You know, Pop," Bryan said, "I'm good at what I do. And I learned it in church. I'm proud of that!"

"And look what you're doin'," snapped Big Rev. "You're taking the gift that God gave you out of the church and for what? For—"

"For the enjoyment of others," Bryan interjected before his father could finish his statement.

"For who?" Big Rev said. "A bunch of drunks, dope addicts, and whores?"

"No! Mannn, not everybody who listens to secular music are all drunks, dope addicts, and whores. And why you actin' so holier than thou about it? You like jazz, don't you? Are you a drunk and a whore?"

Forks plummeted down onto plates. Water glasses, including Daniel's, smacked back down on the table.

"You'd better watch your mouth, son. A college degree don't keep you safe from the back of my hand,"

Big Rev warned almost in a simmering growl. Millie wanted to say something to at least slow the carnage that was happening, but she remained speechless with the rest.

Bryan attempted to cool down to plead his next point. "Music makes me happy, Pop. In the music business is where I belong. And Chocolate Storm is good. It's my creation. You know, like 'D' is yours." Bryan couldn't look at Daniel after he said that. He knew he slashed Daniel, unexpectedly, when really he was aiming his sword at his father.

Daniel's face blushed a deep maroon. Joyce looked over, feeling terrible for him, but she didn't make a move to comfort him. Finally, Mother Millie protested. "Bryan," she shouted once she found her voice, "that was a terrible thing to say."

"Sorry, Mom. Sorry 'D,'" Bryan said, still not looking at Daniel.

"But the truth is, Pop, you got what you want. You get everything you want. You need to let me have what I want. Let me follow my dream."

"And just where do you think this dream is gonna lead you, huh? Besides skid row," Big Rev charged.

"No. To stardom, in my own right. Doing what I love to do."

Big Rev threw his napkin down in his plate and pushed his formidable body away from the table. He made a grand measure of noise doing it. The hardwood floor cried out in pain. "Stardom, huh? Do you know how many fools think that same thing?"

"I'm not a fool."

"Okay, okay." Big Rev stopped his motion and said this to his son, "Let's say you go to New York and record this, this album. Fine, as long as you pull yourself together in the fall and buckle down for divinity school."

Big Rev had conceded and included both Bryan's summer plans and his future serious plans into his realm of reasoning. For the Graystones, this was big. Big Rev never conceded or compromised about much of anything. Big Rev had said his piece and finished removing himself from the dinner table. For him the dilemma was over—worked out, decided, and done. But it wasn't quite over. Right then, Bryan made a split decision that placed him at the point of no return.

"I'm not coming back, Pop."

Big Rev swerved his body back in his son's direction. What he thought he heard him say was incredulous. "What you say, boy?"

"You heard me right, Pop. I'm going to New York, and I'm not coming back. I'm not going to divinity school, either. That's your thing, not mine." Bryan was standing up now, as well.

Big Rev fumed. "You mean you gonna raise your scrawny tail up from *my* table, in *my* house, and defy *me*, boy? Your father?"

"Ain't nobody defying you, Pop. I'm just goin' out after my dream, my way, that's all."

"You're disgracin' this family and my church. You're disgracin' God," Big Rev declared.

Both Daniel and Joyce choked and coughed. They were submerged in fear.

"Ain't nobody disgracin' nobody." Bryan's voice was low and gravelly.

"Oh, naw you talkin' back to me, huh? Well, listen here, Mr. Dreamchaser, if you pack your rags—no, the stuff that I paid for—and walk out of this house, don't you come back, you hear?"

"Tommy!" Mother Millie yelled and gasped. She hurried herself from the table and followed her husband up the stairs and to their bedroom. Round two would happen in private, behind closed doors and without Bryan. Obviously, she needed to talk some sense into him. The kids commenced to clearing the table.

The celebration was over. Everyone but Joyce, Daniel, and Bryan moved. Bryan looked over at the two of them and said, "Well, I guess the two of y'all better watch your butts around here." He laughed sarcastically. They were silent. Bryan salted the fresh revelation, saying, "Y'all see what happens when you do something he don't like." He left the dining room and headed upstairs to pack.

In the fall of 1977, Daniel entered into Morgan's School of Divinity. As expected, he rose to new heights.

Bryan's debut album, *Holy Ghost Funk*, went platinum. It was the first of seven platinum hits. He didn't come home for holidays or even for Joyce's wedding to Derrick Ellis or, later, when she gave birth to her green-apple-eyed son, Derrick, Jr. Li'l 'D' is what everyone grew to call him.

Chapter Seventeen

Pocket Change Payoffs

1996

"I hear your boys are doing a bang-up job collecting the money on Sundays," Crystal said to Daniel with a crooked grin. It was Tuesday. She appeared in his office holding phone messages. Familiar with that smirk on her face, he could sense something was up.

"They've been doing it for a year now. What are you talking about?" he asked. She gloated with satisfaction.

"Your boys. Yo' deacs. Your bang-up finance committee," she said. She cracked herself up.

Okay, trouble's brewing, he calculated in his head. "Come in here and shut the door," Daniel demanded. She had his undivided attention now, which was how she liked it.

"Well, Rev, if you don't put a handle on things, your boys are gonna embarrass you one day."

He darn-near raised his voice at that comment, but caught himself. He raised his eyebrows instead. "Crystal, please," he said in a low, serious tone, "cut it out and explain yourself."

She sat down in the chair opposite his desk and moved in close.

"Are you aware that your boys, excuse me, the *deacons*, are not bothering to count the change that comes in on Sundays?"

Daniel fell back in his chair in total disbelief. "What are you talking about?"

"It's true," Crystal said. "Evidently by the time they get to the money that jingles, they get tired of counting. And I haven't even gotten to the part about how many times the bank slips don't match up with the deposits." She threw herself back in her chair and rolled her eyes to nail in her point.

"Mr. Shapiro, down at the bank, called me three times this month sounding off about it."

"Why didn't you come to me about it?" Daniel asked.

"Because I handled it. That's my job, Boss, remember?"

"So why are you telling me this stuff now?" he said. She smiled. That little boy cuteness came out when he was pissed, horny, or helpless. And right now, she wanted him pissed.

"The answer to that is simple, Boss . . .," she told him. "I'm telling you because this little tidbit is out in the congregation, that's why," Crystal said in mocked seriousness. "And it's gonna embarrass your high-yella heinie if you don't do something about it," she smirked again.

For like a second, Daniel weighed his options. His first preference was to smack that smart-alecky smile off Crystal's face. But that could lead to no good. So, he eased up from his chair and moved around the desk, patientlike. He straddled the arm of her chair. Crystal watched him closely, braced for she didn't know what. He rubbed his thigh on her arm, dipped down, and pecked her forehead with a kiss that dripped of sweet poison. Then he sodomized her ear with his tongue. She tensed up a bit at first, but then relaxed as his words went in after.

"Come on, Crystal . . ." Daniel whispered. He stroked her hair with his chin, then stroked the neck of her silk blouse with his fingers. Her head rolled. Her backbone relaxed like a kitten responding to a nice belly scratch from its master. "Sweetheart," Daniel said with the voice he only used during their Monday morning meetings, "I'm sorry about the other day. I had so much on my mind. I wanted to lie there all afternoon with you," he whispered. "Big Rev spoiled it. I was really mad at him, not you." He inched his fingers to the front of her blouse. "I've always liked the way you look in this dress," he said.

It's a blouse, but what the heck, she made a mental note.

"I like the way you look outta your dress too," he said and smiled in her eyes. Her silent return was his go-ahead to continue the conversation at hand. He was on top, now. He walked back to his seat of authority behind his desk.

"So, Crystal," Daniel said. Tensions had eased. The Monday Morning voice tone evaporated. "What are you talking about? The deacons not counting the change that comes in the collections?"

"Well, they just divvy it up among themselves."

He glared at her.

"Yep." She was relaxed now and had lost her need to torture him.

"How do you know this?"

"You know little Charise, Jayray's daughter?"

"Yeah. I know her. Jayray does my car."

"Yeah. Well, Charise went on a date with Deacon Winston's son, Dante."

"So?"

"Well, Charise told her mother and father at the dinner table how Dante paid for the whole entire date:

movie, Big Macs, even gas for the car in change/loose money/coins."

"And how do you know this, Crystal?" He itched to get at it.

"Well . . .," Crystal said. The gossip juices watered in her mouth. ". . . Charise's little sister, Shelia, told my daughter." Crystal was almost breathless, relaying the revelation. "And that's not all. The other day during the youth basketball game in the park, the Mr. Softy Ice Cream Truck rolled around. Deacon Winston's son volunteered to buy. Rita followed Dante too to hurry them along. You know Rita."

He nodded.

"And Rita . . . you know . . . She's my homegirl. Rita said his ashtray and glove compartment—yes, girlfriend went into his glove compartment—all of that was *full* of change." Crystal's hand swept the air to hammer another nail in her point. "He grabbed up a handful of more than twenty dollars in change. Divvied it up like it wasn't nothing, and the kids bought ice-cream cones, ice pops, whatever they wanted."

"Crystal, how do you know that the change Rita saw in his car came from the Forest Unity offering plates, huh? How can you say that?"

"Daniel, honey, Dante told her it did."

"What!"

"You heard me. Rita asked him, outright, how come he had so much loose change. And he told her. Like it was nothing. He told her that it came from the offering plates on Sundays.

"Ain't nobody made a stink about it yet," Crystal said, "but, you know . . . It's only a matter of time." Daniel had to think a minute. Crystal decided to add to his thoughts. "And while you're thinking on that, let me give you a little more food for thought. I don't know if you're aware of it, but chump change at Forest Unity Church ain't exactly chump change. And those *chumps* you got are padding their pockets with *your* money. Excuse me, Rev . . .," Her smirk widened—kind of like the Joker's. ". . . I mean, *God's* money," she corrected herself.

Daniel yanked the phone receiver off its base, about to tear at its keypad. He stopped himself, pressed it against his chest and inhaled/exhaled a refocused breath. He looked over at Crystal. "Baby, could you get started on those thank-you letters, please?"

"Sure, Rev," she responded as she got up to leave. She knew full well who he was about to call.

"Shut the door behind you."

"Right, Rev." Crystal left.

The phone moved into its third ring. Finally, there was a pick up. "Deacon," Daniel said.

"Hey, Rev," Deacon Charlie Winston answered, using a relaxed homeboy voice.

"Get here in an hour." The call ended, leaving the deacon hanging.

Daniel had a feeling that some financial discrepancies might have been occurring, but he couldn't put his finger on it. So he had kept it to himself. The church paid for his mortgage and car note, which was outside of his salary and not exactly common knowledge. Crystal knew it, Deacon Winston, and of course, Big Rev knew it. But none of that veered out of the usual, and it shouldn't have caused the two-million-dollar check for the down payment for the land to bounce. The check was for the land on which the old Lemel Middle School once stood.

He had gotten a confidential phone call about the insufficient funds from Mr. Shapiro just that morning. Unbeknownst to Daniel, Crystal eavesdropped on the bank's phone call. She eavesdropped on all his calls. Reverend Harris and Forest Unity Church were good and valuable customers of the Foxwoods Bank of North America, and the bank siphoned off a good many customers from its congregation. Mr. Shapiro, first name, Sheldon—Sheldon and Daniel played golf together sometimes. He gladly gave his friend a grace period before he had to inform the city that the check was no good. So first thing on Daniel's agenda was to come up with about $250,000 worth of "pocket change" to make that check good. He fumed.

Chapter Eighteen

Crystal Clear

1996

"Reverend Harris," Crystal announced on the phone using her professional voice, "Deacon Winston is here to see you."

Deacon Winston stood in front of her desk hovering and smiling down at her. If he and Daniel were still enjoying boyhood, he might have a shot at that booty too. There wasn't nothing wrong with sampling Daniel's leftovers. *Shoot! That's how I got my wife*, he thought. He remembered how his little cinnamon beauty, shy and in love, was devastated when Daniel, in hot demand, didn't have the time to coax her out of her virginity.

Deacon Winston fought the image of Crystal, nude and kneeling before the Rev . . .

"Thanks, Crystal." Daniel's voice penetrated the speakerphone.

"You can go in now," she smiled.

He let go a shaky, "ah, huh," and couldn't meet her eyes. She gave him a *you-wish-you-could-tap-this* smile anyway. Crystal watched the deacon walk into Daniel's office.

The entire church speculated. It couldn't help it. From the moment Mrs. Gentry fled the scene, it seemed like

Daniel and Crystal were inseparable. Increasingly, no one could get a word, a message, or a visit with Daniel without having to first go through her. Speculation was only human. Crystal knew it. She liked it. It gave her power. She had no power at home except for the power attached to her hip in the form of a cell phone. It was Daniel's hotline to her at all times. She even placed it on her night table beside her bed when she slept. When folks started whispering about it, they wondered what in the world her husband was thinking.

Deacon Winston burst through the door with a grin. "Hey, Rev, what's up? What's on fire?"

"Come in, Charlie. Close the door behind you."

Deacon Winston did what he was told, walked in deeper, and sat down. He was silent. When Daniel called him "Charlie" instead of 'C,' he knew it was serious.

Daniel cleared his throat before he spoke. "Charlie, what's this about the deacons pocketing the offering change?"

"Where'd you hear something like that? They're counting the money. I'm counting it too." He repositioned himself in the chair and cleared his throat. "In fact, me and the boys are here until five and six o'clock in the evening, every Sunday, counting money."

Daniel kept his eye on him the entire time he spoke, scrutinizing.

"Charlie, I heard y'all are in there counting all the bills and checks, all the paper money, but you're not counting the change."

"Where'd you get that from?" He painted himself vague.

"Is it true, Charlie?"

"Well . . . no . . . yeah . . .," he stuttered now. The deacon continued, "Rev, do you know how much change comes through here on a Sunday?"

"No, Charlie, I don't 'cause you don't count it."

"Shoot, it's the dollars that count, right, man?"

"All of it counts. You boys been stealing my money."

Deacon Winston took some breaths, wiped his forehead with a white embroidered handkerchief he pulled out of his breast pocket, and stood up. "Look, man, ain't Noboby stealin' from you. We just didn't think that noisy money was all that serious. We're working like slaves in that backroom. Anybody ever tell you that?" deacon retorted, wondering who the mole was.

"Okay, Charlie," Daniel said. His jaws loosened up. "What's done is done. But I want that change counted from now on. You got that?"

"Yeah, Rev, I got cha." Charlie sat back down.

"Here's what we gonna do. I know your men have been working their butts off. We're gonna add a few more saints to the list." Daniel let his chair swivel to help him think. "Check out who in the congregation should get the call to become a deacon and let's recruit them."

"The 'Call,'" Deacon Winston said with a sarcastic smile.

"Yeah, boy, 'The Call,' and I'll call them up and asked them to be a deacon," Daniel said. They both laughed.

"Start off by calling Brother Elroy Sallie. He's running the music ministry. Crystal can give you his number."

"Brother Sallie? Why him?"

"He's a good, seasoned, stable brother."

"Didn't Brother Sallie used to go to Big Rev's church?"

"Yeah, that's how I know he's a good brother. He moved his family over to Forest Unity to support me.

I've known that cat all of my life. If there's anybody you can trust, it's Brother Elroy Sallie."

"What you mean is . . .," Deacon Winston said, ". . . since you can't trust me."

"Now, c'mon, 'C,' don't take it like that. You said, yourself, y'all are overworked," Daniel said. Then he smiled to soothe the savage beast. "I'm gonna appoint Deacon Elroy Sallie as your cochair," Daniel slipped in, hopeful it would slide under the wire.

"Cochair!"

"Yeah, you know what I mean, your second lieutenant. Oh, and recruit Brother Mercer too."

"Mercer?" Deacon Winston said, "You mean Reggie Mercer, Crystal's husband?"

"Yeah, Crystal's husband."

Deacon Winston said under his breath, "Keep your friends close and the friends you screwin' over, closer, huh."

"What's that, Charlie?" Daniel asked the question coldly.

"Huh? Nothing, Rev," Deacon Winston said. He got up to leave.

The meeting was over.

Daniel came up with $1,500,000 for the land. The problem was he wrote a $2 million check for the down payment on his $7 million mini-me worship center. Thank God, the coming Sunday was Forest Unity's anniversary Sunday. He was sure he could cover the difference. He rubbed his forehead; then he intercomed Crystal. "Crystal, can you bring me a copy of Sunday's agenda, please? Bring the draft bulletin, if it's ready. Thanks."

She brought them in with a smile. He snatched both, thanked her, and proceeded to peruse the schedules.

He knew the congregation was revved and would show up in record numbers, wearing special colors for the day, presenting a children's play in the morning, and fellowshipping with The Bible Deliverance Church of God for the evening service. The entire day was primed for a great turnout. "Each one, bring one," he recalled saying from the pulpit for the last three Sundays. It was one of the most effective secret weapons, besides the main attraction of Daniel, to pump up the membership and the offering. There would be ecumenical dignitaries invited and city officials, Mr. Shapiro, the works. To top it off, Big Rev was slated as the guest preacher for the entire day. Everyone rushed to see Big Rev and Little Rev put on a show together.

Raising $500,000 would be a stretch, but he thought he could do it. The timing couldn't have been better. Daniel had dinner over at Big Rev's the next evening to discuss the particulars.

"I heard about that scam," Big Rev smirked, "each-one-bring-one crap!"

"It ain't no scam to get people to come to church, raise the bounty—for the church," he stressed, "while they're in the Spirit. I'm just telling you to call an impromptu come-on-down-and-get-your-blessing offering," Daniel said. "That's all."

"That's all, huh? I don't want none of that hocus-pocus crap," Big Rev said, sitting in his La-Z-Boy, shaking his hands in the air. "Just do it the old-fashioned way. Put a table out; set a basket on it, and say, 'This is for the preacher. If you were blessed by what the Lord did through him, then bless the preacher, or the building fund, or whatever.' Is that so hard to do?"

"Well, no, Pop. If you say so, we'll do it that way. But believe me, you'd get more the other way."

"Son, I got all I need. I'm living comfortable. My church takes good care of me and always has. And the Lord has blessed me even with all my faults. One day, you'll realize that that's enough."

Daniel was silent, thinking about what Big Rev said.

"And when you gettin' married, boy?" Big Rev said, half in jest, half-serious.

"Pop," Daniel laughed, "don't start, Pop!"

"You got someone on the hook?" Big Rev probed.

"Well, yeah. Perhaps," Daniel said, slowly, grinning.

"She right for the job?"

"Oh yeah, I'd say she's Ms. Right," Daniel replied.

Chapter Nineteen

There's a-Meetin' in the Ladies' Room

1996

"Saints, I'd like you to meet someone very special to me." Daniel aimed his smile down and out—second row, center. "Stand up, Mother, stand up and let the folks see you," he said from the pulpit. His teeth glistened. Rose, caught off guard, nervously cleared her purse and church program off her lap. Something she couldn't catch fell to the carpet, and she stood to face the crowd. She brandished a timid smile and waved.

Then, she turned in the direction of her son and mouthed the words "thank you." She blew him a kiss. He pretended to catch it. The congregation laughed and clapped. Rose sat down. The syrupy moment made Daniel's stomach queasy. He swallowed hard, determined not to let it disrupt his Academy Award—winning performance.

The occasion was Children's Day. Though the Anniversary Sunday pulled in more than half of the $500,000 he needed to make the down payment check good on his mini-me worship center, he still needed money, and he was pulling out all the stops for the celebration at hand. Daniel knew the saints flocked to church whenever he hinted a further revelation of his private life. So he gladly announced that the church would officially get to meet his mother on that glorious day.

The Sunday also doubled as another Each-One-Bring-One Sunday again. Each-One-Bring-One Sunday happened at least once a month lately. During Daniel's brief three-year tenure, the Forest Unity Church of Baltimore was rounding out a 2,500-member congregation. All of the youth in the church and in the community were encouraged to bring their parents, aunts, uncles, and guardians to the service. A fair number of parents in the community dropped off their children at church and sped off before the Holy Ghost could catch them, Daniel joked in private. But teens and young adults found their way there in droves due to word-of-mouth. Daniel was a magnet.

Folks close to Daniel were starting to ask why his mother had never been to the church. She wasn't even there during his installation service. And Daniel often referred to Millie Graystone as his mother. Most of them knew about Rose, had heard the legendary tales about her that deliciously traveled over from The Bible Deliverance Church of God. The mother-sisters had died within eight months of each other back in 1986. Daniel's Aunt Cille went first. Lucille suffered from Alzheimer's before she passed away. Her death was especially painful to Daniel because toward the end of her life, his aunt Cille not only didn't recognize him as Daniel, but she kept accusing him of murder and screaming out the name Jud Hainey, whenever she saw him. It always stunned him into silence. She'd holler and cry and sometimes curse at him.

Aunt Cille was ninety-three when she died. It seemed that Aunt Mattie, who was ninety-six and very clear-minded, was so heartbroken about losing her sister that she just couldn't live without her. Daniel's Aunt Mattie went to heaven in her sleep, in her home, in her bedroom, sitting in her precious rocking chair. Her Bible laid open to the Twenty-third Psalm, cradled in the well of her lap.

Rose attended both funerals, inappropriately dressed and drunk.

Daniel was becoming quite the politician in the way of being able to sense when it was time to do things. Portraying the good son, he stopped in on his mother from time to time and made sure she had everything she needed. He paid the rent on her apartment and supplemented her barmaid salary. He loved her; but it was a long time ago when he learned to love her at a distance. That's just the way it was. He'd try to minister to her. She told everybody how he was the only thing she did in her life that turned out right. But when it came to church invites, Rose always issued her standard answer, "I'll get down there to that church as soon as I get my life right."

The Friday evening before the church service, Daniel went over to see his mother and he asked, again, about attending the Children's Day celebration. Rose said yes. It surprised both of them.

From that Sunday on, Rose attended Forest Unity on a near regular basis. There was nothing she could do about the past, she knew, but she began to think earnestly about wanting to change her life and wanting to support her son in the present. Prior to the invitation, unbeknownst to her son, Rose had joined an AA group and was trying to get a handle on her drinking. She was still addicted to no-good men. She was just going to have to tackle one thing at a time.

The year was 1996. Rose may have been fifty-eight years old, but she looked good and had a body that could hold its own against any woman twenty years her junior. Rose's drinking, partying, and man-drama, which she still loved because she craved to be the earth's center, hadn't seemed to take its toll at all. She now wore her hair in a short, cropped do. It complemented her face. But she refused to let it go gray. And she liked her clothes tight and revealing. Going a size up on that skirt set presented another major battle. Crystal was ordered to take her shopping.

"Isn't she beautiful?" Daniel said to his congregation. He beamed like a proud son. And he wasn't lying. Rose was beautiful. She blushed, and the congregation laughed and clapped again.

Throughout the Children's Day weekend celebration, more than one hundred children and teens, members of the church, enjoyed events at Daniel's house. There was a prayer breakfast, a basketball tournament, a picnic, complete with a Moon Bounce set up in the backyard for the little ones, a movie shown on Daniel's big screen TV, and a Sunday dinner. Young energy spilled out from everywhere in the house and on the front and back lawns. The house was wall-to-wall children. It looked like a carnival. Church volunteers worked like tireless ants taking care of everything. Daniel roamed around and played with the young ones like he was a kid himself.

"Over here, over here," he jumped up and down, shouting during a pickup game of basketball in his backyard. Daniel waved his hands about, pushed, and shoved his teen opposition, much to their delight, trying to steal the ball. And when he tripped and fell over his own feet, the kids and their bystander parents all fell out on the lawn, howling and laughing. "Foul, foul," he tried to shout, but he was doubled over in hysterics. And when he tried to recount it the next day in church, hysterics abounded once more.

Children's Day was a special occasion, but, actually, a small core of young people often spent time at Daniel's house. He was their Pied Piper. But when Big Rev saw how generally exhausted Daniel was growing, he suggested that perhaps Daniel should move out into one of the surrounding counties.

"So drop-ins won't be so convenient," Big Rev said. On the Thursday before the celebration, The Bible Deliverance Church of God and Forest Unity Church of Baltimore conducted a combined fellowship by taking both youth ministries to an Orioles' game. Big Rev loved baseball, so he and Daniel went along. They sat in box seats, of course, for privacy. Then they got to talking.

"Son, you know, since you say you're gonna marry that little girl you met, I was thinking that maybe you need to get a house farther out."

"What? Where's that coming from? Farther out where and why?" Daniel spoke, dropping and munching on handfuls of popcorn.

"If you're going to be married, a new marriage needs privacy. And let's face it, son, living as close to the church as you do, privacy is one thing you don't have. Them kids are 'round your house 24/7."

"It's not that bad."

"It looks like it to me, boy. And you look tired. You ain't as young as you used to be, you know." Big Rev smiled at the ribbing he dished out.

It was funny to Daniel too. He said, "You know, Pop, first, you tell me to get married, and I'm doin' what you told me to do. And now you're telling me to move out of my house. And where would I move to—if I did decide to move?"

"How'd you meet up with her again . . . With this Lori?" he said. Most of the time, he got her name wrong.

"A blind date," Daniel said. He popped candy-coated peanuts into his mouth this time. "Bryan set us up. She didn't even know I was a pastor," he said.

"Yeah, well, she knows it now," Big Rev chuckled. "She's a bit younger than you, ain't she, boy?"

"Yeah . . . need 'em young," Daniel said, gloating. "She gotta give me some babies." He laughed.

Big Rev laughed too at the rawness of the thought. "Hope she don't give you a fit, instead, like all them other gals you been running with. You said she's a musician?"

"Yep."

"She sings that devil-hollering music my son plays, huh?" Big Rev's forehead wrinkled with disapproval.

"Bryan's music is good, Pop. You ought to give it a chance. Lori was one of Bryan's students. You know . . . when he did his gospel music workshop at Morgan. Remember?"

The Children's Day at Forest Unity was packed. It was standing room only, and turned Daniel's deficit into a surplus. The day was good. Two hours after the service, the church thinned considerably. Only remnants of the insiders' crowd straggled about. Inside the ladies' room, three toilets flushed: one, then two, then three. Crystal came out of one stall and moved toward the line of basins to wash her hands. She checked herself out in the mirror. Shortly after that, Joyce Graystone appeared with the same goal. Moments later, Lori Sparrow appeared. The three were astonished at the sight of the other. Jaws dropped, but only for a second.

"Well, well, well, what is the Lord up to now? Or is it the devil?" Crystal cracked, keeping her eyes on her own reflection in the mirror, freshening up her lipstick.

"Oh no. It's the devil doin' this, and you ought to know that, Crystal, since you're his bastard child," Joyce said, while staring at her reflection, reapplying her rouge.

Crystal and Joyce both shut down their beauty utensils, tossed them in their purses, and turned to face each other. And for a second or two, it seemed that Lori had a ringside seat. Nobody had said anything to her yet. Lori, of course, knew both women, but she had yet to corroborate the backstory gossip about either. That Daniel had a past and perhaps a present relationship with both Crystal and Joyce. Lori knew she didn't like the way Crystal always made demands on Daniel's time right in front of her face. Three months ago, since Monday was Daniel's only full day off, Lori's first official act as his fiancée was to put an end to his Monday morning meetings with Crystal. Now, Mondays were reserved for their time together, and Lori noticed right away how Crystal didn't seem to like it.

Crystal's extracurricular activities ended abruptly when Lori fell into the picture out of nowhere. She was going to get to Lori in a minute, but first she had to straighten out Joyce.

"I know you ain't talkin' about nobody being nobody's bastard child." Crystal's crooked smirk was a mile wide.

"You whorin' witch," Joyce quipped back. Her hand was in the face-slapping position. "Whatya you doin' with all your free time now, Crystal, since you ain't sleepin' with Daniel anymore—just your husband?"

As juicy as the moment was, Lori felt she had primped her hair long enough and that it was time to vacate the ugly scene. Though she was losing her ability to make like it wasn't affecting her, she thought it was best to remain above it. Lori attempted to squeeze past them, but that last comment caused her to freeze, drop her mouth, and drop her purse on the floor. Crystal turned and accidentally/on purpose kicked the purse under the adjacent bathroom stall door. Both Joyce and Crystal blocked Lori's passage. They stood with nasty attitudes smeared all over their faces and their arms folded like barricades.

"Enjoy it while you can, sweetie," Joyce sniped at Lori. "Maybe it's all yours now, but if you know like I know, you'll be sharing it before the honeymoon is over."

Crystal stood there and looked Lori up and down, wondering what Lori had that she didn't. *How come the Rev picked her to marry?* her thoughts raced. One thing that Lori *didn't* have was an unresponsive husband and three bratty kids. "You better be careful, little girl," Crystal said to Lori, "whatever you got, he's gonna get tired of, and—"

"And *what?*" Joyce snapped. She directed her venom at Crystal now, where she really wanted it. ". . . and what? He'll come running back to you? That's what you think? Honey, you ain't nothing but yesterday's filthy rag."

"Why don't you mind your own business?" Crystal whispered through clinched teeth. Her head moved sideways, back and forth on its axis; her lips worked about three inches from Joyce's nose.

"Ahhh, ladies," Lori interrupted. She had collected herself by then and was ready to snipe back. She did the black woman head roll as well and said, "Just a word to both of you two old hags . . ." Lori secured her purse strap on her shoulder, ". . . leave my man alone and stop grabbing at crumbs and sloppy seconds. It's not very becoming of Christian women. Y'all ain't that hungry, are yah?" She said her piece and squeezed between both of them. Lori exited the ladies' room with her heart hurting, but her back was straight.

Crystal and Joyce both were stunned into silence until Lori disappeared out the door. Joyce said, watching the door close, "Poor little girl is in for a rude awakening." Crystal headed for the door as well.

With her back turned to Joyce, she let loose one more zinger. "Huh! You should know." She left.

Joyce stood there gazing at herself in the mirror. "That stupid fool."

Outside, Lori couldn't get to the parking lot fast enough and into her Jaguar before she let her tears fall. *Is he really sleeping with those two witches?* she questioned herself. She gripped her steering wheel, twisting and turning it in dry dock, trying to get out of there as quickly as possible.

"Before I totally trip," she said to herself, trying to calm herself down, "I'll give Daniel a chance to straighten this out. Yeah, that's right. That's what I'll do." She twisted the key and pressed down hard on the gas pedal to let the engine roar. "I need to hear what he's got to say about all this. If his mess is raggedy, I sure don't need to be all up in it." She maneuvered like she was at the starting line of the Indy 500. "My momma told me I can do bad all by myself."

Crystal whipped out her cell phone to speed dial Daniel's cell. It rang and rang until the recorded message kicked in. That was the kind of treatment she got from him lately. He dropped her, cold turkey. She was so mad, anger could have split her in two.

Chapter Twenty

Speak Now or Forever Hold Your Peace

1996

"It's going to be official, Sunday. I just wanted to tell you first before I made the announcement. I figured I at least owed you that."

"You're a grown man, Daniel, you don't owe me anything," Joyce said.

She kicked miscellaneous pebbles around in the sand when she talked.

Daniel had halted their stroll to say what he had to say and study her face after he had said it. Joyce looked out at the water. Her goal was to let the rhythmic roll of the waves hypnotize her, not the concentrated strain in her ex-lover's eyes. It seemed like centuries ago when they strolled that very same strip of beach, arm-in-arm, on a regular basis, during their secret getaways to Solomon's Island. It was their private paradise as far as they were concerned. It belonged to them. Why Daniel had begged for her to meet him there, to tell her this, she'd never understand. She felt it unnecessarily cruel. But she was determined to keep her cool. She'd given him all she had—her body, her love, her dignity. There was nothing left to give. *Don't cry, Joyce. Whatever you do, don't cry*, she commanded herself. *Don't give him that too.*

"You marrying Lori Sparrow is not exactly a news flash, you know," Joyce said. Daniel fanned out the blanket he was holding and spread it atop the sand, maneuvering like Joyce hadn't said what she said at all. They were just two star-crossed lovers sharing a carefree world. The two of them folded their bodies onto it wondering what to do next. She allowed herself to cuddle in his waiting arms because she couldn't help it. They absorbed the beautiful landscape that God had laid out before them, foamy blue and greenish waves in constant motion, white-feathered birds coasting low and dipping their beaks into the water for lunch, and families enjoying a perfectly presummer-drenched day against a backdrop of quaint little shops and restaurants. *Why couldn't this moment be all there is?* she wondered.

Daniel readjusted himself slightly when the awareness of her warmth feeling good and forbidden washed over him. She fell weak to his touch the night before. Their lovemaking ravaged her soul, but titillated her body still. He sat there, gently rubbing her thigh, gazing at a skyline that only replayed their lovemaking in his mind, and made him hopeful for another night of bliss before he had to head back to Baltimore—to the world he inadvertently created for show.

That's it, Joyce had vowed to herself. Their tryst the night before was the end. *I'm heading back to Baltimore today*, she assured her mind and heart. What they did last night would not happen again. She certainly wasn't about to be anybody's tawdry mistress; the adulterous other woman. Maybe some others would, but not her.

"I already asked Lori. We've been planning," Daniel said, "but tomorrow, I'm going to announce the engagement to the church."

Joyce's chuckle had a slight snarl in it. "Oh, if your church could see you now, huh? Why are you marrying her, Daniel? I don't understand. Help me to understand." Her voice was mixed with hurt and anger.

"Big Rev told me to. That's why. It's not proper for me to be single forever. So I'm getting married." He spoke like he had practiced his speech, several times, in fact.

"But, why to her?"

Frustrated, he gently moved her aside and stood up. "Because she fits the image—she can get me into the right circles." He was reaching for an answer that would let him off the hook of absurdity once it hit air, but the hook dug in like a meat hook. "She's teachable, you know?" He twisted and turned and looked dumbfounded.

The previous gentle moment had rushed out with the tide.

"Teachable? What the heck does that mean? Marry me, Daniel. We love each other. Forget about pleasing my father all the time, pleasing a crowd, and please me. Please yourself—with something tangible—your family!"

For years, off and on, her pride helped her to stonewall when he refused to step out on faith. When she stonewalled, he stonewalled too. But a mere unexpected glance or touch between them, and emotions raced to the thin lining of their skin. It was a vicious cycle.

"Perhaps you crossed the line when you married that Derrick guy," Daniel said, low, defensive, and wounded.

"Perhaps you forced my hand when you kept refusing to make a public commitment to me," Joyce's glare pierced. "But that's over now," she said. "Marry me, so we can start over." Her pride lay naked and unprotected. There wasn't a hedge, a fig leaf, nothing in sight, and it broke Daniel's heart—that fear of losing his kingdom would have him stoop so low as to cause this.

Daniel knew he would never love anyone the way he loved Joyce, and he had no inkling to. Yet he couldn't make a move. For a man whose words melted and oozed out of his mouth with flawless effort, he stood there stumped for words.

With all her defenses crumbled into the sand burying her feet, soft and wanting, she said, "All these years, I've been waiting for you to man up. I've been willing to drop everything and anybody for you. And you still can't."

Ashamed, he loosed himself from her touch and her gaze. He turned his back and said, ". . . You're off limits to me. You know that."

She kicked sand. "My God! What kind of hold does my father have on you? We're grown people now, Daniel! Don't make the mistake you're about to make."

Daniel stared at her with pain on his face. His pitiful expression kept the moment silent. Silence was his shield. Finally, he said, "We'd better be getting back."

Tears rolled down Joyce's cheeks. He moved to comfort her. "Back off!" she shouted. She looked into his eyes with an expression that he read very well. It conveyed her total heartbreak. When her words came, she gently, but firmly said, "This won't happen again, Daniel." She threw her hands up in the air around her. She added, "You can marry her, Daniel, but I'll tell you one thing. I won't be your whore, your groupie, your fool. I won't be your anything!"

"I love you, Joyce." Daniel snuck it in, slicing her hurt and rage, but he couldn't defuse it. She didn't respond. Without action, his words meant nothing.

"Forget you, Daniel. Just go burn in hell! And hurry up!"

Joyce walked the line of the sandy beach, alone, ahead of him. He kept his eye on her, but he let the distance between them grow, greater and greater. Joyce walked back to the Stratford Inn's parking lot. She got into her car and drove off—toward the Bay Bridge.

Lori Sparrow was the first girl Daniel at least respected. Sure, she had her mind on herself a little too much, messing around with her music and all that, but she was young and pure and honest. He would marry her and fill her up with babies and concerns for him. Lori had strict values. He knew right away that she'd inherited that from her father, Deacon Jimmy Sparrow. From the moment the Sparrow family got to the church, they walked a tight spiritual line. Mrs. Sparrow listened intently to Daniel's preaching like she was studying it instead of being mesmerized by it. He was bothered by that. He watched her from the pulpit. She wasn't hooting and hollering at everything he said, especially when he threw out his buzz words and praises that were sure to get the hooting and hollering started. Her husband was the same way. Indoctrinating Jimmy Sparrow into the deacon board was the perfect way. But that brother kept getting harder to control. Deacon Sparrow kept messing up the empire with his bothersome questions. The one thing Daniel could count on from Deacon Sparrow was that he did everything in a quiet manner. Daniel knew it was because Sparrow wanted to protect his daughter.

Daniel made his engagement announcement from the pulpit that Sunday. Lori stood there beaming by his side. With her help, he recounted the cute moments of their awkward blind date and subsequent budding, record-setting courtship. The congregation laughed and supped on every juicy detail. Now it had a future first lady to suck up to. Those wanting to get close invited her to lunches, dinners, and the outings they planned. They showered her with gifts. Several women in the congregation, like the woman who always came to Daniel's house to cut his hair, sat there that Sunday, itchy about the news. But they forced themselves to brandish a good convincing game face.

Oh, there'll be a slight cooldown, most of them thought, *but then the extracurricular activities will start up again. What in heaven's name did he see in her in the first place? What's she got between her legs,* they pondered, *gold?*

But Daniel didn't know what Lori had between her legs. Lori took the position that a holy man, naturally, wouldn't ask her to have sex before marriage. He never made a move in that direction. And he liked that. Lori didn't need him to make her look good or feel important. She didn't need him for prestige or arm candy. He liked that too. She was beautiful in her own right, had her own measure of male groupies because her career as a Rhythm and Blues artist was heating up, and she had a strong relationship with God and her family. Her only underlying motive came wrapped in her private consults with God. God had blessed her to make her circle complete, and at twenty-seven, she had fallen in love.

Daniel and Lori had wonderful times together. Conversation flowed easily between them. They shared their personal aspirations and shared interesting tidbits from Lori's life when she toured with Bryan and his band, Chocolate Storm. That intimidated Daniel a bit. It was a new feeling, but he'd keep it to himself, deciding that he'd fix that later. She just needed some retooling. Still, her life was exciting to hear about. She

didn't see a problem with her singing secular music
as long as it was good, mostly about love. Neither did
Daniel. Lori looked sensuous and classy, all at the same
time. It was in the way she carried herself, in the way
that she spoke, and in her manner of dress. She never
once wore anything too provocative or out of place. She
never put her well-defined goods on a meat wagon display. Daniel loved to inhale her too. The scent she wore
was something he'd never come across, a million miles
from that powdery scent.

Lori had a vintage jazz quality to her voice as well
that put her in the category of greats like Sarah Vaughn
and Billie Holiday, even. But Lori also put it down
whenever she sang to her Lord and Savior. She was a
featured soloist at Forest Unity when she was in town.
Her singing just about laid everyone out in the aisles.
Lori's praise and worship came from a place deep inside.

Lori loved Daniel and planned to adhere, as best she
could, to the biblical rules of marriage, but she wasn't
about to lose her career before it even had a chance to
pop off. She hadn't planned on being a bland preacher's wife, a stand-by-your-man kind of wife, dropping
babies as soon as they got married. Of course, she'd
do what she could to help his ministry. That would be
her ministry; the way she served God. All that other
stuff, running committees, teaching Bible studies, etc.,
would come in time, after she had established herself
in the music world and maybe could take a break.
Those were all the details that ran through her mind.

They had a certain kind of chemistry together, and it
was good. There was no need to rock the boat with pid-
dly details, dates, and times. *My mother had a career*,
Lori thought, *and they're coming up on their thirtieth
wedding anniversary*. Daniel was easy to talk to, and

he was from this century. So surely he understood about a woman's need for independence. There was no need to bring all that up when they were busy trying to plan a wedding.

The wedding date was set for Saturday, May 18, 1996, exactly five months from the day of the announcement. They'd been already making arrangements behind the scenes before the announcement. So everything seemed in hand. The ceremony would take place at Forest Unity. Big Rev would perform the service.

Crystal and her family were conspicuously absent for Daniel's big announcement of impending marital bliss. Deacon Mercer needed to be out of town for his job. Crystal had decided to go with him—was the word. Daniel and Lori married in grand style as planned. Privately, for him, it was a public show of confidence that the Lord was working things out.

On their wedding day the sanctuary looked like heaven, bathed in pink and white roses showered with baby's breath. Daniel and his groomsmen: Deacon Winston, Eric Johnson, Reggie Mercer, and Lori's brother, James, Jr., stood decked in black tuxedos. Their waists were wrapped with silk white cummerbunds. Positioned at the altar, the line of silver cuff links shimmered off sunrays gleaming through the stained glass windows. Not a man there stood below six feet. Bryan had his brother's back as best man. As a show of solidarity, Bryan looked at Daniel with a smile and thumped the upper part of his tuxedo jacket with his two fingers. His inside pocket held the wedding couple's circle of love. Secured in a tiny black velvet jewelry box lay matching wedding bands: twenty-four carat white gold, encrusted completely around with huge diamonds to match Lori's engagement ring. The three-ring custom-made set, set a brother back an estimated $27,000, the *Baltimore Sun* would later report, but, "Nothing is too good to show off pure love," Daniel had said.

Five goddesses floated down the aisle on an unrolled path of white satin sprinkled with pink rose petals. The goddesses were dressed in flowing off-the-shoulder pink gowns that celebrated the female form in the most dignified way. A layer of white silk chiffon draped their bare shoulders and danced in the gentle breeze of each woman's ascent to the altar. They stood lined up and perfectly framed in a cherry wood threshold. The ring bearer wore a black top hat and tails. The flower girl, with a head full of bouncy Shirley Temple curls, was a miniature baby doll bride. The guests swooned at the sight of both. They lit up the path to wedded bliss.

Cinderella's silhouette appeared on the other side of the sanctuary's glass double doors. She looked like a doll only suited for the mantle—look, but don't touch. The bodice of Lori's dress, white-on-crystal white, like icing, was contoured to the waist. Her full-length sleeves were created of lace. Each sleeve clung to and stopped abruptly at the bend of each shoulder and hugged her entire arm, clear down to the topside of her hand, where it ended in a triangle dangling a single pearl attached to a tiny crocheted string.

From the bodice, the gown fanned out endless layers of cloth, giving hint of nothing but pure fantasy underneath. No less than 2,500 hand-sewn pearls complemented the dress, though not one outdid the gleam of Lori's smile ornamented by a white sheer veil streaming from her pearl-encrusted crown. Its train, tacked on in dainty pleats, was a flowing five yards long.

The congregation stood and turned on cue of the "Wedding March," and issued a collective gasp of wonderment, her Prince Charming included, as she made way her entrance.

"And now, my son," Big Rev said, flashing a smile. Everyone laughed, "you may kiss your bride." Daniel eagerly turned toward Lori and uncharacteristically fumbled with the layers of her veil.

The couple threw the wedding reception bash in Baltimore's swankiest ballroom, Martin's West. Christian music abounded beneath the twirl of three glittering chandeliers. There seemed no end to the dinner buffet and the dessert carts. The walls of the ballroom, as was each table setting, were adorned with pink and white rose arrangements. Each place setting offered every guest a white ribboned champagne glass to take home. They brandished two statements in gold script: *Reverend and Mrs. Daniel J. Harris* and *May 18, 1996*. Daniel and Lori cut the cake and shared a first dance to a BeBe and CeCe Winans's tune. Lori threw the bouquet at a dozen-and-a-half women gunning for it, most hopeful for a crack at Daniel once he was finished with his bride. Daniel threw the garter. But the couple passed on the tradition of Daniel slipping the garter off his bride's thigh and the lucky man slipping it on a lucky woman. "It's not dignified," Big Rev said during the planning.

The *Baltimore Sun* and the *Baltimore Afro* gave perfect play-by-play rundowns of the nuptials, complete with center-spread color photos. Critics murmured, later, among themselves, that the event was a grand display of narcissism.

Joyce attended the wedding, but reportedly turned her ankle on the church steps and could not attend the reception.

Chapter Twenty-one

The Master's Call via AT&T

1996

"Ahhh, Deacon Sparrow, can we talk to you a minute?" Deacon Winston asked.

"Sure, brothers. What's this all about?" Deacon Sparrow countered.

Deacon Winston did all the talking. The others, the five of them, bunched up around Deacon Sparrow crowding his space—his private aura. The impromptu meeting went down after Sunday service in the vestibule near the staircase. The mood was meant to be intimidating.

"The Rev watched you today and noticed, like we've been noticing, that you didn't stand with us to take up the offerings."

"Yeah, that's right," Deacon Sparrow responded coarsely. His inquisitive smile disappeared because, now, he knew what this was all about. Deacon Winston and the other brothers were sent by Daniel to "straighten him out" on the matter.

Deacon Winston gave Deacon Sparrow a stern, direct eye-to-eye when he said, "For weeks now, you've been avoiding your duty. Today, you seemed to be in bold defiance. That looks bad to the church, Brother."

"Yeah, well, Deac," Deacon Sparrow said, "you know, I've tried to talk to Rev about it several times, but I can't seem to catch him."

"The Rev told me to tell you that you're not being obedient. He's asked you to collect and count the money, and you haven't."

Sparrow looked at the other deacons crowded around him like henchmen. *What y'all flunkies gonna do, kick my butt or somethin'?* he thought.

One Sunday, before the main offering, he leaned over and whispered to Deacon Baylor, "Hey, why we doin' this?"

Deacon Baylor whispered back, "I don't know." Then Baylor got up and grabbed an offering plate and got to work. And that's how it was for all the deacons, the seasoned ones and the new ones who got an AT&T calling to take their place on Deacon's Row. All kinds of demands had come down from on high and when anybody asked a question about it, the only answer was, "Rev said." Deacon Sparrow was sick of the "Rev said" answer. He had complied with everything else, bodyguard duty, running around to every guest-preaching gig Daniel did, running errands, even opening and closing the church sometimes. But with the money-thing, "Uh-uh," he complained to his wife one Sunday. "Everybody's got limits. Money can get funny in an instant. You heard about them givin' away the change and messing up the bank receipts, didn't you?"

"Deacon Winston," Deacon Sparrow said with a large measure of patience, "do you know what the duties of a deacon are?"

"Sure, I do."

"Then you show me in the Bible where it says that deacons are supposed to take up the money."

"A deacon is supposed to serve his pastor," Deacon Winston said coolly.

"A deacon is not supposed to handle the money," Deacon Sparrow threw back, just as calm, "and I'm not qualified to handle the money, sign for the money of this church, or be responsible for where the money goes after it leaves this church." Sparrow could stare down as good as he got. He delivered eyeball as good as he got.

Deacon Winston was steamed. He kept silent and kept his eye in Sparrow's eye. The showdown was sorely unanticipated. The other deacons began to fidget with doubt in their bones.

Deacon Sparrow continued, "I haven't been consulted on why that decision was made, where the money goes, or how it's being spent. So, I don't need to handle the money."

"You're being disobedient, Brother," Deacon Charlie Winston lobbed back.

"No, I'm not. I know what a deacon is, and I'm being that. I received my calling from God, long before I came to this church," Deacon Sparrow assured, "and not from some telephone call in the middle of the night." Deacon Sparrow kept his gaze on Deacon Winston as if the two were alone, but he meant for his comment to snipe at everyone around him.

The confrontation that day signaled the beginning of the end of a budding friendship between Winston and Sparrow. No one ever asked Deacon Sparrow to step down from being a deacon, but the other deacons were instructed to ostracize him every opportunity they got. Perhaps he and his family would leave the church quietly on their own volition. They didn't.

"Looks like this meeting is over, Brothers," Deacon Sparrow said as he looked around. No one wanted to give him eye contact. "Excuse me," he said. The other deacons cleared a path, and he walked away and left them standing there, dumbfounded. Deacon Winston and Deacon Sparrow parted in separate directions. The others coughed and shuffled, avoided looking at one another, then scattered like roaches.

Daniel made the big announcement to the church that it was about to build a new worship center over where the old Lemel Middle School used to stand. He strategically timed his announcement, Big Rev advised, until after he felt that all his ducks were in a row; that way, it would be too late for any naysayers to monkey-wrench his progress. "Among other things," he said from the pulpit, "we'll have satellite services." The sacrificial offerings had begun. Daniel's lawyer, Eric Milton Johnson, had come up with a brilliant plan to get the congregation to contribute more, and more consistently. That was the story for publication. It would financially benefit everyone at the same time. It was going to take an unprecedented $7 million for the project to be completed.

"'Employ a bond company,' Brother Johnson suggested," Daniel explained to the congregation, but that was not really true. Brother Johnson sat on his pew and smiled at the wisdom to which he was accredited, but he hadn't suggested a thing. Daniel and Crystal came up with the brilliant plan. It had been done before at several other churches around the country with great results.

The bond company guaranteed the bank's $7 million loan to Forest Unity and would, in turn, raise the funds by selling interest-yielding bonds from a variety of businesses to members of the congregation. The congregation would get first dibs on purchasing the bonds at a premium rate; then the bond company would open the sale to the community at large, and then nation-wide. Everybody would make money on the deal.

The bond agents who frequented the church propa-gating promotions and paperwork officially dubbed the plan, the Faith Fidelity United Campaign, the FFUC plan. FFUC also stood for Faith in Forest Unity Church. Daniel put the deacons in charge. They weren't qualified for that either. Crystal was the liaison be-tween them and Daniel, with whom he now discussed only business. Daniel, in consultation with Deacon Winston, the bond company agents, construction heads, etc., handed down all major decisions. There was a constant stream of permits and legal papers to be approved and signed. The deacons designated Deacon Cherry to be the official liaison between the church, city officials, and the bond company. He put his "John Hancock" on everything. The congregation and other outside investors were kept informed about the general building progress—only the things that they needed to know.

The progress moved slowly, but without any serious problems until a glitch happened with the house that Daniel had decided to purchase. He'd taken up Big Rev's suggestion about looking into that mansion in Ellicott City. Big Rev rode out there with him to see it. Six spacious bedrooms, a sunken living room, state-of-the-art kitchen, and a shamrock-shaped inground pool and pool house were just some of the perks. *Imagine, a black preacher owning all this. God certainly is good. All the time!* was the thought that skirted through Big Rev's mind.

During the forty-minute ride from the place, Big Rev talked about how important it was for a newly mar-ried couple to have their privacy. "You and Lori need space and time to work things out," he preached. "Let her know who's boss. Come together on your likes and dislikes and on how you're going to run the ministry. Believe me, boy, you may not realize it now, but when there's two heads running things—and that Lori looks like she may be pretty strong-headed—all kinds of problems can crop up and tear your kingdom asunder. You're gonna have to teach her how she's supposed to serve you."

When Daniel saw all that space inside and outside that mansion, he couldn't help seeing visions of filling it up with children—some of his own and from the church. Their loyalty and admiration of him felt different from that of the ho-groupies, the gold diggers, and the suck-ups. All that felt superficial. Right or wrong, he used the wicked lot as sustenance to feed his dirty flesh. But God had placed him in the position of being able to connect with young people and show them that loving and learning about God was not just for old fogies who didn't know how to have fun. It was the best part about being a pastor. It was time for him to be the *Big Rev* of his world, and this was just the place to do it in.

Daniel was anxious. His ready cash was short. He had to move fast because the realtor had two other serious offers on the table, but she was willing to give him an opportunity to outbid them. It was that charisma he had and his favor with women at work. The sale of his present home and a private dip into the church's building fund account would cover the sizable down payment, closing costs, and, of course, the furnishings. That private dip would also ensure that he could pay for the mansion, no matter what happened at the church.

This needed to be a private transaction, so with the discretionary assistance of Mr. Shapiro from the bank, the transfer of the bond money went smoothly. Daniel transferred 10 percent of the $3 million recently raised above and beyond the first $2 million down payment for the church's new land. The cost of the mansion was $2 million. So with 300k in his personal account, everything would be covered, he calculated. The 300k, he would be able to cover in a couple of weeks when his house sold. If things got a little tight with the building project, he could instruct his boys to do a little skimping on the materials and labor. In fact, as a safety net, he had already instructed Deacon Winston to hire some cheaper, unlicensed contractors that Winston could trust for the side jobs like the manual labor: moving bricks, hauling construction equipment, etc.

From the pulpit, Daniel also solicited the free labor of church members, eager to do God's work. The saints, who were electricians, carpenters, painters, and such, rushed to volunteer. However, the chaos they caused drove the building foreman crazy. All that came to light, later, when all the professionals quit.

Church members were ecstatic about the new beginning. Every meeting had them picking out and voting on things like the design of the outer facing of the church, carpet colors and paint colors, bathroom styles, the types of curtains, and where they should purchase pews and Bibles. In meetings, church members passed around architectural drawings, floor plans, brick samples, colorful carpet and fabric swatches. They enthusiastically bickered over what ministry would command what office and workspace, and how those spaces should look. Whatever it took, it would be the best of everything. God had mandated no less, Daniel declared. The congregation agreed. They purchased an abundance of bonds too.

"You need to sign this, Boss," Crystal said, bursting into Daniel's office and throwing some papers on his desk.

"Sign what?" he said. He was busy scratching his head over his bank statements.

"The payroll and some other stuff," she said, feigning efficiency, enjoying the farce.

"Why can't you sign it?"

"Don't think I should," she said, staring at him. Her grin was cocked to the side of her mouth.

"Where's Deacon Cherry?"

"Don't know."

"Winston?"

"He ain't here."

"You sign 'em," Daniel said. He flicked his hand off in the air in her direction.

"Nope."

Exasperated, Daniel sighed, leaned back in his chair, and looked up at the ceiling. These days he never knew when some devilish mood swing would hit Crystal to make her feel like being a pain. More than once, he fantasized about firing her, but that held the potential of wreaking more havoc. She knew too much. And she seemed to always know what he was doing before he was about to do it. The best way to handle it was to wait her out. She'd tire of being ignored and fade away, perhaps back into her husband's arms. He could hope.

But according to how Crystal felt about it, that wasn't about to happen; not even close. What she felt for Daniel had nothing to do with her husband. Daniel had used her and had thrown her away like a filthy rag, and he was going to pay for it. Finally, she'd come up with the perfect plan to ensure her job security and exact a little revenge, if she decided to go through with it.

"Come on, Rev," Crystal said with a shy, playful tone, "sign the payroll sheets. I'd like to get home." Daniel just wanted Crystal out of his sight. He pushed aside what he was doing and signed on the fanned out sheets of checks and papers she placed before him. Only the signature lines were visible on most of them. He hurried through the task.

"Finished. Okay!" Daniel said.

"Okay!" Crystal turned and vacated the office as quickly as she could, laughing and relishing in the fact that she knew how to get him to sign anything she wanted.

Chapter Twenty-two

Money and Its Evil Root

1996

"Crystal! Crystalll!" Daniel yelled. Crystal came running.

"What, Boss?"

"Get me Eric on the phone."

"Okay, Boss, whatever you say."

"And could you please cut that 'Boss' nonsense for a minute. I'm not in the mood for that crap today."

Crystal returned to her desk with a sinister grin on her face. She walked out in silence and sat down at her desk, satisfied about getting on Daniel's nerves. She rang up the church's lawyer, Eric Johnson. She also eavesdropped on Eric and Daniel's conversation.

"Look, man," Daniel said. He yelled a desperate whisper. He didn't want Crystal overhearing him. "I've been trying to get in touch with the bond company for two weeks now. And when I called this morning, the doggone phone was disconnected. Naw, you tell me, what kind of mess is that? Huh?"

"Well, I'm sure there's a logical explanation for it before we get all upset and jump to conclusions. Rev, let me make a few inquiries and check some things out, okay?"

"Eric, my neck's on the line if that darn bond company done jumped up and absconded with my church's money. You gotta darn well clear this mess up for me, mannn."

Eric heard the abrupt click in his ear. The conversation was over. He was ticked at the way his boy, Daniel, spoke to him, but he put his anger aside because he knew Daniel was excitable—nothing personal.

Daniel had some legitimate concerns, Eric couldn't deny it. Here, the calendar steadily moved closer and closer to the due date for the completion of the church edifice. And yet, even to the laymen's eye, it could be deduced that completion wasn't even close. Breezes freely blew in and through the building's skeleton, dirt piles had started to sprout weeds, and construction equipment lay in the sun, minus the human touch needed to work them. This revealed a lot.

A lot *was* happening, just not at the construction site. First off, church members who ventured out reported what they had found.

"Girrrl," one member whispered to another, "all that's missing out there is some tumbleweed. That site is a desert!" They'd shake their heads and laugh—in disgust.

Church dissention grew because the laymen news reports conflicted with what was being told from the pulpit and in the church meetings. For a time, "all is well" was the only message for publication. But all wasn't well. Daniel and the deacons didn't mean to lie outright—that wasn't their intention at all. They just needed some stalling time to clear up a few trouble spots and various misunderstandings before some real negative publicity got out. An angry congregation or an angry concerted mob in the congregation, usually all the empty-headed know-it-alls, can dry up the tithing in a heartbeat; and then where would the church be, and the purchase of Daniel's mansion?

The construction had stopped because the construction foreman couldn't take the confusion anymore. Church members were milling around messing things up and acting like they had no one to answer to except Daniel. But Daniel didn't know how to put up a building. "You can't talk the talk or walk the walk," the foreman let Daniel know during a private shouting match. And to top that, a couple of payments bounced. There was seemingly no good reason for it. None was given.

When the third payment bounced, the ABC construction company pulled out and threatened to sue for unpaid wages and breach of contract. An inexperienced church crew moved in to save the day. It kicked up the level of chaos a hundred notches until finally the site resembled a ghost town with gravel and dust blowing in the breeze. The pulpit supplied various explanations for why the construction had stalled. The best explanation was the one about a city ordinance that said the church must supply a paved parking lot before any more work on the building could be done. That was a good one—good for about three or four separate sacrificial offerings, alone.

"Paving the parking lot was one of the many extra expenses the church had not prepared for," Daniel explained. "After all, this building process stuff is new to most everyone, isn't it?" The congregation winched, but agreed. "And those pesky strict building codes, about one thing or the next, kept cropping up. Some jealous sinner downtown," Daniel said, "had it in for Forest Unity Church. But if the church will just hold on and continue the fight, God will see to it that we will prevail. Amen?" he preached.

The parking lot offerings were good for several obedient saints to come running to the altar with $1,000 in hand. Another time, the saints were asked to "sacrifice to God one week's salary. Just one week!" Daniel preached. Then he sealed the deal between them and God. "You do this and not only will the church be blessed, but your own personal finances will be blessed. Remember, God will not pour favor into your pocketbooks if you rob Him. Amen, Church? Amen."

The lack of evidence of tar, black paint, or even shoeblack anywhere near the building site caused some members to leave the church completely. The same thing happened to more members when other sacrificial offerings failed to deliver on promises of completed building work. And word got out, in the press, that the ABC Construction Company had filed suit for breach of contract.

"I'll be da—! What the heck is that boy doin' over there?" was Big Rev's commentary when he read the *Baltimore Sun* that morning.

Daniel didn't have much of a lucid answer when he was later summoned to Big Rev's office for an inquiry. So they focused on damage control. Forest Unity wouldn't put up a fight. It would simply settle out of court. "It was just a misunderstanding, coupled with the efforts of some mean-spirited people, that's all," explained Big Rev in a Forest Unity Church meeting. For everyone who loved Daniel and loved the church, that explanation was enough, Big Rev implied. Anyone who wanted more of an explanation obviously didn't love Daniel and didn't love the church, and they were no different than those mean-spirited people who were willfully trying to sabotage the church. They were disobedient to God and headed straight to hell in a handbasket, Big Rev dared to declare.

Glitches, large and small, each one lethal, fell on the building project. It was like toppled dominos on a card table. The press had a field day. The problems began to split families. Husbands and wives, grown children and their parents and grandparents divvied up sides to do battle at their dinner tables. Those with blind unyielding loyalty to Daniel and the church fell on one side of the mashed potatoes. Those determined to ask questions and dig until plausible explanations could be unearthed, and perhaps rectified, were on the other side. And that was the side that usually stopped their tithes unless they could ascertain where the money went. There was a third faction too. It dipped and stirred among the first two factions. The members of this group, in faith, cashed in their IRA accounts, their retirement nest eggs, and their children's college funds to purchase bonds and cash in on a great deal. This group of investors also included the community at large and beyond.

Daniel wasn't sure just when circumstances had relegated him from offense to defense, but he found himself having to make new kinds of decisions—for public relations' sake. He did not purchase the mansion. He and Big Rev deliberated and concluded that with all the bad publicity surrounding the church construction debacle, it wasn't the right time to flaunt a mansion. Besides, another glitch transpired having to do with the sale of his house. Every time a serious buyer materialized who happened to be white, Daniel refused to entertain his or her bid—without explanation.

"Hey," his realtor said to Daniel. She was so excited, she came to his house to tell the news, "I've got a guy who wants to put in a contract for your house."

Daniel, unexcited, asked, "Yeah? What's his name?"

She was puzzled, but answered, "Dembrosky. He's very excited."

Daniel looked over her head and said, "Naw. No. I'm not selling to him."

"What?" she said. "You've got to be kidding. This is the third buyer you've turned down." Daniel was silent. "I'd like to know why."

"I just don't like him."

With that, the realtor turned her high heel on a dime and without looking back, she said, "You know what? I've got better things to do with my time." When she reached her Mercedes, she said, "I don't care how fine you are. Shoot!"

At any rate, not buying the mansion was a good decision. Once the decision was made, Daniel should have put the transferred money right back into the church's building fund. But he didn't. Frankly, the money just plain ole looked good sitting in his account. No harm intended. And after all the mess blew over, another mansion opportunity would arise. He wanted to be ready. But a new problem arose instead. The $3 million he'd siphoned off, total, began to dwindle. Somehow . . . for this reason and for that reason, most of the set-aside money evaporated into thin air. A time or two, an essential staff member faced foreclosure, or maybe a church member's relative needed a bailing out, etc. Those troubles had to be fixed, pronto. Repentance could come after.

Especially noted by the Prosecution . . . later . . . was Daniel's fortieth birthday bash before his wedding. Several families from The Bible Deliverance Church of God and Forest Unity, including Big Rev, Daniel, and Crystal, as "administrative assistant," got together and celebrated in the Holy Land. First, they made a stop in Rome, which included a lovely train ride to and from

Paris. Stateside, Crystal needed a new sports car to keep her mouth shut. Deacon Winston's wife's car died and that had to be handled. She worked at the church. There was an array of problems that popped up and could only be handled with ready cash.

And now this. The bond company seemed to have vanished into thin air. Mr. Shapiro, at the bank, had been frantically calling the church. The bond company missed three loan payments and was now in default. Mr. Shapiro had had enough. He was catching flack from his superiors. "The entire $7 million, plus interest, is due," Mr. Shapiro shouted, "and failure to comply will level criminal charges of fraud and an array of relatable offenses," he clarified over the phone to Daniel. Golf dates were long over. The offense carried with it a possible maximum twenty-year sentence, plus restitution.

"Somebody is going to have to get up off their behind with the bank's money," Mr. Shapiro said on the phone. Daniel couldn't believe that his friend had gotten that raw with it.

Just to be sure, Daniel checked Crystal's file when she was not in the office to read over the church's contract with the bond company. He hunted for loopholes. *Surely, there is some way to get off this sinking ship*, he thought while in the middle of his ransacking. *A way to stall the bank, hold the bond company to the fire, while I replenish the kitty with a few more sacrificial offerings.* Daniel almost hit the floor when he deciphered the contract, bearing his signature and making him personally liable for all the bonds. He couldn't believe it. He was almost certain he hadn't remembered it that way. He'd delegated the signing chores to Deacon Cherry. *When the heck did I sign this?* he wondered.

Word got out about the bond company's disappearance. Church members stopped receiving dividends from their bonds all of a sudden and without explanation. More members jumped ship. Some threatened lawsuits before they left. Daniel was beyond humiliation. He was angry to the tenth power. He directed his anger more at the absconding bond company than at anyone else, but he was not oblivious to a few individuals who may have had it in for him. They were mostly discarded ex-lovers, some driven-off church members, and fired church employees.

"That's how stuff keeps getting leaked to the press," he surmised to himself. The devil was trying to kill him, he knew that, but he would stand on that mount and fight the devil to his dying breath.

"Bryan's on the phone," Big Rev said to Daniel during one of their many consultations in Big Rev's study.

"We'll get to the bottom of all this," Big Rev said to Daniel, "but right now, we need some time. Boy, you've got criminal charges breathing down your neck. We got to get some money in there, immediately. Bryan's got star power, now, with his band and teaching at Morgan and all. He can throw a couple of concerts and pick up the slack, quick-fast." Daniel knew it to be true. He reached for the phone.

Bryan came in like the cavalry. In just two celebrity-filled concerts, plus a few celebrity donations, a whopping $3 million of free money materialized. Bryan's star power, reputation, and influence in the music world were nothing to sneeze at. He and Lori worked closely on several projects. They found that they worked well together, on stage and backstage. They got a standing ovation every time they performed their duet together. There was even talk of Bryan recording a few songs with Lori. Still trying to help his brother,

Daniel, he and Lori took the show on the road along the East Coast. Success would ensure getting Forest Unity and Daniel out of hot water and back on the building course for sure. Daniel was nothing but grateful for Bryan's help, even though he confided to his brother, "Mannn, I'll tell you the truth. I wouldn't attempt to build a doghouse after this." The two laughed.

But it was too late. The district attorney's office was tracking the whole situation. DA Anthony L. Barone had been on the job for more than twenty successful years, and he had a propensity for nabbing ne'er-do-well uppity ministers, white or black, but especially, "uppity nigger ministers," as he called them in private. But nothing this big had crossed his path prior to this. Barone hated how ministers preyed on unsuspecting folk who just wanted to be good, do good, and live good. Barone sped up the clock on any possible grace period that Daniel might have had to pay the money back, and he secretly fed the press mill.

Chapter Twenty-three

Trouble in Paradise

1996

"You know . . . I'm tired of all your stinky-behind crap. Sick and tired!" Lori snapped.

"Oh, Lordy," Daniel looked up at the ceiling in disgust, "Lori, please don't start that same old crap again. I really don't have time for it right now, okay? Some white joker's tryin' to put my butt in jail—if you haven't noticed."

"You're the same old whiney little brat you always been too," she shouted. "Ain't thinkin' about nothing or nobody but your sorry self. I tried to overlook your baby-fied ways, but you make it impossible to do that. Huh!" She folded her arms across her chest and steadied her stance. "How come every time I come home from a tour—and might I add, this last little tour was to help *your* behind out—How come . . ."

Daniel stormed out of the kitchen in the middle of her point and galloped the main stairs to the master bedroom. Lori followed him, stomping her feet all the way.

"Quit runnin' away from me, you little worm," she said once she got to the bedroom. "How come," she screamed, "every time I come home, you got this house full of your concubines? That's what I'd like to know."

"Faith Banks ain't what you tryin' to call her—"

"She's a *darn* whore! Did I get it right that time?"

"She's a hairstylist and an old friend, and she ain't done nothin' to you."

"Oooh, you don't count sleepin' with my husband every time she gets the chance as doin' somethin' to me? And how come you can't take your high-yella, fake-negro behind to the freakin' barbershop like every other freakin' man in Baltimore, huh?"

"'Cause I don't freakin' feel like it," Daniel yelled back. "You know, you got some crazy-behind jealousy issues. Ha! You need to take care of that mess. I think you need Jesus." With that, Daniel walked into the bathroom and shut the door. She pushed the door open while he was standing over the toilet, holding the family jewels.

"Does she cut the hairs around your little privates as well?"

"Maybe. And my privates ain't little, and you know it," Daniel snapped back, unable to fully enjoy the release of bodily fluids. He flushed and washed his hands.

She watched him. Visions of her clutching the butcher knife from that nice set they got for a wedding present danced in her head like sugarplums. *You ain't even worth the effort*, she thought to herself. "Daniel, I'm tired of finding out that you got women runnin' all up and through here when I'm not home."

"You're exaggerating *and* hallucinating. You talkin' about the nice mothers at the church." He had walked up to her, slowly, and towered over her. His green-apple eyes stared cold and threatening.

Lori wasn't about to back down. "You lyin' through your sleazy teeth."

He ignored the accusation. "Somebody's gotta take care of me while you're out doin' God knows what. It ain't proper for a woman not to be beside her man. You been disrespectful from the get-go." He backed off her, pitiful.

"You'd better come up out of the dark ages with that stupid nonsense," Lori said. Then she changed the subject back to where she had it. "I'm tired of the rumors and the snickering behind my back, and the jokes square-dead in front of my face. And I'm sick and tired of your lies, and your scandals. This ride has been one for the books. You know that, you jackleg son-of-a . . .? And you know what else?"

"No, what?"

"It's over," she said in a smooth voice.

"You know where your soul is goin', right, Lori?"

"My body's already there."

Daniel was sitting on the bed feigning interest in her ongoing threats. He'd heard them before. She stood across from him bellowing. As soon as she took a breath and he could get a word in edgewise, he interjected, calmly, "You know, if you acted like a real first lady and got active in the church, and acted like a real wife and had some babies, you wouldn't have all this time for all that fantasizing you always doin'." It was as close as he could come to trying to roll back the argument. But as far as Lori was concerned, he was being a smart-behind. She saw fire. They had been around that fence countless times, and they never failed to not end up on opposite sides. To bring it up again, now, was ludicrous to her. While he spoke, she wanted to bash his face in with her shoe.

"Ughhh! I don't believe you have the nerve to push that nonsensical yin-yang out of your mouth. What kind of a husband have you been to me, you slut?" Lori smirked real good when she said that.

He cut a glare at the attack on his manhood.

She continued, "Have a baby! With who? With you? You must be out your dusty mind for sure. I think you done fell and bumped yo' head. You ain't even no father to that bastard you had with that dummy, Joyce! But I guess it takes a bastard to birth a bastard, huh?"

Lori conquered his full attention now. In his heart of hearts, he felt that Joyce's boy was his. Sometimes he even prayed it to be so. But the fact remained that he wasn't man enough to ask the question—get it straight, once and for all. He still couldn't own the consequences. He knew she could read all that in his wounded-looking expression. It angered him to be vulnerable.

He jumped up from the bed, catapulted his body toward her, and grabbed her by both her shoulders. He wanted to rip her body clean in two. Instead, he shook her good and took some joy in seeing her body flex like a rag doll. Her teeth and jewelry clanked like cold water pipes. When she should have been afraid of his sudden move of aggressiveness because she knew she cut deep with that last remark, she wasn't. To her, his bark was still absent of bite. She feared nothing.

"What the heck are you talkin' about?" he yelled.

Lori mimicked him. "What the heck are you talkin' about, stupid? Everybody knows Joyce's boy is yours. That ain't top secret. Shoot, he looks just like your dumb-behind. Too bad for him. And you know what? I'm gonna do just like Joyce's poor husband, Derrick, did. I'm gettin' out of here before I lose my mind. 'Cause like I said, I'm sick and tired of your bull. I don't care whether you go to jail or not, either. And I surely don't care where you go or what you do—'Pretty Boy' Floyd." Lori uttered the last part of her little speech in a calm, controlled tone.

After she said the "Everybody knows Joyce's baby is yours" part, Daniel let go of her shoulders and just

stood there listening like a bad little boy being scolded
by his mommy. He really didn't care much whether she
left him or stayed with him, except for the fact that she
had started up with Bryan, probably while they were on
tour to save his behind, he surmised. With all the moving and sticking he had done, he knew he didn't dare
squawk about it. And deep down, he knew that Lori
deserved to have someone who really cared about her
and that wasn't him. She knocked the wind out of his
sail, though, with that last comment.

Lori maneuvered herself to the bedroom door in the
ready-to-vacate position when she threw her husband
another little bone to suck on. She declared, "And I
can't wait to make a little phone call to your precious
Big Rev too—let 'em know that little bastard is yours!
You slimy whorin' jellyfish wimp!" And there, in a
flash, she was gone—out of his life.

Later, new news would surface that Lori would seek
an annulment and after a respectable passage of time,
she and Bryan would wed in Maui in a modest fashion.
They'd have babies too, musician babies. But all that
waited down the pike of juicy gossip. But for right then,
the revelation getting out that Li'l 'D' was Daniel's flesh
and blood, that was something to contend with in the
present. Near or around conception, Daniel played
with the semantics of knowing for sure that the boy was
his. Back then, he wouldn't let himself travel anywhere
near the truth. Apparently, though, over the years, the
lineage was plain to everybody except him. It was obvious to everyone except Big Rev too.

The next day was Sunday. Daniel preached his heart
out. He preached, and what was left of his congregation stretched out in the aisles, slain in the Holy Spirit.
It was a respectable amount, about 700, if one counted
the newcomers who were always drawn by Daniel's

charisma and the curiosity seekers drawn by all the bad publicity. Add those to the church member diehards and it was a good decent crowd—for any other church besides FU. Daniel ran and jumped and cried God's Word until his back sweat soaked clear through his robe. The first lady was conspicuously absent only because her absence came without any explanation from the pulpit, like usual. Bryan was in the congregation, though. Daniel looked out and spied him in one of the middle rows. He couldn't believe it. After the service, Daniel sent one of the deacons out to fetch him. Bryan was heading that way anyway.

They both stood in Daniel's office facing each other like two cowboy Western duelers. Daniel got right to the point. "Hey, brother, I can't believe you're doing it to me."

"Doing what?" Bryan said. His look conveyed pure puzzlement, but Daniel didn't buy it.

"You stealin' my wife right from under me like that. How could you do it, bro?"

Bryan took the puzzled look off his face, shook his head, and stepped back—now amazed at Daniel's gall. He said, "Now wait a minute; hold on, Daniel. You got this all wrong."

"How can that be, brother?" Daniel said sarcastically. "How can that be when you went out on tour with my wife and came back with her as your woman?"

Bryan got a little more perturbed at Daniel's nerve. His defensive smile was gone.

"First of all, brother, do not ever talk to me like I don't *know* you and—know *all* about you." Bryan poked his index finger in the air toward Daniel and cocked his head to the side, and brought it back for emphasis. "You got me, right!" Bryan continued after a breath. "You gotta be somebody's husband before somebody can come up and even try to steal your wife. Don't be tryin' to act like Big Rev, naw." That was a punch under the belt, and it was meant to be. "Lori is not and was never your possession. She's a person, a flesh-and-blood woman."

"I don't know what the heck you're talkin' about."

"I'm talkin' about you ain't never loved Lori. Shoot, you were only following Pop's orders to marry somebody. I wished I'da known that crap; then I would have never introduced a nice girl like that to somebody as messed up as you. Stupid me, huh? I thought a good woman wouldda calmed your tail down . . . since you jacked everything up with my sister."

Daniel looked floored, then wounded.

"Oh, c'mon, naw. My sister and Phadra confided in me, desperate to keep her standing after all the hurt you put on her 'cause you were so worried about your precious image," Bryan said, aiming for his words to slice Daniel wide open.

Daniel tried to cut just as deep too. He sniped, "So that's yo' reason for lickin' up my sloppy seconds."

That comment almost netted Daniel a punch in his face. Bryan drew back his fist, ready to give it to him. But Bryan caught his rage and dropped his arms. Daniel dropped his too. They were in the house of the Lord.

"You know what, pretty Ricky?" Bryan said, shaking his head. Daniel didn't answer. He just stood there with his eyes clouded with jealousy. "You a sad case. Always tryin' to be something that you ain't. You ain't even worth a punch in the face. You just pitiful. And you gonna end up all alone and even more crazy than you already are—if you don't start checkin' yourself."

"What the heck are you talkin' about?"

"That's pitiful too. That you don't even know," Bryan said. He walked out and slammed the door. The conversation was over.

***

Lori made good on her promise to drop a bomb-
shell on Big Rev. Ironically, the call from an enraged
Big Rev and a knock on Daniel's door from a process
server both came at the same time. A process server
stood waiting to hand Daniel a subpoena laced with
several counts of fraud. A hearing was scheduled to determine if there was enough evidence to formally indict
him. The press came along with the process server to
document images of Daniel's shocked look. It was an
orgasmic coup for the metro tabloids. Daniel snatched
the paper, signed for it, and slammed the door in the
process server's face. Camera flashes exploded wildly
even past the moment the door slammed shut. Then he
ran to answer the phone.

"You mean to tell me that you had my daughter all
mixed up in your harem of whores?" Big Rev was so
mad that by the time he'd gotten to the end of his sentence his baritone voice cracked.

"Listen, Pop, it's not like that. It wasn't like that."
Daniel stood in the middle of his living room, crum-
pling up the legal papers. He threw them to the floor. A
couple of days later, Deacon Winston and Eric Johnson
would stop by the house. They would pick the papers
up, smooth them out, and read them to Daniel, and
ask him if he understood what he had to do. Then
they would lead him to the shower and to a fresh set
of clothes. But for right then, he was alone, barricaded
and uninformed. The press camped out in his front
yard waiting for a chance to pummel him with questions and snap some more great photos. They were on
safari for more front-page news.

"I loved Joyce, Pop. It all just happened. I still love
her. She never told me about the baby!" Now Daniel's
voice cracked.

"If you love her, then why haven't I heard about it all this time? Why haven't you stepped up like a man to tell the truth? How could you lie to me . . . you bastard?"

The word "bastard" coming from Big Rev pierced multiple wounds all over Daniel's body.

Big Rev flinched a little when he said it, but his anger moved forward. "Here, I take you in, like you were my own son, my own flesh and blood, and you lied to me under my own roof?" Big Rev just couldn't believe it. "Boy," he said, "if you wasn't my grandson's sorry excuse for a father, I'd come over there and blow your brains out. You hear me?"

Daniel stood frozen, lifeless on his feet, crucified by every word.

"But I'll tell you this, boy, the Lord will have His way with you, and I won't have to lift a finger. If He sends you to hell for all the conniving crap you did, that will be fine with me!" Big Rev yelled.

There was an abrupt click in Daniel's ear.

There was perhaps one observation Daniel took time out to notice during the melee at his front door and on the phone with Big Rev. His world as he knew it had fallen down around him. He felt like he was two minutes from a front seat in purgatory. Big Rev and Joyce hated him. Lori had left him for Bryan. And the State of Maryland wanted to throw him in jail. *Lord, just let the crap kill me*, was the passing thought that flew by.

Just as Big Rev hung up the phone, Millie appeared, oblivious to what had just happened. "Hurry up, Grandpa, we're running late for Li'l 'D's birthday party."

Big Rev's mood struggled to switch gears, but he managed. "Oh, my goodness, Mother, you know I clean forgot. Give me a minute. I'll be ready." But instead, he stood up from his seat and pulled her over to the couch and guided her body to sit down beside him.

"What in the world are you doing, Daddy? You know we ain't got no time for this foolishness." She giggled out a playful, "Later, Big Daddy, later!"

Big Rev got serious. "Look, woman," he said affectionately, "I got something to tell you, and it won't take more than a minute. I promise."

She dropped the fun and games and looked worried. "What? What is it?"

Big Rev cleared his throat before he spoke. "Daniel is Li'l 'D's father; not Derrick, Joyce's ex." He laid his concentrated gaze into her eyes waiting to rescue her from shock, anger, disbelief, or something, but her look was only one of resolution.

"Is that what you had to tell me, sweetie?" she said.

Puzzled, Big Rev replied, "Well . . . yeah, isn't that enough?" Now he was the one who needed rescuing. Millie pulled herself to her feet and looked down adoringly at her husband.

"Sweetie, I've known that for a while. Our daughter *does* talk to me."

Big Rev screamed in his head, *Secrets! Secrets all around me!*

Millie paused a second to read his mind and his facial expression.

"And, shoot," she continued, "nobody had to tell me anyway. Daniel pops up in that boy's face and mannerisms every time I'm with our grandson. That boy is ten years old today. You mean you haven't seen it?"

Big Rev was nearly speechless. "No. I didn't see anything. Why didn't you say something to me?" he asked.

"Because it wasn't my place," Millie settled on. She bent down and puffed up the couch pillows Big Rev had squished. She decided to skip over the finer points of the revelation. "What's done is done," she said to that.

"After Joyce and Derrick broke up, it's been only my prayer that maybe Joyce and Daniel would somehow find their way back together . . . so that the three of them can be a real family. That's what's important, now," Millie sighed and continued. "I guess you haven't seen the way those two look at each other whenever they're in a room together, either, huh? Or the way they try so hard not to look at each other." Big Rev was ashamed he had not realized any of this. "But you never did see anything you didn't want to see," she said without looking at him.

When he could speak, he said, "You know, Mother, I just called that boy up and threatened to kill him."

"Daddy," Millie said in a disappointing tone, "now, you know you were wrong. You're a man of God," she reminded him, "not God Himself. You ain't never gonna know everything, and it's not your place to hand down the punishment—or set the rules on who should love each other and who shouldn't." Her eyes narrowed. "Now, didn't you learn anything from your own teaching? And everybody ain't gonna do what you want 'em to do. Those kids made a mistake, that's true. But you mean to tell me that you're gonna hold them to the fire for the rest of their lives? Did God hold you to the fire for the wrongs you've done?"

Millie had vowed to God that she would love, honor, and cherish her husband for life, and to the best of her ability. She was doing that. But it didn't make her stupid or blind to any of his faults, nor did it make her less vulnerable to the hurt. She just loved him in spite of it all. "I don't know about you, but my God forgives me for the mistakes I've made whenever I go to Him in pure repentance."

For a moment, Big Rev's mind shouted out, *What mistakes?* but he forced himself to let it pass. His wife continued.

"And look at our precious grandson. God put Daniel in our lives when he was a little boy. Now, you could be lookin' at a third-generation holy man. You're gonna turn your back on that too?" Millie was laying him out good, but she did it so sweetly, which was her style of handling him, that all he could do was take it and be grateful.

You're right! That's what he said to her in his look. She nodded in agreement.

Then she leaned down and planted a wet kiss on his big forehead and said, "Now, let's get to our grand-baby's birthday party."

Big Rev stood up and ceremoniously bowed to her will, saying, "Yes, dear." They headed out the door on their way to the car.

Chapter Twenty-Four

Guilty

1996

"Your Honor, the State plans to show the court that the defendant, Daniel Judah Harris, willfully and blatantly acted to commit fraud against the City of Baltimore and its citizens, who trusted him and placed him at the helm of the historic Forest Unity Church of Baltimore," said Prosecutor Anthony L. Barone during his opening statement. He methodically paced back and forth, taking up nearly the full length of the judge's bench as he spoke. "Harris boldly violated city code ordinances and attempted to bribe city officials in the process. He purported to extract and embezzle a total amount of $7 million by way of soliciting and selling fake bonds. And from his pulpit, he extorted cold hard cash under false pretenses.

"The Prosecution has more than sufficient evidence to prove the aforementioned charges. Among other exhibits of evidence, Your Honor, I will submit to the court two separate accounting ledgers maintained by the Forest Unity Church." Barone said all that and more in his opening statement at Daniel's indictment hearing.

Later, further into the hearing, when Barone produced the two bookkeeping ledgers, the spectators gasped and murmured. Even Daniel had a look of surprise plastered on his face. He didn't know anything about a second set of books at the church. He never even heard anyone infer that such a thing existed. And yet, there it was.

Inside the hidden ledger, Crystal's personal one, she kept meticulous records of how every penny and every dime was spent, including the loose change offerings that the deacons weren't counting. She had harbored a good estimate of that. It was labeled under miscellaneous funds along with an explanation for its existence and the reprimand that Daniel had issued to the deacon board. Where Daniel was fuzzy on the when and where's, and the specifics about how money was spent, Crystal was crystal clear. When she was called to testify, she said that the reverend, her boss, had instructed her to keep and maintain the second ledger, "just for their clarification, only." She fought not to blink her lie, since she was under oath. She purposely avoided looking over in Daniel's direction the entire time she was on the witness stand. His eyes could have burned a hole in her forehead.

To strengthen the assertion of Daniel's frivolous handling of the church's money and his criminal intentions, Barone showered the court with an array of names of people who received money, above and under the table, the dispensed amounts as well as the purchased items and luxuries. And if Daniel had discreetly rescued a church member from the penalty of a utility shut-off notice, kept a good teen out of jail, or saved a family from certain eviction, which was the case on many occasions, both Crystal and Barone placed them under a suspicious cloak of nepotism.

It seemed that most of the deacons, the essential staff members like Crystal and her secretary, and several of the in-crowd church members were having a grand old time in the name of Jesus. The list included vacations, cars, car rentals, hotel rooms, a $5,000 round brass bed (that belonged to Daniel), Rolex watches, jewelry, a wedding, a seven-day honeymoon in Greece, and more. All of the staff's salaries and huge benefit packages were laid bare for public scrutiny as well.

Barone and his assistant left no stone unturned. Then the prosecutor dug into the meat of the matter. Barone dissected the bank's loan to the church, which was now in default and drenched with late fees and penalties. He called Mr. Sheldon Shapiro and his superior to testify. That revealed Daniel's secret money transfers into his private checking and savings accounts, and his mansion-purchasing prospects in Ellicott City. Barone called Lori Sparrow Harris to the stand. Barone called Derrick Ellis, Joyce's ex-husband, and some angry bondholders to testify. He even dug up a few members of the Wicker clan to spice up the soup. They all hammered their own private nails into Daniel's coffin.

"You're looking at a man who is capable of anything that begins with deceit," Barone alleged. His index finger repeatedly stabbed the air above his head as he spoke. By the time the hearing ended, sexual affairs were no longer secret. Faith, the hairstylist, and the prophesying choir member were among the parade of concubines called to the stand. And then came the big question. Barone, standing behind his counsel table, giving glaring eye-to-eye, asked Joyce, "Did you and Reverend Harris have an affair?"

Her body felt like a sack of cement plopped on the witness stand. She took her time to answer, but finally, she said, "Yes." The spectators gasped.

Barone kept going. "Who is the father of your son, Ms. Graystone?" At this moment, if a pin had fallen to the floor it could be heard loud and clear. "Answer the question, Ms. Graystone," Barone said. "Is Reverend Daniel Harris the father of your one and only child—your son?"

Joyce's eyes moistened, then welled up. "Yes," she said faintly.

"Come again, Ms. Graystone?" Barone said.

"I said, yes!" Joyce yelled. Tears fell down her cheeks.

"Thank you, Ms. Graystone. I have no more questions, Your Honor," Barone said. Joyce got up and fled the scene, crying. Her girl, Phadra, consoled and shielded.

Rose erupted into tears. Still seated behind her son, she yearned to offer him some kind of comfort but felt helpless to do so. It broke her heart not only to know that she could do nothing about this "public lynching," as she called it, but also it grieved her to know that he would shun her comfort if she offered it.

It was mid-December and Rose sat there dressed in a too-tight pale pink pant suit with matching patent leather stiletto heels and purse. She couldn't help herself. She sat there reminiscing about years forever gone—and how she messed up.

"All you ever did was drop little negative hints about who my father was," Daniel threw up at her once during one of their arguments. "You never ever went into any real detail about him. Details I could use. How could you not bother to tell me if he loved me or wanted me?"

"I never meant you no harm," was all the explanation Rose could muster up.

***

During the court hearing, Barone had yet to hammer the final nail in Daniel's coffin—that came when he pulled out the infamous contract, "Signed by the Reverend Daniel J. Harris," he asserted, "which states in black and white that Harris, and Harris alone, is financially responsible for the fake bonds he sold and the payment of accrued dividends, current and overdue. Why would an intelligent, savvy man such as the defendant you see sitting over there sign such a bold agreement, Your Honor, if he had not already worked out a secret, dubious agreement with the said bond company?" Barone worked the entire courtroom with his comments. On his next point, he walked directly over to Daniel and lodged his accusations right to his face.

"It was to steal the $7 million and vanish into thin air, along with the bond company, of which this office has not been able to uncover a trace. At this juncture, Your Honor, the only evidence that the bond company ever existed is the tangible presence of bogus paperwork belonging to the bondholders and the absence of most of their life savings," Barone said. He kept his gaze on Daniel who stared right back at him.

"And let me remind the court, Your Honor, that those bonds were peddled nationwide. If such a plan were not true, why did the defendant feel the need to stash a little away—please excuse me . . ."

Barone paused for the sake of dramatics and began to work the courtroom again. Then he continued his seemingly impromptu observation, ". . . $3 million could hardly be classified as 'a little.' To most of us hardworking citizens, that's more than any of us will ever see in a lifetime. Why would the reverend stash that money away if he were not planning to need it in a hurry? Perhaps it would be to purchase a ticket and a new lifestyle somewhere outside of the United States? I also propose that the building of his imaginary church was nothing more than a mere smokescreen to dupe those poor, trusting people out of their lifesavings. The Prosecution rests, Your Honor." Barone sat down.

It was Eric Milton Johnson's turn to speak. He had his work cut out for him. He was loaded with character witnesses. In the end, they were much more than Barone could come up with to defame Daniel. So that was good. Daniel was shocked when Eric called Big Rev to the stand. Big Rev arrived late. He testified, "I love Daniel like a son, and I believe in him wholeheartedly." That was good, but the overall problem with Eric's character witnesses was that they failed to produce as much evidence juice as Barone's lethal witnesses, just faith. There was a little heartstring tugging here and there, but not nearly enough. When he spoke, Eric got up and slowly moved from behind the desk to position himself on center stage.

"Your Honor, the Reverend Daniel Judah Harris is not the calculating, dishonest monster that the Prosecution portrays him to be. He has been an upstanding member of this community his entire life. He has been a bona fide man of God, preaching the Word of God since the age of fourteen. His only crime is that he is a man, of mere flesh and blood, not perfect, and victim of common mistakes that men can make," Eric declared, rendering a look of compassionate hurt to the judge and the crowd.

He continued, "Mistakes such as misjudging the character of the bond company. Reverend Harris did not commit fraud. He did not set out to dupe anyone out of his or her lifesavings. He merely set out to expand the reach of the great legacy of the Forest Unity Church of Baltimore, an institution of which he had

come to love. He had nothing to do with the bond
company's current disappearance, nor did he have any
plans to leave the country, as Mr. Barone so boldly ac-
cuses without a decent shred of hard evidence. What he
alleges is purely absurd. Half of what Barone proposes
is strictly circumstantial, meaning the chief executive
officer of the bond company, and not Reverend Daniel
J. Harris, is the one who should be the subject of this
hearing. That is the culprit who sought out to commit
fraud and to dupe people out of their money."

Eric Milton Johnson worked that courtroom just as
good as Barone had, but on most of it, he was bluffing
and talking a good game. Behind the scenes, he had his
law firm working night and day trying to uncover the
whereabouts of the bond company. If he found it or
them, he was certain he could deflect the fraud charge
away from Daniel and onto the bond company—but
first things first. He did have one big blessing to work
with though. Deacon Cherry came up with the original
contract—a copy of the original contract that he had
made right after signing it. Apparently, Crystal had
missed that little nugget. It was dated prior to the one
with Daniel's signature and was minus the dubious
financial responsibility clause that Eric, himself, had
negotiated out of the contract's terms. Whether the
court would accept the first contract as legal and bind-
ing remained to be seen.

The crowd ooooohed and ahhhed again at this latest
contract revelation. Whether this thing went to trial
or not, Johnson planned to hunt down the bond company. After all, he did feel partially responsible, since
he allowed Daniel to publicly make him responsible
for bringing the bond company to the church in the
first place. It was the only way Daniel, and the church,
could get out from under its present threat of fore-

closure and place the church in the position to repay the bank loan. But as it stood now, instead of having a brand-new edifice to look forward to, one in which to expand its Christian outreach, Forest Unity was about to be homeless. And Daniel was looking at stiff fines and certain prison time.

The judge pounded her gavel and declared, "Court is adjourned until three o'clock. I'll announce my decision at that time."

"All rise," the bailiff shouted.

It was the longest three hours ever to take place, Daniel had decided. He and Eric stole away to have a private lunch and strategize in a little greasy spoon up the street from the courthouse. Thankfully, no one they knew happened to walk in, and they managed to avoid the press. They ate slowly. Neither of them had much of an appetite, really. They picked at their food, and they talked.

"Look, don't worry, mannn. This thing won't go to trial. It's impossible," Eric said.

Daniel just looked at his friend and counsel and thought, *Don't worry seems kind of ludicrous.* "I know I've done things wrong," Daniel said, "and perhaps I deserve to pay for them, but I just can't understand all this. Am I holier than thou to ask God why He's punishing me, Jerusalem, with Babylon?" He let go a weak, sarcastic chuckle. "I mean, I've done some stupid things, but you know the system. Ain't those cats worse than me?" He was referring to the white man.

"Yeah, man, I hear you. But you know, like with all of us, the rules ain't fair," Eric said. Then he hated to do it, but he had to open a different can of worms. "Look mannn, if you got any other bombshells in your closet, like fathering children, you need to let a brother know. You get me, right?"

"Yeah, I get you. I guess you might as well know that I had a little thing with Crystal Mercer too. Now, that was a trash bin."

"I know," Eric said like it was nothing and kept on eating, "I know that on both counts." He said it like perhaps he'd poked it too.

Daniel was shocked to hear it and looked up at Eric with a frozen stare. Eric started laughing. "Come on, mannn, let's face it; your business has been raggedy for a while, naw, dawg."

At three on the dot, the bailiff spoke. "All rise for Her Honor Grace McPhever."

The honorable judge sat on her perch and began to speak. "The Court has listened with great care to both the Prosecution and the Defense. And it is my decision that there is sufficient cause for this case to move to trial. Will the defendant, Daniel Judah Harris, please stand?" She looked directly at Daniel. He stood up straight, buttoned the middle button of his suit jacket and, with respect, returned her direct look. Eric stood with him. The judge continued, "... You are hereby formally indicted by the powers invested in me by the State of Maryland, on five counts of fraud, two counts of misappropriation of funds, and nine counts of breach of trust." The spectators gasped. "If you are convicted of these charges, they carry a combined punishable sentence of up to twenty years, plus fines. Counsel for the Defense, what say you?"

"Your Honor, my client pleads not guilty to these charges. I also petition the court to release him under his own recognizance," Eric said, presenting an attentive face to the judge.

Barone jumped up from his seat like someone had pulled his chair out from under him. "Your Honor, this defendant could be considered a flight risk. He has the means, and he has the motive. I motion the court that it at least set high bail on Mr. Harris to ensure his return to stand trial."

"Motion granted," Judge McPhever said. "The bail is set for $700,000. The trial will take place exactly three weeks from today at 9:00 A.M. Court is adjourned." She pounded her gavel. As far as Daniel was concerned, she might as well have pounded it right upside his head.

Chapter Twenty-Five

The Last Mile

1996

Daniel heard the indictment. Instead of feeling an incredible doom or fear, he felt a strange sensation of light release. Stressors left his body. Bryan put up bail. Daniel was shocked and thankful.

During Daniel's solitary ride home, he'd decided that he had exactly three weeks to resolve any issues left unfinished and to set his house in order. That should also take him through a solitary New Year's Eve to think about his three-minute marriage, his pending prison time, and his public disgrace—denying his son. He could think clear through to mid-January of 1997.

But he wasn't going to show up for that trial, he'd decided. He wasn't about to become a fugitive on the run, either. Daniel had had a good run of it in this life. That's what the preacher now summed up. Most of it was good. It was too bad that he couldn't go out in a blaze of honorable glory, but those were the breaks. He'd come from nothing, and he would go back to nothing. He had run out of wiggle room. He couldn't move forward, and he couldn't go backward. *Shoot*, he thought to himself, turning into his driveway, *I guess Billy Preston was right. Huh. Nothin' from nothin' does leave nothin'.*

"Devil, this is a bunch of bull. You can have *all* this drama," Daniel said, officially conceding the battle and the war.

For days leading up to the first Sunday after the hearing, Daniel refused to make contact with anyone, not even with God. He couldn't have cared less. For the first time in his life, Daniel refused to pray or to preach. As far as he was concerned, he and the Lord had done all that they could do together. They had no more business to conduct. Why God had chosen to turn His back on him, he didn't know, but He had, and that was that. The rest of the week, Daniel wanted to be left alone, and he was alone. He didn't answer the phone or the door.

But then, Sunday came and at the stroke of midnight, he awoke. And a decision was made that he would go to Forest Unity and preach later that day.

Not a soul had heard from him since the hearing. No one expected him to show up at the church on Sunday. The trustees made other arrangements. They summoned Reverend Archer to come and preach in Daniel's place. When Daniel appeared around the altar's bend out of nowhere, right in the middle of praise and worship, Reverend Archer was surprised and wide-eyed. He discreetly conceded the pulpit. The visiting reverend spouted out some gobbledygook about being there to support his longtime friend and colleague and the church. He then took his seat. The congregation gasped and applauded Daniel into position.

The Reverend Daniel J. Harris stood up and moved toward the podium without hesitation of speech. He preached the tightest lesson on Job to which the congregation had ever been privy. It was breathless and passionate, and desperate, even. Nearing his final point, Daniel screamed out his words with teardrops flooding his pupils.

Throughout his sermon, his mouth moved, his voice rang out, and the truth reigned in its power, but he didn't want it to. He no longer agreed with the message he found himself shouting except for when he shouted the part, "Job was blameless and punished for no good reason!" And he had some other points to make like how God just stood there and let it happen. Also, he thought, the sermon wouldn't have been complete without tongue-slashing a few folks in the congregation. Daniel's head ached. His hands trembled. Sweat mixed with his tears made his buttercream cheeks glow. He shouted, "'Why don't you just curse God and die?' That's what Job's wife told him." *Cursing God,* he thought, *that's what I wanna say. And I'll end it right there,* he concluded in his mind. But that was not where he ended it.

The struggle within him made his body weak. His tears refused to dry up. His feet took him running down off the pulpit and planted him on the altar, front and center. He shouted with all the might left within him, "Job had preplanned on being faithful to the end—come rain or shine. And let me remind you, precious saints, faith that ain't been tested is false. Real faith moves in when real grace appears to have run out. Job, the faithful servant, adamantly refused to curse God."

There was a hush throughout the sanctuary. Anybody who failed to see a correlation between the message and what the church was going through had to be deaf, dumb, and blind. Still, it was an unintended revelation on Daniel's part. And it had sprung forth intended for the people of the great Forest Unity branch of Zion, not for Daniel.

Forest Unity was Job, God was God, and Daniel was merely the messenger that both God and the devil chose to use. Daniel was nowhere near the center of attention he thought he was during the entire church mess. As he preached, the revelation washed clearer and clearer for those who wanted to see it. God and Satan made a dollar bet to see if God's faithful would fold under the pressure of evil. If it folded under this lightweight mess, then how in the world could it become a superpower of Christianity, responsible for nurturing and transforming the multitudes of sin-sick around it? The answer was, Daniel unwillingly preached, "It couldn't."

And so, the object of the dollar bet wasn't Daniel J. Harris. It was the Forest Unity Church of Baltimore.

On the pulpit, Daniel tried to align his situation with Job's situation, but he failed. He was angry about it too. *That double-crossing son of a bit—*His mind stopped short. He was trapped in utter inner turmoil because to curse God was all he had planned to do. He yearned to get back at the Lord for turning His back on him. But it didn't go down like that. The voice inside him no longer belonged to him. Daniel's thoughts worked laps around his head, while Daniel's soul filled with all he'd learned his entire life. He was running on autopilot. Here he had entered into the final days of his life and revelation projectiled out of the preacher's mouth like vomit.

Idol worship, gazing up at the golden calf that offered them a pretty smile from the pulpit instead of keeping their eyes on God, leveled a death sentence to the church that it deserved. However, in light of this, what should it do? Some tried to ask, but the body of Christ had been broadsided by the question. Some were paralyzed from the waist down by the blame game, and they could neither move backward nor forward. Some who were hurt in the wreckage cut their losses and took flight. But there would be a few, perhaps, who would stay to clean up the carnage and fight the good fight needed to survive. First, the survivors would have to cast off their rose-colored glasses, trash any leftover idolatry, and refocus on God.

When his sermon was all over, Daniel wiped his drenched forehead with a hand towel someone had handed to him. He adjourned himself back to the pulpit and allowed his body to fall into his seat. Reverend Archer performed the altar call. Twenty people ran down to the altar to give their lives to Christ and to join the church in spite of all the church's bad publicity.

For the first week in between Sunday number one and Sunday number two, Daniel kept himself in seclusion again. And he wasn't planning on preaching again; that was a given. *Let Reverend Archer handle it or whoever. I don't give a flying fig,* he thought while he shredded some personal papers in his home office. Daniel was too busy with housecleaning chores to be annoyed by anyone.

Big Rev, Mother Millie, Bryan, Eric, Deacon Winston called incessantly—even Rose called about three times before she gave up. They came by, banged on the door, but Daniel wouldn't answer. After three days, Big Rev returned with the police in tow. Daniel answered the door with an attitude. He ignored Big Rev's presence and only addressed the police. "I'm all right," he said, "no trouble, here, officers." Then he slammed the door in their faces. Daniel planned on seeing all of them, but it was going to have to be on his terms; no one else's.

"Give the boy some room. He's been through a lot." That was Big Rev's final announcement. "He'll come around soon enough."

Monday morning week two Daniel walked into the church's office like he had been reporting for work all along and nothing unusual had gone on in the least.

Crystal was leaning back comfortably in her chair, gab-
bing on the phone to one of her girlfriends when Daniel
slipped into her peripheral vision. She thought he was
a ghost, a vision, or something. It also came to her to
fear for her safety because now he was aware of her
setup and switcheroo of the bond company contracts.
She dropped the phone and toppled out of her chair.
Daniel stood there with a measure of uncalculated
pleasure watching his former mistress, behind up,
panties showing, and struggling hard to pull herself together. He offered her no assistance. The idea crossed
him to yell out, "Pink ones, huh?" but he held it.

"Crystal, come in my office. We need to talk." Assured that she would follow his command, he headed
into his office without looking back. He took his seat
behind his desk.

"So what's up, Boss?" She hadn't intended on sarcasm, but it slipped out. He neither flinched nor ac-
knowledged her behavior. He looked in her eyes and
smiled the kind of smile when a person is actually glad
to see the person they're looking at.

"Crystal, I would like to sincerely apologize for everything I've done to you."

Crystal's mouth flew open. Her eyes bugged. Then
she said, "Apologize for what?"

But Daniel did not acknowledge the question. He
strained to fight arrogance, but to him, her question
seemed stupid. He went on with his speech. "I took
unfair advantage of you and your situation at home.
We committed sin, but as your shepherd, I am held to
a higher level of accountability for what I did—and for
what I caused you to do. I sincerely hope that you have
asked God for forgiveness and that you try to make it
work with Deacon Mercer to give your family a healthy,
loving household."

Crystal sat there, paralyzed in the chair, fixed on Daniel's face as he spoke. He continued, "But more than that, Crystal . . ." He paused, got up, and moved from behind his desk to kneel down in front of her. He gently took hold of her hands. Her body responded with a flood of mixed hot and cold emotions. The power of his touch on her flesh had not diminished in spite of her hurt and rage. He spoke to her in a soft, sincere voice. "I'm sorry, Crystal. I am. And I know that's not enough. But I want you to know that. You didn't deserve my disrespectful behavior. And if it means anything at all, hurting you was not what I set out to do. If anything, I was seeking to defile my own flesh, not yours." He laughed a little. "As wrong as that attraction was, Crystal, you are captivating. But you need to know that it was because of my self-doubt and lack of integrity that allowed me to go after your soul and your integrity. I guess I needed someone else's integrity to cover my shortcomings. I am so sorry. You deserve God's best."

He let go of her hands that had been resting in her lap. He got up and leaned against his desk in front of her. He kept his eyes on her. She returned his gaze, and his silence told her to say whatever was in her heart or head to say. If she needed to curse him out, so be it. She got that, but she remained speechless. After a minute or two of that, he said, "See ya around," and he headed for the door. Without looking back, he yelled out, kind of flippantly, "Hold my calls."

Daniel answered a heavy knock on the door. He opened it and found Big Rev standing there ready for battle. *Great,* Daniel thought, *I didn't even have to call you.* "Come on in, Pop. What's goin' on?" he said like it was no big deal. Big Rev followed him in beyond the foyer and into the living room. Daniel plopped down on his couch and spread-eagled his arms atop the rim of the couch as if to say, *The world is my oyster*. Big Rev sat down in the La-Z-Boy Daniel had bought for him to sit in whenever he visited.

"What do you mean, 'What's goin' on?' What's going on with you? How ya been, boy? Folks are worried about ya," Big Rev said, incredulous.

Daniel replied, "Ahhh, no need for that. I'm fine. You can pass the word that I'm fine."

"Look, boy. I don't want no foolin' around. I wanna know what you've been up to, barricaded in this house. What you been thinkin'?"

"I been cleanin' and thinkin'. That good enough for you? I'm fine, I told you." Daniel's voice got a little rugged.

"Listen, son, a lot of people care about you. I care about you. We're gonna get through this thing. Don't you worry about that, but you've got to hold on, Daniel. You've got to stay in the fight."

Big Rev wasn't demanding; he was pleading. This was new. Daniel was taken aback.

"I love you, son, not like you were a son of mine; I love you because you *are* my son. And there is something else you need to remember . . ."

"What's that's supposed to mean?" Daniel asked, earnestly trying to figure out just where this was going.

"You're God's son too."

The answer let him down. He did not want to hear any yin-yang about God right now from Big Rev or anybody else. But Big Rev had one last thing to say as he got up to leave. Daniel walked with him to the door.

"And you're a father too, Daniel. Li'l 'D' needs you. He needs his father. Don't do to him what you think

Jud Hainey did to you. Don't act like he doesn't exist and check out of his life. You're too good of a man for that, boy. Too good."

Daniel was speechless and could only eye Big Rev's meaty lips as he spoke. He hadn't heard anyone speak his father's name except his aunt Mattie.

Big Rev's eyes were warm and direct. "Your Aunt Mattie confided in me, son. We all loved you very much. Look, you're a man of God, whether you like it or not. And you know better than anyone that you cannot reconcile the past; just forgive it. Walk away from it, son, and move on."

Daniel stood there. His arms hung at his sides. They felt like lead. He was no longer the Reverend Daniel J. Harris. He wasn't Little Rev. He was a hurting and confused fourteen-year-old boy wanting to know where he'd come from.

Big Rev went on. "The best thing about love and redemption, boy, is that it has no memory. I realize your son was made from love, and I know that he has no knowledge of the pain you come from. If you leave him now, son, he won't understand. So, you think about that."

Big Rev took one more long look into Daniel's eyes as if he'd never see them again. Then he turned and shut the front door behind him. "Jud Hainey," the name pricked his ears. Until that moment, Daniel was never sure, but always wondered if anybody else beside Rose and Aunt Mattie knew anything about his true lineage.

He stepped in the memory of his aunt Mattie about a couple of months before Aunt Cille died, revealing to him his father's name and the awful origin of Aunt Cille's broken heart. "Keep it to yo'self," Aunt Mattie whispered to him. "Keep it from yo' aunt Cille, 'specially so."

He was crushed. Lost for words. They embraced in a hug. She broke to look at him and say something else, but someone knocked on the front door and the opportunity evaporated as suddenly as it had materialized. They never spoke about it again.

Daniel went to Bryan's house to apologize to him for his behavior at the church that Sunday they almost came to blows. He also wanted to apologize for always trying to take his place as Big Rev's number-one son, or for, at least, wishing that it could happen. When he got there, he found Lori there. *Good*, he thought, fighting an extra serving of sarcasm, *I can kill two songbirds with one stone.*

"Hey, guys," Daniel said, hugging both of them at the door of Bryan's apartment. "Thanks for letting me come over."

"No problem, man. You my boy; you know that," Bryan said, trying to keep the mood light.

It was the Saturday before the trial on Monday. Daniel sat down on the couch. He took note of his former wife's casual dress. She looked good in those cutoff jeans. As good as she looked when she tried them on in Hecht's during one of their shopping trips and he'd bought them for her. During the money-was-no-object excursion, they giggled and played with each other, teasing about the fact that he had just purchased a pair of cutoff jeans for the first lady of Forest Unity Church. *It was a good day, but, oh well.* Bryan sat in a chair across from Daniel. Lori sat on the arm of Bryan's chair and put her arm around the chair's back, marking her new territory and making a point.

Daniel pretended he didn't notice the turf or the point. He got right to his point. "Look, since both of you are here . . ."

Lori twitched a little. Bryan remained fixed on Daniel's face.

". . . I just came over here to say that I'm terribly sorry for my behavior, past and past." He let out an embarrassed chuckle at his slight attempt of a joke that rested on truth. "Lori, you are a great woman. I didn't deserve you. I thought I did. I wanted to. But I didn't. I wasn't ready for you yet. And I'm sorry for that. Bryan, mannn, thanks. You tried to do me a solid by giving me a chance with the woman you should have had all along, and I love you for it. I know you've always given me the unconditional love of a brother—even though I had no blood claim to that love. Mannn," Daniel smiled at his brother, ". . . you gotta be the most secure cat on earth." They all laughed.

Then it got serious. Daniel went on. "You two cats deserve to find happiness together." He stood up to leave. "I love you both, and I'm sorry." He headed for the door without giving them time to say anything. Lori was about to open her mouth to say something, but Bryan gestured and tugged at her hand. He understood his brother, and he understood that nothing else needed to be said. They heard the door slam shut from down the hall.

The day progressed to evening. The last person he needed to see was Rose. And she really was the last person that Daniel wanted to see—on earth. It wasn't that he hated Rose because he was convinced that he didn't. In fact, he knew that he loved her. She was his mother, and that was enough. All of his life he craved her closeness, her presence in his. The prospects soothed him maternally, even though she never really acted in the way that he wanted.

When Rose opened the door, she hugged him like always. She smelled like cigarettes, but Daniel's delicate senses could also smell the baby powder that perfumed her breasts. It was her trademark, even after all these years. And he could always detect it.

"Come on in, baby, sit down," Rose said. He followed her into the kitchen. They sat at a little round, wobbly kitchen table that only had two wobbly seats. The kitchen itself was barely big enough to turn around in.

"You want something to eat, honey? There's some fried chicken warming in the oven and some macaroni and cheese and corn over there." Rose pointed to the stovetop. She wasn't much of a cook, and what she really meant was a box of preprepared frozen fried chicken was warming in the oven and some TV dinner-type servings of macaroni and cheese had already been thawed out and heated, along with the canned cream corn that had been sitting on the stovetop, probably for most of the day and the night before.

"No, thanks, Mom," Daniel said, fully aware of her culinary skills and what she really meant.

Rose gave him a slight head nod that said, *Suit yourself,* and lit another cigarette. She took a long first drag for strength because being alone with her son made her nervous. Whenever they were this close he was always staring at her, she felt, like he was judging her. She stole a glance at him while she inhaled, and this time was no different. He sat across from her, detailing her every move. He wasn't smiling, just looking at her deeply. Rose hated when he didn't smile. He looked like his daddy.

Finally she asked, "So what's up, Daniel? To what do I owe the pleasure of your company?" Saying it properlike tickled her. He was always trying to be proper, hanging around those uppity Graystones, so she was mocking him. He caught the joke. He smiled. Rose smiled. But it was a nervous smile.

"I love you, Mom," Daniel said.

Uh-oh, Rose thought. "I love you too, son," she said. She put out her cigarette and reached for her pack to grab another. The next logical thing to say was to ask Daniel what brought this on. She knew that's what he wanted. That's what he needed, but she refused. She was not in the mood for a deep conversation right now. She got up and walked over to the stove and started fiddling with the food.

Finally, she said, leaning on the stove, her back toward him, "Daniel, let's not go there, okay? I love you, and you love me, all right? I ain't really in the mood for none of ya—"

"I'm not going to ask you about anything you don't want to talk about. I know you don't want to talk about my father. I got that, okay? All I'm trying to tell you is that I love you. That's it. That's all. As you are. No strings. No questions. It doesn't matter anymore. I know you gave me all that you had to give. And I'm all right with that."

In the middle of his little speech, she stopped fiddling with the boxed fried chicken and turned around to face him with tears running down her face. If she could find her voice to speak, she wanted to make the sound that says, "I'm sorry." But she couldn't find her voice, so she said it with her eyes. He stood up and hugged her.

"Well, look, Ma, I gotta get goin'. So I'ma get outta here, okay?"

"Okay, son." Her voice quivered. He hugged her again; and then he left. And he left eight twenty-dollar bills on her kitchen table. Rose watched him jump into his car from her front window. She wiped her eyes as she watched his car disappear from her sight. She stood there with not a clue about what had just happened. When she discovered what he left on the table, she folded the bills in a tight roll, smiled, and stuffed them in her bra.

That night, Daniel slept heavy. Before he fell asleep, he toyed with the idea of it being his last night of sleep. Flashes of Jesus praying in Gethsemane illuminated in his mind. After all, he was doing what he had to do to save his congregation, to save the church, etc. But before Daniel could rest on that noble truth, truer notions of fear and saving himself from embarrassment moved in. Quickly, he discarded all rhyme and reason. *Ain't no sense in being blasphemous* was the afterthought. Then he concluded that thinking about the last-night thing—period—was not only too morbid, but also too dramatic. And he really wasn't trying to be dramatic or trying to feel sorry for himself; nothing like that. If anything, he enjoyed the fact that he had taken charge of his life back from Big Rev, back from the church, and especially, he had taken it back from God or whoever else wanted to run it. He would meet his end on his terms.

Earlier that day, Daniel had taken a nice long drive out to the county to purchase his assurance of a solid night's sleep—a fifth of vodka. Night came on. His eyes closed.

When Daniel awoke on his last Sunday before the trial, he still hadn't changed his mind on what he planned to do at daylight, during the 11 o'clock hour, the church hour. He planned to drive to the construction site of the unfinished church, ascend its barren scaffolding, and jump to his death. It would be his final apology to the congregation of Forest Unity Church of Baltimore. He was certain, in a warped way, that the sensational publicity, alone, would drum up enough support and donations to finish what he failed to finish. The church could then move on with its mission.

He slept until 9:30 Sunday morning. Better than he had felt in weeks, his body was light and airy upon awakening. The world and its problems, his problems, had not disappeared, but he felt changed inside. There was a sense of responsibility and honor. Somehow, he felt that he held no grudges against anyone. The revelation of a good night's sleep taught him that his existence was not an accident, but well in God's plan and overall picture. But he must stick to the original plan. His death had to bring about a good end for the church, for him, for his son—Joyce and her parents would take good care of him.

He got dressed and drove to the Lemel land site. Then he got out of his car, stumbled a few yards over pebbles, gravel, and stone, and began to climb the scaffolding that looked like a steel skeleton braced against the sky. Falling three floors into a pit of solid rock and dirt, damp from a previous rain, should do the trick. To leave an ugly, disfigured, and mangled corpse was poetic justice.

"Come on down from there, son," a voice yelled up. It startled Daniel so much, his sneaker almost lost its footing before he was ready to let go. He could have just let go and been done with it, but he was in control of this thing. He'd let go when he was ready to let go. Daniel looked down and saw Bryan calling up at him. He was shocked. *How did he know?* he thought.

"Get away from me, mannn. This ain't got nothing to do with you."

"The heck it ain't. You're doin' the wrong thing. Just come on down or I'm comin' up," Bryan yelled. With that, he took hold of the bottom tier like he was commandeering the monkey bars from a bunch of kids at the playground. Bryan made his way up the structure of gray bolts and steel, and it was the only time Daniel took his eyes off the jagged rocks below.

"I'll jump before you get up here," Daniel yelled down.

"Well, then, I'll jump right behind you. I freakin' swear it. And Pop and the family can find both of our bodies and try to figure out what happened." That little bit of reasoning sucker punched Daniel in the gut. His conviction quivered. Bryan picked up on the vibe and followed his first jab with an uppercut. He'd landed on the top by then. "Is this your good-bye to Joyce and your son? Because I talked to Joyce, mannn, and she said she ain't seen you since the hearing. Why is that, Daniel? You said good-bye to me, to Lori, to Rose, to Pop. How come you ain't said good-bye to Joyce? I thought you loved her, man. How come you couldn't even let your son know how you felt about him? How come?"

Bryan kept jabbing, and it pulverized Daniel. "What you think he's gonna grow up to feel about you? How you think he's gonna see you, man? *Like this?* Let's talk about it, man."

Daniel just clung to the steel beam and refocused on the pit below. He sensed he was running out of time. But the questions about his son had baffled him. How dare he repeat history he struggled hard not to hash over. Bryan silently prayed for the opposite straight to the heavens and it bought him time. Finally, he made his way over and wrapped himself around Daniel and the steel beam Daniel seemed cemented to. Both men were panting. The cold wind rustled about them and made billowing sails of their shirts.

When Daniel broke down in tears, Bryan whispered, "The best thing about life is that you can start over." The brothers were pelted by flying bits of gravel. It stuck between their teeth and felt gritty on their tongues.

Daniel yielded to Bryan's strength and released himself in it. The two men descended off the towering minime monument back to common ground. Not a word was said. None was needed. The two men walked to Bryan's car. "Get in, man, so I can keep my eye on you," he laughed. Daniel just did what he was told. They got in and drove back to Daniel's house. They walked into the living room and the first thing Bryan spied was the fifth of vodka. Daniel fell onto the couch, whipped.

"Vodka!" Bryan said, "Mannn, you stupid, you know that?" They both began to laugh the laugh of irony—the preacher boy trying to drink at this late date. "And let me tell you something—orange juice goes with vodka, not coke, you fool!" The tension lifted. Daniel looked helplessly at Bryan and asked, "How'd you know, man?"

Bryan responded, "Mannn—jumpin' off your unfinished church building? Boy, have you forgotten that I know all about your grandstanding behind? Boy, I knew you were over there doing something crazy." Then Bryan said to his brother seriously. "We're gonna get through this, mannn." He chuckled at another irony and said, "Don't let me have to teach *you* about faith. Remember, I'm the one gettin' rich off that devil music."

They both let out a weak I-know-that's-right laugh.

"Yeah," Daniel said, "I thought Big Rev was gonna kill you for that one."

"Oh, you got jokes, huh?" Bryan smiled, then got serious again. "You must be feelin' better already."

There was a knock on the door. The visitor was responding to a Mayday call Bryan had made earlier.

"I heard you forgot to say good-bye to me," Joyce said. A shocked Daniel stood motionless at the front door. She moved in and embraced him as if her life depended on it. He slowly moved his arms up to squeeze her tightly because at that moment, his life surely did. Her skin against his own was about as soft and pleasurable as he could remember. Her body was the softest pillow in the world. Her cheek against his felt like heaven; and then her soft hands cradled his face—her lips warmed his lips when she kissed him. The world shrank down to the two of them.

There would be a lot to talk about, but later. Right now, this felt like unconditional love and redemption surging from one body into another and back again. Bryan politely excused himself out.

Daniel didn't preach that Sunday. He and Joyce drove to Solomon's Island to talk, to cry, to repent—to talk.

Monday morning came. Daniel had resolved to face whatever. Eric called at 6:30 A.M. "Rev, you up?"

"Whatya think?"

Eric laughed. "I think you're up. Look, I'm on my way to pick you up. I hav—"

Daniel interrupted. "Don't think I'm gonna need a ride home, huh?"

"Hey, don't even go there, mannn," Eric said, then he thought a minute and continued, "Oh, that's right. You ain't been taking calls. The bond company turned up. Crystal gave me a lead and my private investigators worked it. It seems the homeboys were chilling in Ocho Rios before setting up new in Detroit. We've got something to work with now. You ready to put up a fight? Ready for round two?"

"Oh, I'm more than ready. In fact, I'm ready to kick some—"

"Heyyyy, glad to see you've got your fire back," Eric said. "You and God made up, huh?" he joked. Then the joking ceased. "Rev," Eric said in a monotone voice, "I know you know this is serious. But I'm your counsel, and I've got to say it—"

Interrupting, Daniel said, "I know. What's up? Spill it, man."

"The prosecutor is after you. For him, you're a test case and quite a feather in his cap." Eric paused so that they both could correctly process the moment. He continued, "Let's face it, you're no angel in this thing, but Barone pulled out a cannon to kill a flea."

"Yeah, I know all that," Daniel said. There was gravel in his voice.

"But don't lose faith," Eric said. "We've got some bullets of our own, and we're gonna use them."

Daniel sighed, but kept silent.

"But as I said, I'm your counsel, and I've got to tell you this—straight up," Eric said. "The outcome might not be fair, as we see it, and you're looking at some serious time—five to fifteen years." Processing time abounded. Eric broke in, "Can you handle it, Pastor? I mean, come what may?"

"Brother, lemme tell you somethin'," Daniel declared into the phone, "Me and God—we're on one accord! So let's do this."

They laughed—a kind of dry, sobering laugh. The conversation was over.

The End

About the Author

Yvonne J. Medley is a features writer and photographer, currently concentrating on her sequel to *God in Wingtip Shoes* and her screenplay titled *Sandwiched*. She has worked on staff at the *Washington Times* and freelanced for several publications, such as the *Washington Post*, *People* Magazine, *Gospel Today* Magazine, *A Time to Love* Magazine, and other national and local publications. Medley garnered recognition for controversial pieces on racism and the church and the psychology of sexually abusive clergy. Her work has been cited in online encyclopedias and Wikipedia.

Medley travels the country, interviewing and writing about intriguing personalities as well as *everyday* heroes, proving that everyone has a riveting and beneficial story to tell. One only needs to make a quality effort to unearth it.

She conducts her *Life Journeys Writing* workshops, designed to empower and encourage incarcerated men and women, as well as youth and adults and fellow writers within the general population. Some of these workshops have been supported by the Maryland Humanities Council's One Maryland: One Book program. Medley is the founder of The Life Journeys Writers Club, serving writers in Southern Maryland and beyond. She also teaches ESL (English as a Second Language) and ABE (Adult Basic Education) adult learners. Medley is a Point of Change Jail & Street Ministry,

About The Author

Inc., volunteer, dedicated to uplift and impact the lives of incarcerated men and women, their families, and provide aftercare support and life skills training.

Medley conducted Life Journeys Writing workshops for The Maryland Writers' Association's 22nd Annual Writers' Conference, the State of Maryland's Big Read, featuring Ray Bradbury's science fiction masterpiece *Fahrenheit 451* (sponsored by the National Endowment for the Arts), and The Reginald F. Lewis Museum of African American History & Culture, as well as various educational programs and churches.

Medley is a wife and mother of four and lives in Waldorf, Maryland.

UC HIS GLORY BOOK CLUB!

www.uchisglorybookclub.net

UC His Glory Book Club is the spirit-inspired brain-child of Joylynn Jossel, Author and Acquisitions Editor of Urban Christian, and Kendra Norman-Bellamy, Author for Urban Christian. This is an online book club that hosts authors of Urban Christian. We welcome as members all men and women who have a passion for reading Christian-based fiction.

UC His Glory Book Club pledges our commitment to provide support, positive feedback, encouragement, and a forum whereby members can openly discuss and review the literary works of Urban Christian authors.

There is no membership fee associated with UC His Glory Book Club; however, we do ask that you support the authors through purchasing, encouraging, providing book reviews, and of course, your prayers. We also ask that you respect our beliefs and follow the guidelines of the book club. We hope to receive your valuable input, opinions, and reviews that build up, rather than tear down our authors.

WHAT WE BELIEVE

—We believe that Jesus is the Christ, Son of the Living God.

—We believe the Bible is the true, living Word of God.

—We believe all Urban Christian authors should use their God-given writing abilities to honor God and share the message of the written word God has given to each of them uniquely.

—We believe in supporting Urban Christian authors in their literary endeavors by reading, purchasing and sharing their titles with our online community.

—We believe that in everything we do in our literary arena should be done in a manner that will lead to God being glorified and honored.

—We look forward to the online fellowship with you. Please visit us often at *www.uchisglorybookclub.net*.

Many Blessings to You!

Shelia E. Lipsey,
President, UC His Glory Book Club